Cat and the *Countess*

Casey Claybourne

BERKLEY BOOKS, NEW YORK

CAT AND THE COUNTESS

A Berkley Book / published by arrangement with
the author

PRINTING HISTORY
Berkley edition / February 2000

The Penguin Putnam Inc. World Wide Web site address is
http://www.penguinputnam.com

ISBN: 0-425-17335-6

BERKLEY®
Berkley Books are published by The Berkley Publishing Group,
a division of Penguin Putnam Inc.,
375 Hudson Street, New York, New York 10014.
BERKLEY and the "B" logo are trademarks
belonging to Penguin Putnam Inc.

PRINTED IN THE UNITED STATES OF AMERICA

10 9 8 7 6 5 4 3 2 1

Special thanks to Annette Ketchum of Bartlesville, Oklahoma, for sharing her knowledge of the Lenape bandolier bag

For Collins Stephens
(whose aliases include Steve, Papaw,
and the Big Ole Turkey Bird)
with buckets of love
and thanks for being there when we needed you

One

❧❧❧

As a rule, Niankwe "Wildcat" MacInnes never posed much objection to a woman putting her hand down his pants. In fact, he generally tried to encourage that sort of activity. However, at this particular moment, on this particular day, the sensation of dainty fingers creeping across his upper buttocks just plain got him mad.

He went completely still, feeling those trespassing digits skim over his hip, as the oily smell of ink scented the air of the dusty stationer's shop. Like all of London, the shop was congested and cramped, with scarcely enough room for a man to draw breath. Only a few days earlier, news of Wellington's victory at Fuentes de Onoro had reached the capital city, sending the English people out into the markets and onto the streets with a renewed sense of optimism, their faith in the undying supremacy of the Holy British Empire once again restored.

Although Wildcat cared almost nothing about England's war with the French, he did need to purchase sealing wax and so found himself crammed, along with a dozen others, into the dark, narrow stationer's shop, vying for the attention of the sole and harried salesclerk.

As his rear end was being explored.

For a very brief moment, he asked himself if perhaps he was jumping to a hasty and inaccurate conclusion. Perhaps the touch was merely accidental. Perhaps some innocent woman had inadvertently brushed up behind him amid the shop's crowded confines. A woman with slender, dexterous fingers . . .

Then a faint, almost imperceptible, tug near his waist convinced him that the contact was neither unintentional nor innocent. That pinch had purpose.

Angrily he spun around, his feathered braid a flash of bright, whirling crimson against the dull grays of the poorly lit shop.

"What the hell do you th—"

His voice shriveled up somewhere near his Adam's apple as his gaze came into contact with a pair of amazingly blue eyes. Cornflower blue. Ingenuous and dewy. Confusion flickered through him as he swung his head first left, then right; but no other person was standing within arm's reach. No one but this completely unexpected woman, clinging to the hand of a skinny, tow-headed boy.

Shifting his weight from one scuffed boot to the other, he gave the woman a quick, yet thorough, once-over. Though untrained, even *his* eye was able to recognize the wealth in the delicate lace and luxurious satin of the woman's dress, in the swansdown-trimmed bonnet resting atop her flaxen hair, and in the emerald chips sparkling demurely at her earlobes. This was not merely a woman, fercrissake, this was a *lady*. A society jewel, a blue-blooded aristocrat, a member of London's elite *ton* . . . But a pickpocket?

"What do you think you're doing?" he blurted out, taken aback by the woman's appearance when he'd been expecting to find some dirty street urchin or gypsy thief hovering behind him.

"I—" The lady blinked, her gold-tipped lashes fanning up and down in a motion so fast it was as if her eyelids were moving at treble speed. "I beg your pardon?"

Her voice was pleasant, a rich, almost musical warble. Wildcat liked the sound of it, and liked the funny way her lips puckered and stretched, moving with careful precision to form her words. Not really beautiful, she was nonetheless handsome, her features put together in an intriguing fashion, in a manner that held a man's interest even as he questioned if her eyebrows weren't just a touch too bushy or her nose just a hint too abrupt.

Short—she stood no higher than his heart—she was not what Wildcat would have described as petite. Round and full and plump and white, the woman reminded him of a downy snowshoe hare, all quivery and alert.

Her hands, he noticed, were encased in ivory kid gloves that looked to be as soft and supple as freshly churned butter. With her left hand, she held on to a child, a frail-looking boy of about eight or nine years whose calm, owlish stare and sickly pallor were in marked contrast to her own twittery robustness. The child's sober regard left Wildcat feeling oddly unsettled and he hastily transferred his gaze from the boy to the woman's right

hand, which was hanging open at her side. Open and
. . . empty.

Now, wait a minute.

"Look here, lady, I know I felt someone digging
around in my drawers just now—"

Nearby an old woman emitted a loud gasp. Wildcat
silenced the eavesdropper with a bone-chilling glare that
turned the woman's wrinkled face a deep and mottled
crimson that matched her hat. She clamped her mouth
shut, swallowed hard, and hurriedly moved off to examine a set of pastels on the other side of the shop. None
of the other patrons appeared to have taken notice; they
were too intent on their midday shopping.

Nonetheless, Wildcat was suddenly drawn into a
keener awareness of his situation and surroundings. He
cast a wary glance around the stationer's before shaking
his head in disgust.

*Just what the hell are you thinking, MacInnes? Have
you completely lost your wits?* To suspect this rich,
white lady of stealing from him was nothing short of
ludicrous. Insane. *Kpitscha.*

He gave another self-derisive shake of his head, his
braid swaying across his shoulder like a beaded pendu-
lum. Heck, only a frothing-at-the-mouth lunatic would
be crazy enough to accuse this woman of thievery when
it was perfectly obvious she had no need of his few
measly pieces of gold. He, a Delaware-Scots crossbreed,
charging this bejeweled snow princess with trying to lift
his coin purse . . .

Uh-huh. Kpitscha.

Nodding slowly, thoughtfully, to himself, Wildcat decided that the woman must have had another objective—
one physical, not fiscal. Odds were the lady did this sort

of thing all the time, getting her jollies out of groping the asses of unsuspecting strangers in stationer's shops. For all he knew, this was probably her idea of some damned fine entertainment; instead of rubbing elbows with the common folk, she rubbed parts of the anatomy decidedly more intimate.

Yeah, that has to be it, he decided. In fact, hadn't he met her type a hundred times before? Most likely, she was one of those society women who enjoyed pursuing men outside of her social circle. Men like him. Men whose appearance promised something just a little bit different. Just a little bit dangerous.

For a moment, as he watched the filtered sunlight reflect off her silver-blond curls, Wildcat allowed himself to entertain the notion of such a dalliance. After all, the woman sure was easy on the eyes. *And hard on what counts,* he added, surreptitiously adjusting himself beneath his leggings.

But her blood ran blue, probably even bluer than those mesmerizing eyes of hers. In other words, she was taboo. Off-limits. *Kwitelittowagan.*

Furthermore, he had sworn off women for a while, all except for the working kind, that is. During the last few months, he had begun to notice that one-night "relationships" had lost their appeal. What once had been fun— damned good fun—had become empty, meaningless. Tedious even. At a mere thirty-four years of age, he was already so jaded and so cynical that even *sex* wasn't what it used to be, frevvinsake.

Now, that's pitiful, Wildcat murmured to himself. *Goddamned pitiful.*

But pitiful or not, he knew he had absolutely no intention of tangling with the rich bunny-woman, no mat-

ter how big and luscious her *nunagan* were, no matter
how many times she squeezed his rear end. He appreciated her efforts at a flirtation, but he'd learned his lesson about the fairer sex. Learned it well.

"I, uh—" He sent a cautious glance to the boy, before
telling her, "I'm not interested, but thanks."

She blinked.

Wildcat was still trying to figure out how she got her
lashes to move so fast, when the boy blurted out, "Are
you an Indian?"

"Oliver!" Her cheeks gone instantly pink, she leaned
over the child to whisper, affording Wildcat a dizzying
glance of her endowments. Until then, Wildcat had been
unaffected by the warm air in the shop.

"I—I apologize," she said, after sharing a word with
the child. "He did not mean to give offense."

With a wink at the shamefaced boy, Wildcat drawled,
"None taken."

He was just about to turn away and forget the whole
episode when he noticed that he and the blonde had
drawn the attention of two young military officers who
were entering the shop.

Brass buttons gleaming, scarlet coats tight across their
puffed-out chests, the pair of soldiers came sauntering
toward them, boot heels marking their progress in sharp,
staccato bursts across the scarred wooden floor. Fuzzy-
cheeked and full of youthful swagger, the two appeared
to be freshly commissioned and spoiling for trouble,
their sights set directly on Wildcat.

Even from a few yards away, Wildcat could smell
their bloodlust, their need to prove themselves as men.
He sighed quietly, wondering if the two young pups had
any idea what they were getting themselves into. A Le-

nape brave simply wasn't the sort of fella to sharpen one's teeth on. Especially not a Lenape brave who'd had Wildcat's recent run of bad luck.

As the soldiers drew alongside the woman, the two men studied Wildcat with undisguised hostility. He responded with the same degree of warmth, giving them a grim, tight smile. He knew what these English officers saw when they looked at him. They saw a dark-skinned, feather-wearing, buckskin-clad savage in a limp cravat, an old coat, and frayed leather leggings. They saw an outsider, a man who did not belong in their white world, talking to their soft, white women. A man who did not belong anywhere.

The soldiers saluted the blond woman and the heavier of the two greeted her by name, sweeping his tasseled hat from his head. "Lady Pemsley, how do you do?"

She acknowledged him with a quivery dip of her chin. "Captain Cummings."

At the back of his mind, Wildcat noticed that, though she seemed to be constantly alert—almost skittish—she kept her voice controlled and tranquil.

"Might we be of some assistance here, m'lady?"

"Assistance?" At the base of her throat, her pulse fluttered against her translucent skin.

"Is this *person* disturbing you?" The captain jerked his head in Wildcat's direction.

As if she'd forgotten he was even standing there, a hitch formed between the lady's pale winged brows, her bewildered gaze drifting toward him. Their eyes met. Wildcat's questioned. Hers . . . pleaded?

Now, why in the blazes was she looking at him like that? Was that guilt he saw in her face? Confusion? Or did she merely have a gift for making a man's insides twist up with that sweet, wounded expression of hers?

Cummings, who must have taken the lady's silence as an assent, indicated the door with his peach-fuzz chin. "Perhaps you had best be on your way, Indian man."

Wildcat sized the captain up from head to toe. The lad might have been twenty-two. An infant.

"Thanks," he said, "but I'm in no rush."

Shocked affront twisted Cummings's features, and he took an aggressive step forward. His smaller companion did the same. Once again, Wildcat questioned if the two men had been drinking or simply were in need of a dose of common sense. After all, neither of them looked as if he'd had any real experience with blood or pain or death.

At least, not yet.

"Do we need to hurry you along, then?" Cummings threatened, puffing his chest out another inch or two till he looked ready to burst.

Wildcat only gave a lazy scratch to the side of his mouth, aware of how the other shoppers had all grown still and silent. The tension was palpable, the heat of the day pronounced, as evidenced by the sweat beginning to bead Cummings's heavy brow.

"Well, you're welcome to try," Wildcat drawled in his finest American twang as he shifted a few inches to the right so that his hunting knife rested more securely against his front hip.

Cummings bristled and drew himself up to launch an attack. Wildcat settled his weight evenly between his feet, anticipating the first blow.

"No!"

Eyes wide, Lady Pemsley placed a restraining hand on the officer's coat sleeve just as he began to raise his arm. Though no more than a touch, it was powerful enough to freeze the man in his tracks.

"Captain, please," she murmured, sending a pointed glance to the child hovering at her side.

Wildcat followed her nod to the somber-faced boy, who was studying them all with a disquieting intensity.

"Captain, I fear there has been some misunderstanding. You see, Mister . . . um—" Lady Pemsley drew Wildcat's attention back to her with a commanding wave of her fingertips.

"MacInnes," he curtly supplied. "Wildcat MacInnes."

"Mr. MacInnes is not at fault here, I assure you," she said, flattening a diminutive hand to a not-so-diminutive bosom. "In fact, *I* am the one who has proved an annoyance to *him.*"

Wildcat quirked a mocking brow. Was the woman actually going to confess to fondling his posterior?

"You see," she said, her fingers twiddling at the ribbon on her bodice, "I cannot seem to manage these new boots and I stumbled over my own feet directly into poor Mr. MacInnes, almost sending him straight to the floor."

She laughed then, a nervous, bunnylike, nose-wriggling laugh, before glancing to Wildcat as if to seek his confirmation. He shrugged, thinking that only the most brainless of twits—maybe someone like a Captain Cummings—would believe that his six-foot-tall frame had nearly been toppled by the tiny Lady Pemsley.

"Oh dear, I am so very sorry about all the fuss. A terrific amount of bother over a pair of boots, wouldn't you agree?"

Trembling just beneath the surface of her skin, she wrapped a protective arm around her son's shoulders, while her gaze flitted to the shop's window. "Ah, and I see my ride has arrived at last. Again, my apologies, Mr. MacInnes. Clumsy, clumsy me. Gentlemen, I must bid you a good day."

She smiled once more, her lips a fraction too tight for the gesture to be natural, and quickly spun toward the exit in a rustling mass of creamy satin. Before Cummings had found the time to push the words "good day" from his own lips, the lady was already sashaying out the door.

Wildcat watched her go, a pensive frown carved into his forehead. There was something about that woman. Something undeniably intriguing . . .

He listened with half an ear as the two soldiers muttered listless apologies before scurrying away like naughty schoolboys, his eyes all the while continuing to follow the Lady Pemsley until she passed out of view.

Damn, but she was tempting.

Grimacing with regret, Wildcat turned around to make one last search for the sealing wax when he noticed—

His bandolier bag was missing.

Two

❧

"*Mother, that man* in the stationer's shop. Who do you suppose he was?"

Her heart skipping along at a frantic and frenzied pace, Elizabeth fought her way through the swarming Bond Street masses while virtually dragging poor Oliver behind her.

"Wh-which man?"

"The one you were talking with. The Indian. Who was he?"

"I—" She gave a nervous lick to her lips. "Goodness, Oliver, I haven't any idea. He was no one. No one we know, that is."

"I would *like* to know him," Oliver said gravely. "He looks interesting."

Elizabeth arched a brow, unable to take issue with her son's observation. Although loath to confess it, she had to admit that the man named MacInnes looked interesting to the point of being edible.

"Mother, why do you think he wore his hair like that? Loose with that one braid on the side?"

"Oliver, really," Elizabeth said in exasperation, tugging him ever farther from the shop. "You heard the man say he was an Indian. That must be the fashion where he comes from. Apparently he does not mind being stared at, of appearing different from everyone else."

And even as the words left her mouth, Elizabeth felt a spurt of admiration for his boldness, his defiance. There was someone unafraid to reveal his true self.

Tilting up onto the tips of her toes, Elizabeth searched the street for Valerie's carriage, praying that her friend had not instructed the coachman to drive on without them.

"Oh, thank heavens," she murmured, squinting into the afternoon sunshine.

Only two vehicles away, a berline approached bearing the famous Ballatine crest, a laurel wreath encircling a medieval lance. With a spirited wave of her parasol, Elizabeth signaled the driver, who succeeded in navigating a course to the side of the thoroughfare. The young footman jumped down from his perch to pull down the steps.

"Let us look lively now, darling," Elizabeth said, guiding Oliver forward with a light hand to his back. "I fear we have kept Lady Valerie waiting long enough as it is."

Oliver balked at climbing into the carriage, instead turning his face up to her to ask, "May I please sit above, Mother? Please?"

"Oh, Oliver, I don't—" Elizabeth bit into the side of

her cheek, and gave her foot an impatient wiggle. "I don't know, poppets, it is so dangerous. What if you were to lose your balance and fall?"

"I'll be careful," he said, his gray eyes earnest. "I promise."

Frowning, Elizabeth shot another look behind her as the breeze whipped a stray blond hair from beneath her bonnet to dance across her vision. The door to the stationer's was starting to swing open—

"Yes, yes," she abruptly relented. "You may sit above, but do make haste."

Oliver, beaming from ear to ear, scrambled to join the coachman as Elizabeth hoisted her weighty skirts and hastened up the carriage steps. As she took her seat across from her friend, she could not resist sneaking another last peek out the berline's window. Instantly her gaze alit on a dark, uncovered head towering above the crowd. Goodness, was that a red feather she spied? Was it that man MacInnes? Had he followed her from the shop?

"By Jove, Elizabeth, if you do not pull that pretty head of yours into the coach, you're likely to lose it on a lamppost, you know." Valerie's frankly worded warning was accompanied by a vigorous shake of carroty curls. "If you're worried about Oliver, I assure you he is perfectly safe with John Coachman, and will far enjoy watching the sights over sitting in here with us, listening to our dull women's prattle."

Elizabeth nodded absently, watching from the corner of her eye as the dark head appeared to scan the street in both directions before turning toward the Ballatine carriage. Was he staring after them? Or could it be that her overactive imagination was playing tricks on her again?

"Oh, La-a-dy Pem-sley?" Valerie brandished a hand in front of Elizabeth's face. "What on earth has come over you?"

Elizabeth drew away from the window, yanking closed the fringed velvet curtain.

"And where is Oliver's pen set?"

"Oh." *The pen set.* "I forgot to purchase it."

"Forgot? But you came out today expressly for the purpose of purchasing one."

"Yes, I know." Chagrined, Elizabeth chewed at the corner of her lip, noticing that she'd somehow torn open the seam on her glove's forefinger. "I was distracted."

"Apparently so," Valerie agreed with an arch look. "What distracted you so thoroughly that you managed to overlook your shopping?"

"Um . . ." Elizabeth did not want to spend too much thought on the handsome stranger she'd just met. He had unsettled her, unnerved her. Even in broad daylight in the safety of a stationer's shop, he had seemed somehow dangerous and uncivilized. She could not speak of him. She did not wish to.

"I, um, ran into Lady Gupper's son, do you remember? The gentleman we met in Bath a few months ago? At the time, he was desperate for a commission, talking of nothing else."

Valerie's lower lip jutted forward as she tried to recollect. Then a mischievous smile pulled her mouth wide. "Why, of course! Mr. Shortcomings."

Elizabeth frowned, afraid she'd addressed the captain by the wrong name. "His name was Cummings, was it not?"

"Yes, well, according to Eleanor Morse, who knows him intimately, 'Short' Cummings more accurately describes the man's *attributes*."

Elizabeth glanced to her lap.

"Now I've shocked you," Val said, and gave a light laugh of unconcern. "Are you appalled?"

"No, not appalled, of course not." Valerie tended to think her priggish. "However, you must know that Eleanor Morse is considered fast and thus not received by many of London's better families. I would urge you to have a care for your reputation, since a gentleman may consort with whomever he pleases, but a lady is judged by the company she keeps."

Smoothing a hand over her skirts, Elizabeth hoped that she didn't sound too awfully preachy. She loved Valerie dearly, and so worried about her friend's impulsive nature.

"Of course, you do know that you can always speak freely with me, Valerie. Always. I am your friend and will guard your secrets, even from Cresting. But, dearest, when you are out in public, you really ought to consider curbing that acerbic tongue of yours. I fear it will land you in trouble someday."

"By Jove, I hope so," Valerie said, with a lascivious wink. "My tongue needs more adventure."

Elizabeth pursed her lips to keep herself from laughing out loud. It was simply impossible to talk to Valerie of propriety. Incorrigible, outrageous, and softhearted to a fault, Valerie Ballatine was a woman unbridled by society's restrictions.

"I daresay I can be naughty at times," Valerie said, running a hand across her mop of orange curls, "but, at least, I have fun. Honestly, I would go mad if I had to behave as you do, Elizabeth, forever mindful of your manners, and careful to say just the right thing to all the right people. And, truthfully, what has it done for you, being such a paragon?" She made a disdainful poofing sound behind her teeth. "It seems your reward is to be my colorless old brother, who'll bore you to death before you've even seen thirty years of age."

Unable to meet Valerie's gaze, Elizabeth studied the small rip at the side of her gloved finger. "Your brother is not old."

"Compared to Pemsley, I suppose not—" Val caught her breath before clamping a hand over her mouth. "Omigosh, Elizabeth, I am sorry. That was truly terrible of me."

Elizabeth managed a smile. "It does not matter."

And it had not mattered to her that her late husband had been a full twenty-five years her senior, for Oscar Langham, the third Earl Pemsley, had been almost sainted in her eyes, a man without equal. A man too good for this earth.

"I *am* sorry," Valerie repeated penitently. "I am far too rash and thoughtless, and I honestly don't know how you can suffer my company sometimes."

"What do you mean by 'sometimes'?" Elizabeth teased. "I suffer you *all* the time."

Valerie grinned, then playfully thwacked Elizabeth's knee with her closed fan.

"In all seriousness, as much as I would love to have you for a sister, I must wonder, Elizabeth, how you can bear the idea of spending the rest of your days as the Marchioness of Cresting. Peter is a grand fellow and a first-rate brother, but you still cannot convince me that you are in love with him—you can't. Frankly, I doubt the old stick could inspire passion in anyone, with the possible exception of his banker perhaps."

"Now, Val, that is unkind of you. I am immensely fond of Lord Cresting."

Her friend rolled her eyes in an exaggerated circle. "*Fond?* La, Elizabeth, now you sound like Cresting. Dry, dry, dry. What about passion, hmm? What about love in its rawest, most uncivilized form? Or must you always seek out those domineering, austere types? Now, now," she said, warding off Elizabeth's objections with two raised hands, "I know how you fly into the boughs if I dare speak a word against your late husband, but, honestly, darling, if you cannot appreciate the unbalanced nature of that relationsh—"

"Valerie," Elizabeth warned, feeling herself start to bristle.

"Very well," Valerie said nonchalantly. "No more about the sainted Oscar, I promise. Nonetheless, I say, give me a man who appreciates an independent, hot-blooded woman."

Avoiding the questions Valerie had raised regarding "love" and "passion," Elizabeth answered, "I think you undervalue your brother, Valerie. Cresting might not be the next Don Juan, but he would make a wonderful catch for any woman. Even more important, he would serve as an excellent father. Particularly for a boy like Oliver. He could teach my son the responsibilities of the title, instruct him in his duties and such."

"Hmm-mm," Valerie answered with a skeptical waggle of auburn brows.

"In any case, this discussion is pointless." Elizabeth shoved irritably at the same lock of hair that earlier had fallen loose from her bonnet. "Your brother and I have no agreement of any sort. We are . . . friends."

"Fustian!" Valerie cried. "You and I both know that
Peter is only waiting until Mother can meet you and give
you her regal stamp of approval. Then"—Valerie
snapped her slender fingers—"as soon as that's done,
Peter will be on his knees, begging for your hand and
all those other pertinent parts."

"Have you had news from the marchioness?"

"Are you asking when the old witch is expected to fly
into town?" Val shuddered, her Vandyke ruff rippling
atop the mint-green walking gown. "Although I hate to
be the bearer of ill tidings, I must confess I had a note
from her this very morning." Valerie's face curdled, as
if she'd just eaten something distasteful, while atop her
nose, unfashionable freckles stood out like strawberry
dots. "Mama is expected tomorrow or the day after."

"Oh, my," Elizabeth breathed, and sank limply against
the banquette. A flush warmed her as she pressed a hand
to her unsteady heart. "Such little notice," she murmured.

"Come now, you needn't fly into the boughs. She will
adore you."

"Do you think so?"

"Absolutely, that is, I believe, um . . ."

Although Valerie was capable of relating the most
sensational clankers without so much as a telltale blink
of an eye, Elizabeth knew that her friend would give her
the truth and only the truth.

"Very well, maybe not adore you," Val conceded,
"since only the perfect Peter has ever measured up to
her impossibly high standards, but I am sure she will
find you unobjectionable. Your character is sound, your
name without blemish, and you're not coming to the

marriage penniless, which should mean a great deal to the notoriously frugal Flavia Ballatine."

"Your brother tells me that your mother is a woman of deep faith," Elizabeth said hesitantly, recalling with guilt her own sporadic visits to church these last months. "He mentioned that the marchioness is an ardent supporter of your local bishopric."

"Bah. Just as you or I would go to the mantua makers to purchase fabric—in Mother's case, she attends church to buy herself salvation. Honestly, the woman could squeeze blood from a ha'penny, yet she's lavished money on that Devonshire clergy, I think as a way to atone for her disagreeable nature. But I tell you, there's not enough gold in the world to atone for *her* nasty disposition."

Elizabeth sincerely hoped that the marchioness was not as difficult to rub along with as Valerie suggested. Peter, she knew, maintained a very close relationship with his mother. Very close.

"I do hope to make a good impression," Elizabeth said, giving a self-conscious tug to her overly snug bodice.

"Oh, you will," Valerie assured airily.

"If only I hadn't grown so plump this last year—"

"Hah! Standing beside Mother, you will look nothing short of sylphlike, I promise you. Now enough of *your* concerns," Valerie said with a petulant flip of her fingers. "In fact, it is frightfully selfish of you to be thinking only of yourself, Elizabeth, when you ought to be fretting on my behalf, you know. Just watch. The moment she lands, Mama will embark yet again on her mission to see me wed to anything male and breathing. It pains her very soul to see me march merrily into spinsterhood.

By Jove, when I remember what a close call I had with Lord Skye at home last summer . . . The poor sot hadn't figured out Mother's purpose until she had already applied for the reading of the banns!"

"I daresay the marchioness seeks only your happiness, as any mother does for her child."

"Then she ought to let me be happy as I choose," Valerie argued, slapping her fan into her palm with a belligerent glower. "I am barely two-and-twenty. Let me have my fun, I say."

Elizabeth deliberately withheld comment, for she doubted quite seriously that the Marchioness Cresting would approve of her daughter's notion of "fun." Although society had yet to condemn her openly, Valerie walked a very fine line between social disgrace and acceptance.

"Do you disapprove?" Valerie asked, taking note of Elizabeth's silence.

"It is not my place to approve or disapprove. I would never stand in judgment of you, Valerie. I am your friend."

Nodding uncertainly like a bashful schoolgirl, Valerie plucked at the sleeve of her gown. Despite her daring ways and brushes with impropriety, she truly did care about the opinion of others.

"So when does Oliver leave for school?" Valerie asked, deftly turning the subject.

"When?" A pang lanced through Elizabeth's middle, and she raised her gaze to the carriage roof. "Too soon. He leaves the day after tomorrow."

"You've decided against Eton, then?"

"I have. Peter felt that Oliver should attend his father's alma mater, but I simply could not reconcile my-self to the idea."

"My, my," Valerie said softly.

Was her friend surprised that she'd not yielded to Cresting's advice?

Wondering, Elizabeth continued, "As you well know, Oliver's health is so fragile, I did not see how he could survive the rigors of public school. And since Mr. Fra-zer's Academy did come highly recommended from Pemsley's solicitor, well, I would like to think that the smaller, more secure setting—Mr. Frazer takes in only a dozen boys—will better suit Oliver's disposition."

"The country air is bound to be good for him."

"Yes," Elizabeth agreed, though she had to bite at her lips to hide their trembling.

"Come now, I know this isn't easy for you," Valerie said, reaching over to give Elizabeth's hand a bracing pat. "Nonetheless, you must admit that this is the best course for Oliver. We all can see how you adore the little fellow, but you cannot keep him clinging to your apron strings forever."

"I know. I had hoped to wait at least until next term to send him, but the headmaster convinced me that a mid-year transition would be less painful."

"Less painful for you or for Oliver?" Valerie asked with a sympathetic grin.

Try as she might, Elizabeth was unable to muster an answering smile. After losing her husband sixteen months earlier, the thought of now bidding good-bye to her precious son seemed a purely unbearable task. *Un-bearable.*

A shuddering sigh pushed her corset tight as the car-riage pulled to a stop outside her Bedford Square town

house. For a moment, as Elizabeth gazed out onto its
weathered stone facade and rows of sweetly budding
azalea, she felt herself drawn back to that day, twelve
long years ago, when she'd first laid eyes on this house.
Long before there had been an Oliver. Long before there
had been an Elizabeth Langham.

She'd just seen her fourteenth birthday, a young
woman-child, awkward in her new-sprung maturity and
wary of its effects on those around her—especially men.
The carriage had driven up to the Bedford Square home
in the fresh light of morning, with the sun shining directly on the front door's gleaming brass knocker. She
had been awestruck; not merely by the house's size and
grandeur, by its towering colonnades and black iron bal-
conies, but even more by its cleanliness. It had seemed
to her perfect, pristine. A haven for all things pure and
clean.

She remembered how the windows had looked like
diamond-kissed squares of crystal set against the dignified gray stone, and how even the stoop appeared freshly
polished, not a cobweb or shoe scuff to be seen. Of
course, she'd hidden her wonder, not wishing to be
viewed as naive or unsophisticated—yet that sense of
awe had never really left her. Even after all these years.

Not that the house was grand by today's standards. In
reality, one would call it a modest residence for an earl.
But Oscar hadn't wanted any of the pomp of Mayfair,
preferring to be removed from society's hub. He wasn't
one to like much fuss.

"I hope you won't be offended if I don't come in,"
Valerie said as the footman came around to the coach
door. "But I am running late for an appointment with a
most intriguing Dutch artist." Her gray eyes sparkled as

she batted the fan coyly in front of her face. "He is altogether improper—Mother would simply die if she knew—but he's very pretty and wildly in love with me and has asked me to pose for him. *Au naturel,*" she added with another excited flutter of the fan.

Elizabeth answered with only a quiet "ah." Some time ago she had learned not to interfere in Valerie's affairs of the heart, for it seemed that they rarely ended happily or well. For whatever reason, her friend had a penchant for seeking out the most inappropriate of men.

"Of course, I understand and I thank you for your company. You are a dear to go out with me, Val, when you know how I dislike shopping."

"My pleasure, whenever you like. Now go on, be off with you," Valerie said, shooing her out the door, "or Hendrick will be in a nasty pout when I arrive late."

Elizabeth pressed her cheek to her friend's, then accepted the footman's hand. As she descended, her protective gaze followed Oliver, who was racing ahead to the town house door. Boyles, their one-eyed butler, stood waiting to receive him.

She started toward the house, then abruptly spun back around again to squint anxiously into the coach's interior.

"You will contact me as soon as the marchioness arrives, won't you?"

"Lord, yes, the minute she lands," Valerie agreed, her tone impatient. "Although I told you you've no reason to be concerned. If anyone is nearly as perfect as my brother, it is you, Elizabeth Langham. So will you please stop jabbering and allow me to meet my Dutchman?"

Valerie waved, the footman shut the coach door, and by the time Elizabeth reached the threshold of her home, the Ballatine horses were rattling off down the street in a flurry of blue-gray dust, taking Valerie off to her secret rendezvous.

As a turtledove cooed melodiously from the eaves above, Elizabeth lingered in the open doorway, watching the dust settle back onto the street. Deep inside, a tiny, wistful voice questioned if she might never do something so outrageous as race off to an illicit tryst with an intriguing and inappropriate man. One dark and tall with eyes that seemed able to delve into one's very soul . . .

"M'lady?"

Boyles stood at her side, regarding her with a politely quizzical look, as he waited to close the front door behind her. Blinking, Elizabeth shook herself back to the present, embarrassed at her daydreaming and wayward thoughts. She did not know what had come over her of late, but she'd been terribly absentminded and prone to all sorts of unlikely fancies. Could it be due to her grief over Oliver's impending departure? Or was it nerves as she anticipated the long-awaited offer of marriage from the Marquess of Cresting?

"Was your afternoon enjoyable, m'lady?"

"Yes, lovely," she answered without thinking, fumbling with her tangled bonnet strings. "Although I will need you to send Mrs. Warring out to purchase a stationery set for Oliver later today. I, um, was not able to."

"Yes, m'lady. I'll see to it right away."

He bowed, giving Elizabeth a clear view of the U-shaped bald spot expanding atop his head. Her softly nostalgic smile recalled how, at fourteen, when she'd first met Pemsley House's butler, she'd thought Boyles positively dashing and exotic, rather like a pirate with his black eye patch, strong shoulders, and long, curling hair. Alas, while the eye patch yet remained, the butler's shoulders had become stooped over the years, and the generous bounty of chestnut locks was now no more than a distant memory.

"Goodness, where has the time gone, Boyles?"

"The time? Why, it's not yet three, Lady Pemsley."

She smiled and wagged her head, her gaze sweeping up the foyer's twenty-foot ceilings to the frescoed cupola that topped the massive entryway. Suddenly, and without reason, she felt very alone in her home. Very alone and somehow . . . lost.

Rubbing a hand to her forehead, Elizabeth felt the snag in her torn glove catch at her brow. "I am going to have a rest, I think, Boyles. When Oliver finishes his lessons, tell him that we can take a ride in the park before tea if he is feeling well."

"Yes, m'lady."

Upstairs, Elizabeth entered her new bedchamber, the one she had moved into following her husband's passing. Though smaller than her previous suite, the room's yellow-and-cream decor was cheerful, and did not serve as a constant reminder of the life she'd once had with Lord Pemsley. A life of security, serenity . . .

She closed the door to her bedroom, and carefully turned the key in the lock, her hand lingering on the cool solidity of the iron, its firm yet elegant shape. She smiled slightly at the absurdity of taking comfort from the feel of a key while wryly acknowledging that much in her life had been shifting toward the absurd.

After walking across the room to the far wall, she slowly lowered herself to her knees on the thick Persian carpet, her skirts swelling about her like creamy puffs of meringue. She tugged free of her gloves, making a mental note to have her maid repair the torn seam. A span of mahogany paneling spread eye level before her.

With the accuracy of a motion oft-rehearsed, she reached forward and expertly skimmed her fingers along the paneling until they brushed over a tiny hooked latch. She pressed it toward her. A miniature door swung open, revealing a secret compartment hidden within the wall.

Sighing, Elizabeth drew from the niche a chest nicked and stained with age. She then reached into her bodice, wriggled her fingers, and withdrew from between her corset and shift a colorfully beaded bag. Her nose wrinkled with regret as she tossed the bag on top of a jumbled assortment of jewelry, handkerchiefs, thimble cases, hat pins, and snuffboxes.

"The perfect Lady Pemsley, indeed."

Three

Improbable *as it* seemed, the St. Martin's Lane Inn looked even less appealing than it had the day before, Wildcat thought grimly as his gaze raked over the Scabbard's mossy, soot-blackened exterior. Above the entrance, the inn's sign swung crookedly from a broken chain, forcing Wildcat to duck low as he pushed open the door lest he risk a blackened eye or a lump on the head.

Entering the front tavern, he was careful to keep his eyes averted from those lingering in the murky darkness. In his current foul mood, he knew that even the merest hint of a sneer or challenge from one of the Scabbard's patrons might set off his temper, and *that* he did not need. Already today, he had managed to sidestep one brawl; he sure as blazes didn't need to go looking for another. So as he passed by the tables peopled with shifty-eyed seamen and pockmarked whores, he held himself aloof, his hand never far from the hilt of his knife as he made his way toward the stairs that led to the lodgings above.

In spite of himself, Wildcat knew a moment's regret when he entered his quarters on the alley side of the inn. Musty, dark, and smelling of old boots, the room was one step up from a ship's brig. Barely. Faded yellow wall covering was peeling away from the ceiling in fat, moldy strips, and the mattress on the bed . . . Well, Wildcat didn't like to think about it too closely, but he suspected he'd been sleeping last night with an unsavory assortment of multilegged critters.

He grimaced as his gaze touched the four corners of the room, and he wondered if maybe he'd been a bit hasty in declining the use of the Taggarts' Mayfair town house. Will and Melisande Taggart owned and operated a whiskey distillery just south of Edinburgh, where he had been working these last few months. Close friends— of which Wildcat could count only a handful—the Taggarts had insisted that Wildcat stay at their rarely used Mayfair home, particularly since it was distillery business that had brought him all the way to London.

But, no. *Oh, no.* Wildcat had refused the offer flat out. After all, he couldn't let anyone start to think he'd gone soft, now could he? *Uh-huh.* He had to prove that a clean bed and decent eats were white-man luxuries he could do without.

"Yeah, I showed them, all right," he muttered, batting a stray cobweb from his path. "Showed them I'm a brainless, flea-bitten fool."

With a low growl, and a silent promise to think twice before he let his pride stand in the way of his comfort again, he kicked the door shut with the back of his heel and slid home the squeaky metal bolt. Shrugging out of his coat jacket, he first withdrew his knife from its leather sheath and lay the weapon on the side of the cracked washstand. He then reached for his bandolier bag—

"Damn."

He still didn't quite believe it. Despite having spent the last hour in a lengthy, internal debate, Wildcat still couldn't convince himself that the blonde from the stationer's shop had stolen his bandolier bag.

After racing from the shop, he had watched her drive away in her fancy black carriage, and thought to himself, *Impossible.* For it was just about impossible for him to believe that the soft, round, bunnylike Lady Pemsley would have had any interest in stealing his *pindachsenakan.* Much less have been able to.

So, upon leaving the stationer's, he had retraced his steps of that morning, wondering if perhaps a strap had broken and the bag had dropped from his shoulder without his notice. But, as inconceivable as it was to imagine that the Pemsley woman had stolen his *pindachsenakan,* it was just as impossible—if not more so—to believe that he could have lost his bandolier bag and not been aware of the loss. His bandolier was the symbol of his manhood, his spirit, his Lenape heritage. He had worn that bag across his chest every day of his life these past twenty years and now . . . Now he was supposed to believe that he had simply lost it?

Rolling his shoulders to ease the tension in his neck, Wildcat plopped down on the edge of the mattress. Beneath him, the bed ropes groaned and grumbled, as if echoing his surly mood.

"Dammit," he muttered, "it makes no sense."

—

What reason would the woman have for stealing his pouch? Obviously she could not have been searching for money, for if one were to judge from her appearance, the lady had money enough to finance her own army. Why, then, would she have taken it? Why?

His eyes narrowed thoughtfully as he caught his rippling reflection in the tiny window glass. *Could it be . . . ?* Had she taken the bag as a ploy to draw his attention? Though it seemed a far-fetched method of initiating a liaison, he had to confess that it would not have been the first time he'd attracted the interest of a genuine English "lady." By his reckoning, it would have been . . . the third? Fourth?

Not that it mattered, he told himself, rubbing his palm across the back of his neck. He had already figured out—courtesy of a promiscuous baroness and her two country-bound friends—that these English "ladies" were not as interested in having sex with a man as they were in having sex with a "red" man. War whoops and bondage games . . . It got to be a bore after a while. And although Wildcat wasn't the kind of man to walk away from a spirited tumble, he did have his dignity to consider. He *was* a Lenape brave.

In fact, more than once during the last months, he had suspected that his aristocratic lovers had been disappointed to discover that, with the exception of his tattooed arms, he was put together just like any other man—white or red. He had no extra appendages, no feathers growing from him, no wampum decorating his private parts. He came with the standard male equipment, capable of performing the standard male functions. Albeit performing them well.

"You know, I bet that's it," Wildcat said, scratching

at the underside of his bristled chin. "That's got to be it."

The Pemsley woman probably stole the bag as a way to draw his interest. Maybe she was planning to pretend to have found the bag lying on the floor in order to force an introduction. Then, when the two officers intervened, she became flustered and gave up on her plan, fleeing the stationer's shop with his bandolier.

Bold, Wildcat thought to himself. *Especially since she had the boy with her. Yet maybe these crazy, rich white women like bold and reckless. That baroness from Edinburgh sure seemed to.*

He shook his head, muttering a softly scornful "women" under his breath.

Unfortunately for him, however, the word "women" led his thoughts to one particular woman, and, against his will, his gaze was pulled across the room to a crumpled letter lying atop his traveling bag. It was the letter from Moonface, Watching Leaves' father.

Threading his fingers together, Wildcat dropped his elbows to his knees and stared at the varied scars dotting his knuckles. Hell, he ought to have thrown that letter away days ago. After all, what possible reason could he have for hanging on to it? Did he need to read again and again—as Moonface had described it—of his "unsuitability"? Of how the Lenni Lenape spoke of Niankwe Wildcat MacInnes as one "lost to the People"?

When the letter had arrived in Scotland a fortnight earlier, he had not spoken of it to anyone, not to Melisande nor to Will. He had simply read the letter—once—and set it aside. A day later, he had then used the excuse of the cask shipment as a means of buying himself some time. Time alone. Time alone to think.

Sighing, Wildcat rose and walked across the room to retrieve the letter, stained and smudged. He stared at the unevenly penned lines for a long moment before slowly crushing the paper into a tight little ball that left spots of sable ink spotting his fingers.

Then, with an unerring flick of his wrist, he sent the balled-up paper through the crack of the opened casement window, watching with half an eye as it rolled down the alley to ultimately land in a fetid-looking puddle.

One side of his mouth lifted in a wry, satisfied grin. *Who do you think you are kidding, MacInnes?*

Admittedly, his pride had taken a blow, but he couldn't in good conscience blame Watching Leaves for having broken off their betrothal. Nearly a year had passed since he'd last bothered to write to the girl—two since last he'd seen her. Had he honestly expected her to wait for him forever? Heck, had he even wanted her to?

If he were to be honest, it was the rejection that had stung, not the loss of the beautiful Watching Leaves. For although born and raised a Lenape in his mother's Turtle clan, Wildcat had never been able to forget that half his blood originated from a strange and distant land far on the other side of the Atlantic Ocean. The land of his father. The land of Andrew MacInnes, the adventurous Scots trapper who had died before ever having seen his son take his first steps.

Throughout his life, Wildcat had told himself that once he set foot on the peaty soil of Scotland, once he'd stood eye to eye with his Scots ancestors, then he would know who he was and where he had come from. But during this last year, he had been to Scotland and had been welcomed by his father's family with open arms and open hearts. Yet still . . . he did not know.

He was not really a Scot. And, dammit, according to Watching Leaves, he was no longer enough of a Lenape. So who was he?

His brow furrowed, he let his hand splay over the empty space at his hip where his bandolier bag ought to have been resting. The bag that his mother had painstakingly beaded and gifted to him on the eve of his manhood ceremony.

He had to get it back. He had to. It represented too much, too much of who Niankwe MacInnes was supposed to be.

In a sudden burst of determination, he turned for the door, grabbing his knife from the washstand in one smooth, arcing movement. By God, he was going hunting. Hunting for a woman. And not just any woman, either, but a small, round white one with quick, slender fingers.

On the other side of town, Valerie Ballatine awoke grumpy and groggy in a strange, cold bed. It took her a few seconds to recall her whereabouts as she rubbed grit from her eyes and wondered at the depth of her unusual lethargy. Blinking slowly, her lashes heavy, she glanced to the far wall, noting in sleepy confusion how the late-afternoon sunshine was pushing stubbornly around the fringed edges of the masculine-looking window hangings. *Masculine . . . ?*

"Oh, yes," she murmured, without lifting her head from the pillow. She was at the Hanover Street home of Christian Morse.

Since Hendrick had been too ashamed of his modest

lodgings to rendezvous there, it had been necessary to find another location for their first romantic assignation. Valerie had flatly refused to go to a hotel, believing rented rooms a banal setting in which to surrender her long-guarded, much-vaunted virginity. And she had refused to meet at her own home, knowing that had Peter somehow discovered them, her brother's misguided notion of honor would have resulted in pistols at dawn and Hendrick's death.

So into the dilemma had then rushed Eleanor Morse, the friend of whom Elizabeth so strongly disapproved, who had arranged for Valerie to use her cousin's town house as a trysting site while Christian Morse was away hunting partridge in the northern hills. It had taken some planning and a half-dozen coded messages carried about town by trusted servants, but a date had eventually been set for Valerie to lose her chastity.

She'd nearly backed out. Dozens of times. But the knowledge that her mother was coming into town had served as an impetus. At any rate, twenty-two seemed as good an age as any to surrender one's maidenhead.

Yet . . . Why couldn't she recall having done so?

Studying the quilted canopy above her, she tried to focus, to reconstruct the inexplicably hazy events of the afternoon.

Their meeting had begun promisingly enough, she remembered: a bottle of wine, heated glances tossed back and forth, followed by a playful disrobing. But then once her handsome Dutch artist had finished his sketching and the business of lovemaking had begun . . . Well, evidently the creativity and passion with which Hendrick wielded a paintbrush were somewhat lacking when the man turned his hand to seduction. In fact—

Valerie glanced to the empty space on the other half of the bed. *Could it be that she had actually fallen asleep during her own deflowering?*

She rolled onto her side. "Hendrick?"

Her voice was swallowed up by the dense damask curtains framing the four-poster bed. *Christian Morse's four-poster bed,* she reminded herself with an expanding sense of embarrassment. Christian Morse, a young man well respected and much admired for his distinguished military record. A man with whom her brother regularly played whist!

Valerie pushed up onto her elbow, her stomach suddenly spewing acid. Good Lord, what had she been thinking? Whatever had caused her to accept Eleanor's offer? Had Hendrick been, in truth, so very alluring or had her motives been less pure? Had she perhaps been trying to prove something to her mother? And how, pray tell, would she ever again be able to look Christian Morse in the eye without simply expiring of shame?

Desperate now to vacate the premises, Valerie lunged for the edge of the mattress. Nausea pushed into her throat, sharp and sour. She groaned, her head whirling in dizzying circles as if it had lost all relation to her neck and shoulders. But she had not drunk that much— had she?

She glanced at the single champagne bottle she and Hendrick had emptied and left propped alongside the fireplace bellows. One bottle. Yet, then, why did her head and stomach feel as if she had just been party to a weeklong bacchanal?

"Hendrick?" she called again, this time more loudly. There was no answer, but for the faint tick of an unseen timepiece.

Without fully understanding her motivation, Valerie peeked beneath the tangled bedcovers. The linens were fresh and unstained. There was no evidence of a maidenhead breached.

Her pulse quickened as her gaze shot to the curved leg of the clothespress where Hendrick had earlier tossed his clothing onto the floor. The clothes were gone, as was his sketchpad—

The sketchpad.

Valerie's blood chilled to instant ice. She knew. Lord help her, she knew.

Her fingers tore at her throat, feverishly pressing up and down the length of her collarbone, searching for a velvet ribbon. It was gone. The ribbon was gone, as well as the famous Ballatine brooch.

She sank back onto the bed, surrendering to her vertigo.

Purported to have been gifted to the family by none other than Russia's own Catherine the Great, the hideously ugly mass of oversized diamonds and rubies was known throughout England as the most prized possession in the Ballatine jewelry collection. And the brooch was especially prized by her mother, Flavia. Flavia, who was, at that very moment, winging her way to London for the Regent's gala ball to be held within the month.

"Oh, hell."

Valerie knew she was to blame. Entirely. It was her fault, her folly. In the middle of the night, she had stolen into Peter's study and snatched the brooch from its resting place in the family vault. She had known full well that she had no business borrowing the jewels; they were not hers to take. But the idea of posing for her artist-lover clad only in the Ballatine gems had struck her as so deliciously vulgar, so wonderfully obscene—it was just the sort of thing her mother would abhor.

And she had wanted to impress Hendrick, to flaunt her wealth and social standing before him so that he would appreciate what a tremendous gift she made in bestowing upon him her virginity. Alas, it seemed that she had impressed him only too well.

Clasping a hand over her eyes, Valerie let out a low, anguished cry. "Oh, Hendrick, you bastard. Do you know what you've done?"

"M'lady."

Elizabeth looked up from the book she was sharing with Oliver, disappointed to feel her son's head lift from the side of her shoulder. "Oliver's time," as she called the hour preceding her son's bedtime, was the high point of Elizabeth's day, a very special time between mother and child that the Pemsley House staff knew was not to be interrupted.

Tonight was particularly poignant, as earlier Oliver had suffered another one of his infrequent, yet disturbing, megrim episodes. When he became ill like that, only Elizabeth was capable of soothing him. She had rubbed his back and pressed cool compresses to his brow and sung to him until finally the megrim had passed. Now they sat side by side, Elizabeth hovering happily over her son as he read to her in his sweet child's voice. Until the interruption, that is.

"Yes, Boyles, what is it?" she asked, unable to keep a note of sharpness from her tone.

"I do apologize for disturbing you, m'lady, but there is a caller who insists upon seeing you on a matter he describes as urgent."

"A caller?" Oliver asked. "At this hour?" He turned

toward Elizabeth, his gray eyes intent and intelligent, and somehow far too large for his little face. "Who do you think it could be, Mother?"

A shiver of premonition shook Elizabeth's spine and she clutched hard to the book in her fingers. "I—I do not know."

"If you will excuse the presumption, m'lady, the gentleman"—Boyles gave a delicate cough beneath his gloved fist—"is not the sort we would normally receive at Pemsley House."

"What do you mean?" Oliver asked. "Whom do we not receive?"

"Ah." Boyles glanced uncomfortably to Elizabeth. "The man is a foreigner, m'lord, and not the—"

"A foreigner?" The light of interest kindled in Oliver's gaze. Earlier that afternoon, he had peppered Elizabeth with questions about the "very interesting" Indian they had met at the stationer's shop. Questions about tribes and weapons and "counting coup" and war parties. So many questions that Elizabeth had ultimately been forced to divert him with a trip across town for a flavored ice.

Since she had no flavored ice readily available, and since Oliver looked ready to hop down from the divan and greet the visitor himself, Elizabeth hastened to intervene. She did not *want* to know who was calling. She did not want to know.

"Boyles, if you say the man is not fit to be received, then he's not fit to be received."

"But, Mother—"

She did not so much as spare a look in Oliver's direction.

"Give the man a guinea and send him away," she instructed the butler, her voice unnaturally high as she made shooing motions with her hand. "Send him away and tell him not to return or . . . *or else.*"

Four

~*~

"*Oh, my goodness,*" Elizabeth gasped. "I vow the periwinkle was not nearly so snug when it was fitted last month."

Holding to the back of a tufted boudoir chair for support, Elizabeth blinked until the stars cleared from her vision. In the mirror, she watched as her sturdy Cheapside-born maid labored to truss her up tighter than a holiday roast.

"Marjorie, do you think Madame Truffaut made an error in the measurements?"

"Aye, she must have," the maid lied with ease. "Those French don't know numbers from nubbies." She gave another forceful—and painful—yank to Elizabeth's laces. "There now, m'lady, don't move. We've got it now."

"Got what?" Elizabeth wheezed. "Cracked ribs?"

Marjorie merely clucked her tongue and retrieved the

periwinkle taffeta for which her mistress was evidently willing to sacrifice the ability to breathe for the remainder of the evening.

"The dress sure is flatterin', m'lady," the maid offered consolingly as she squeezed Elizabeth into the too small evening gown. "You see if the marquess's jaw doesn't drop straight to the floor once he lays eyes on you in this fetchin' new frock."

Elizabeth's lips quirked as she pictured Peter Ballatine's regal and clean-shaven jaw falling to her Axminster carpet. In truth, the marquess's jaw never clenched nor gritted—nor fell—but always held a serene and soothing position beneath a serene and soothing smile. Gawking was not the type of behavior to be seen from the Marquess of Cresting; although, curse her vanity, just once, Elizabeth would have liked to draw forth from her suitor a "jaw-dropping" response. Just once, she would have liked Peter to greet her with a sentiment more impassioned and admiring than "I say, you're looking rather well, Elizabeth."

"Thank you, Marjorie," Elizabeth demurred, running her fingers across the bodice's intricate beadwork. "Even if she misjudged the size, Madame has not disappointed."

The abigail circled around to Elizabeth's front, tugging and tucking as she came. "Eh, now, what's this?" she suddenly exclaimed, leaning forward to peer into Elizabeth's face. "You've shadows under your eyes, m'lady. Did you not sleep last night?"

"Ah, this infernal heat is to blame. I declare I cannot recall when we've had a warmer spring." Elizabeth wafted a hand past her flushed cheeks, sending the scent of her lemon hand cream snaking through the air. "I confess I did pass a difficult night."

Yet even as the words left her lips, Elizabeth questioned the fairness of faulting the unseasonable weather for her fitful rest. True, it had been very hot and she had thrashed fretfully atop the bedsheets for what seemed hours and hours upon end, her mind full, her thoughts agitated. Restless and overheated, she had found herself plagued with worries about the marchioness's arrival and Oliver's departure and Valerie's happiness and . . .

And about a stranger's blue eyes.

"Marjorie." Elizabeth fingered a row of shimmering glass beads along her décolletage. "Tell me, what color eyes would you expect to find on an Indian from the Americas?"

The servant made a baffled poofing sound. "Faith, Lady Pemsley, I haven't no idea. Black, I s'pose."

"Yes, one would think black, wouldn't one? Or brown, perhaps?"

Nose wrinkled in deliberation, Elizabeth glanced to the cheval glass, seeing not her own face, but one harsh and craggy and indisputably masculine—the same face that had risen before her so many times during the night. She had to assume that it was the novelty of meeting such an exotic-looking character that had kept Mr. Mac-Innes's image fresh in her mind. The novelty, of course, and the unanswered question of whether or not he had been yesterday evening's mystery caller.

She had nearly convinced herself that he had *not* been the caller, if only because she needed to believe as much. Elizabeth did not want to imagine that man standing at her very doorstep, that man with his astonishingly beautiful eyes set against that fierce, dark visage. It was a peculiar and unsettling combination, that beauty and that fierceness. A sort of frightening splendor.

Elizabeth's fingers flitted over the beadwork again. "Marjorie, would you describe Lord Cresting as a comely man?"

The maid paused in the act of fastening a tape. "Well, now, I'd say the marquess is pleasin' to look at as far as gentlemen go. He's got all his teeth and his smile is right kind."

"Yes." Elizabeth nodded slowly. "His smile is kind, isn't it? There is nothing frightening about the marquess. Nothing to make a person uncomfortable."

"Not unless buckets and buckets of quid make you squeamish. Speakin' for meself, I've got no trouble with a fella who's plump in the pocket." Marjorie underscored her statement with a familiar nudge to Elizabeth's elbow.

A knock at the bedroom door preceded the announcement that the Marquess of Cresting had arrived and awaited the countess in the parlor.

"Cresting? Already?" Elizabeth tried to spin toward the mantel clock, but Marjorie had her secured by the skirts as the abigail made final adjustments to the silk slip overlay. "Goodness, am I late?"

" 'Bout a half hour now," the maid said with equanimity. "I'd imagine his lordship is used to it after courtin' you all these months."

"Gracious, not again! He must think me completely wanting in manners." Elizabeth tried to free herself, but Marjorie went right on fussing with her toilette.

"You best stop pullin' or this silk will tear," the maid admonished. "Besides, won't do him no harm to sit for a spell. Keeps a man honest. And, if you don't mind my

sayin' so, his lordship has kept you waiting long enough
for an offer of marriage, now, hasn't he?"

Elizabeth's forehead creased, her gaze slanting to the
silhouette of her late husband sitting atop her dressing
table. "I was in mourning," she explained, as if Marjorie
didn't already know as much. "Understandably, Cresting
and I are both very concerned about maintaining ap-
pearances—the very last thing I would want is to appear
insensitive to the memory of Oliver's father."

The abigail said nothing, though she fluffed a bow
with more vigor than was needed.

"That will have to do, Marjorie," Elizabeth said,
breaking free of the maid's ministrations. "I really must
be off or Lord Cresting will leave for the party without
me."

"Do you want me to wait up for you, m'lady?"

"Oh . . ." Elizabeth bit guiltily into her lip, refusing to
look in the direction of the secret compartment. "You
better not—that is, er, no. I will manage on my own
tonight, I think."

After snatching up her cloak and gloves, and casting
a distressed look toward the clock, Elizabeth scurried
from the room, her too tight corset causing her to pant
like a winded hound as she minced her way down the
corridor. She was still somewhat out of breath when she
entered the parlor to find Peter flipping through a book
on Chinese history.

He glanced up as she entered, his long, narrow face
revealing none of the impatience she knew he must be
feeling. He was, as always, attired in the most conser-
vative of fashions and groomed to within an inch of his
life. His sister called him the "professor"—behind his
back—because of his staid dress and intelligent brow,

as well as for his well-documented love of all subjects historical. All in all, Peter Ballatine was the very finest example of a gentleman.

Peter returned the book to the shelf before doffing his high-crowned beaver. "I say, Elizabeth, you are looking well this evening."

She fought the unexpected urge to laugh out loud. Dare she hope her suitor had put more emphasis on the "well" tonight?

"Thank you, Peter. And I am sorry to have kept you waiting—yet again—but time and I never seem to be in accord." She shrugged an apology. "Whenever I believe it should be a certain hour, the clocks want to insist it is another."

"I don't believe it should matter if we are a few minutes late," he answered, crossing the room to assist with her cloak. His movements, she noticed, were economical and clean, devoid of the swagger and strut often seen in the younger members of their social set.

"In fact," he said, taking the cloak from her hands, "we are probably fortunate to have missed the worst of the crush."

Elizabeth smiled. Trust Peter to find the silver lining within every cloud.

"Is Valerie not joining us tonight?" she asked.

An almost invisible tic caught at the corner of his eye. "Ah, no. She's driving with Lady Hughes, I believe."

As his long fingers brushed over her shoulders, Elizabeth was suddenly moved to an act of uncharacteristic foolishness. She did not know whether to blame it on her restless night or on the inexplicable fantasies that had overtaken her lately. But, on impulse, she leaned back into the marquess, affording him the opportunity to skim a kiss across her cheek—if he so wished. Unfortunately, when he did not immediately seize upon the opportunity, she remained too long leaning against him, creating a brief moment of awkwardness.

Embarrassed, she jerked away just as he appeared to grasp her purpose. "I—I—"

He pulled back, covering the moment with his customary ease. "I understand that Lady Hollister is planning a special celebration this evening to honor Wellington's recent victory. What do you think it might be?"

Her cheeks still warm with shame, Elizabeth endeavored to make her response lighthearted. "As long as she does not encourage her daughter to sing for us again, I shall be delighted."

The marquess chuckled and the awkward moment was dispelled.

Nonetheless, during the short carriage ride to Lady Hollister's home, Elizabeth wondered at Peter's decision not to kiss her when she had made it quite clear she would have welcomed his embrace. He *had* kissed her in the past and she'd not discouraged him, even though his kisses had been something less than stirring. Had he, too, been left unmoved by their previous intimacy? Or had he been offended by her forwardness this evening? Or . . . had she merely caught him off guard when he'd been preoccupied by the news of his mother's imminent arrival?

As they stood ready to enter the Hollister ballroom, Elizabeth could contain herself no longer. "Valerie tells me the marchioness is expected into town."

Peter's step missed a beat. "Yes," he confirmed. Though with marked hesitation.

That hesitation, that single second of pause, sent a jolt of alarm into Elizabeth's stomach. Was he having second thoughts about her as an intended? Did he no longer wish for her to meet with the dowager?

Naturally, he can make no assurances, she attempted to rationalize, *and he's too much the gentleman to lead me on with false promises.* After all, everyone knew that Cresting would not marry without his mother's approval, and the mere fact that the marchioness was coming to look Elizabeth over was assuredly a portent for the good.

But then why that moment of uncertainty just now? And why had he not kissed her in the parlor at home?

As she and Peter were swallowed up by the horde of party goers, Elizabeth tried to let go of her concerns, but they proceeded to eat away at her calm, like an insistent plaguing voice nattering away inside her head.

"Oh, dear," she murmured, fidgeting with her ear bob. "Oh, dear."

For as her anxieties mounted minute upon minute, her fingers—God save her—started to itch.

From the deepest shadows of the town house courtyard, Wildcat watched as London's elite continued to pour into the Hollister ballroom, filling every inch of the cathedrallike space with plumed and bejeweled ostentation. Diamonds glittered, as did false smiles, while ladies preened and gentlemen postured. Silk fans did battle with the heat as linen kerchiefs swabbed frequently at sweat-dampened brows, and servants scampered about with chilled champagne to quench the seemingly unquenchable thirst of so many guests.

The windows to the ballroom had all been opened, allowing the delicate strains of the orchestra, combined with the din of conversation, to drift out to the gardens as a discordant clamor of voices and violins.

On the other side of those windows, Wildcat stood. And watched and waited. Waited for a glimpse of the Countess Pemsley.

It had not been difficult tracking her down—in fact, it had been far too easy. A shilling here, a quiet word there, and he'd learned not only her plans for the evening, but also the name and age of her son, the number of months she'd been widowed, the fact that her escort tonight was related to England's foreign minister, and the far more trivial detail that she dined on lamb every Friday night.

Wildcat, a man of few words and even fewer confidences, had been taken aback by how willingly the butcher's apprentice and the neighborhood lamplighter had parted with their information. Generally speaking, Wildcat's facade—the feathers, tattoos, etc.—did not inspire a whole lot of trust in the typical English citizen. (Or in the typical Scots or American, for that matter.) Nonetheless, once the gold had made an appearance, the two men had proved only too willing to tell Wildcat all that he needed to know about the lovely and intriguing Lady Pemsley.

With a small, self-conscious frown, Wildcat jerked at the sleeves of his borrowed evening coat, the black silk fabric slippery and soft between his gloved fingers. The coat, which belonged to his friend Will, pulled at his shoulders and arms, constraining his movements. Why, he wondered, had he gone to the effort to dress himself like some kind of carnival clown? Why had he not simply chosen to linger in the darkness, in his usual buck-

skin leggings and vest, until presented with an
opportunity to speak with the countess?

Although he wanted to believe that, in this setting, the
black coat and cream-colored pantaloons were practical,
serving as camouflage just as his deerskin clothing
would have done in the forest, Wildcat didn't need to
lie to himself. There was a small part of him—a part of
him he scorned—that was curious to mingle with these
highbrow English, curious to take a closer look at a life
so very removed from his own.

Inside the ballroom, the party had begun to spill over
into adjacent apartments as people continued to pour into
the Hollister home, filling the ballroom and beyond.
Rooms, previously unlit along the back of the house, had
started to come to life with candlelight and merriment,
and even the gardens had begun to be invaded by groups
of clandestine lovers seeking shadowed corners.

After barely eluding yet another amorous couple,
Wildcat decided that the time was right to seek out Lady
Pemsley. The crowd was now thick enough to conceal
him, and the spirits had been flowing for over two hours,
deadening wits and clouding common sense. No one was
likely to notice an overdressed half-breed, were they?

Skirting along the rear of the house, Wildcat passed
first a music room and then a study already taken over
by boisterous party goers. The third chamber was as yet
unoccupied, and he passed it by to continue to the one
on the corner, dark with curtains drawn. It took no more
than a second for him to slip through the unlatched window and enter what appeared to be some sort of weaving
room.

As he stepped around two large looms and assorted
baskets of wool, Wildcat recognized the smell of dye in

the air, the pungent aroma reminiscent of his Lenape childhood. His mother, Kschichpekat, had been an expert weaver among their tribe, and often in his younger days he had helped her in the preparation of the colorful dyes.

Occupied by those distant memories, Wildcat was jerked back to the present when the door unexpectedly flew open and, into the room, stumbled a young, well-dressed woman. She appeared to be fighting to regain her balance as if she'd leaned into the door and then had it fall open beneath her weight.

Teetering back and forth, she finally righted herself on the threshold. Her silhouette was slim, her hair a fiery, red nimbus as backlit by the corridor sconces. She went still, suddenly realizing that she was not alone. Neither of them spoke for the space of a few, surprised seconds.

Then the woman giggled, and the giggle expanded into laughter, the sound giddy and uncontrolled, suggesting to Wildcat that she'd been enjoying more than her fair share of champagne that evening.

"My, oh my, what do we have here?" She tittered, listing drunkenly to the side in an effort to peer past him into the shadowed room. "Are you waiting for someone in particular, dark knight, or dare I hope this is to be my lucky evening?"

Wildcat made a hasty move to pass. "Excuse me."

"Heavens, what is your hurry? A moment, please." With a brazenness that perturbed him, she flattened her hand against his chest.

Instinct forced him back a step into the room. Undeterred, she followed, leaving the door ajar and the corridor light full on their faces. An attractive woman, she was nonetheless a bit too thin and sharp-featured for Wildcat's taste.

"I do not believe we have met," she said, her smoke-colored eyes shining bright as she appraised him with open and frank admiration.

"No." He hooked his thumb into the waistband of his dress trousers, his stance wary. "We haven't."

"Are you perhaps a friend of Harry's?"

"Harry?" He squinted his eyes. "Mmm, can't say that I am."

"A friend of Lily's, then?"

"Nope."

"Her sister, Mary?"

He smiled slightly, saying nothing.

"Aha." The woman's auburn brows lifted as she tapped the closed fan against the point of her chin. Curious, her gaze wandered to the shoulder-length hair he'd pulled back in a queue. "So you are not acquainted with any of the Hollisters. How very fascinating . . ."

Wildcat cast a disinterested glance to the tips of his shoes.

"You know, as fate would have it," she said with a sanguine smile, "I actually assisted Lily Hollister in composing the guest list for tonight's soiree."

"Did you?"

"Indeed, and, as I recall, I knew every person on the list of invitees."

Wildcat answered on a half grunt as he mentally gauged the narrow doorway. He had no chance of getting by without first physically removing the woman from where she stood blocking his exit.

"But perhaps I have erred," the redhead said, sliding her fan suggestively along his forearm. "Perhaps you were on the list, and I have simply forgotten. What did you say your name was again?"

"I didn't."

"Oh." Her forehead furrowed, and she feigned a pout. "Dear heavens, I do not know what I ought then to do. If you refuse to give me your name, I must be fairly certain you were not properly invited, and equally as certain that I should not allow you to pass.

"On the other hand . . ." Suddenly her eyes grew round as the tip of her fan settled above his breastbone. "Goodness me, of course! Why, you might be precisely what I am looking for!"

Oh, hell, not another one. He had already played this game and not found it to his liking.

"Indeed, I would imagine you'd have all the qualifications necessary for just this sort of endeavor," she said, leaning close so that her spicy, overblown perfume filled his nose and taste buds, her too bright eyes measuring the breadth of his shoulders.

"Tell me, dark knight," she whispered, "might you be interested in earning an effortless one hundred pounds?"

Effortless? He didn't know who she'd been with before, but "effortless" wasn't a term that reflected well on a man's . . . talents. And he had damned sure never been *paid* for it before.

"Look, lady, no matter what you might think about the way I look, I'm not the kind of—"

"Please." The woman's mood abruptly swung from tipsy coquettishness to earnest desperation as she clawed at his wrist with one gloved hand. "Please, hear me out before you refuse. I am in the midst of a frightful predicament, and I do not know where to turn for help."

Not here, Wildcat thought to himself, her fingers gripping him with a painful urgency.

"A very valuable piece of jewelry has been stolen from me," the woman explained in a breathless rush. "A brooch that has been in my family for generations. It is terribly important that it be returned to me immediately."

Wildcat started to pry her grip from his arm, wondering what manner of woman poured out her woes to a complete stranger. *A drunk one, I guess.*

"Lady, I sure as hell don't know why you're telling me this," Wildcat said. "Two minutes ago, you didn't know me from Adam."

"I know," she agreed, her puppy-dog eyes leaving Wildcat wholly unmoved. "But what am I to do? There is no one else to turn to."

"Well, then I'd say you're in a heap of trouble."

"But I am not asking all that much," she pleaded. "If you could find this man for me—"

Wildcat reared back and she rushed on.

"I can provide you with the name of the thief. And I know for a fact that the man is still residing in London, so it should not be all that difficult for you to locate him." Her powdered nose wrinkled as she confessed under her breath, "Although, blast it all, I have not yet been able to find the wretched creature."

His instant distaste for the woman aside, Wildcat was thinking that her story sounded just a shade too similar to his own. "Wait a minute. You *know* who stole the brooch?"

"Oh, I am certain. You see, the man was a friend of mine. A rather . . . close friend."

From her crimson cheeks and defiantly tilted chin, Wildcat inferred just how close this friend had been. So why the hell was the woman sleeping around with a swindling *sschkak* like that?

"So turn him in to the authorities and be done with it." Wildcat moved to edge around her.

"But, I cannot!" She swayed like a cattail in the wind. "You see, the brooch belongs to my mother. And she is unlikely to be forgiving."

"That's too bad," Wildcat said flatly, edging ever farther away.

"No, no, you don't understand. My mother—" She gave an exaggerated shudder. "Well, she is beside the point because, in any event, I do not dare risk the public scandal of an official investigation nor do I have the time to wait for one. I must have the brooch back in my possession before the Regent's gala."

From the other end of the hallway, voices floated toward them. Wildcat frowned, his patience wearing thin. The way he saw it, he had his own thief to track down and sure didn't need to take on the hunt for another.

"If you would only—"

"Sorry, lady, but you don't know me and I don't know you and this isn't any of my damned business."

He slipped around her, but she grabbed at him with both hands, her fan clattering to the floor.

"I'll pay you whatever you want."

"Sorry." Wildcat tried to shake himself loose, but the woman was clinging to him with the determination of a hungry leech.

"Will you not at least consider helping me?" she asked. "Give my proposal some thought?"

As her alcohol-hot breath wafted over him, Wildcat realized that the woman had drunk enough champagne to float an entire fleet of schooners. Come morning, she wasn't likely to remember having met him, much less having had this conversation. So what did it matter what he told her?

"Sure. I'll think about it."

"You will?" Delighted, she clapped her hands together, finally giving him the freedom he sought.

He darted past her.

"But where shall I contact you? You didn't give me your name and you don't know mine."

"Don't worry," he called back to her, without turning around. "If I decide to help out, I'll be the one to find you."

Five

After the marquess had gone to speak with Valerie about her excessive consumption of champagne, Elizabeth slipped away to loosen her stays, for fear she was about to pass out in the Hollister ballroom. She knew herself silly and vain for insisting on wearing the gown. The entire night she'd done naught but suffer—suffer and worry that her corset would pop under the strain.

Too embarrassed to reveal to her peers the extent of her discomfort, she had eschewed the room set aside for the ladies, and had instead snuck upstairs in the hopes of finding an unoccupied chamber. After fumbling at two or three locked doors, she finally found a guest room at the front of the house that opened to her. Before the door clicked shut behind her, she was scrambling for her laces.

"Bloody hell," she muttered, tearing at the gown's fastenings. "How will I ever get out of this punishing thing!"

"Need some help?"

Whirling around, Elizabeth gasped, and would have screamed had she enough air in her lungs to make a scream possible.

Against the bedroom door—the same door she would have sworn she'd firmly closed only seconds earlier—leaned the mysterious stranger from the stationer's shop. Though he had reined in his long hair and changed his attire, she recognized him immediately. Recognized his falsely casual slumping posture and his strong, unmistakable profile. Recognized his self-confidence and poise and arrogant appeal.

"Mr. MacInnes."

One side of his mouth quirked, either in surprise or amusement that she'd remembered his name.

"Wh-what—" Her gaze flickered over his black evening dress, and she thought that he brought her to mind of a villain from one of the cheap chapbooks Oliver liked to read: A man, swarthy and forbidding, living his life among the shadows.

"Wh-what are you doing here?" she stammered, recognizing how very inane her question sounded.

The quirk of his lips blossomed into a full-blown smile, one that made Elizabeth's toes curl in her satin slippers.

"I think you know."

The force of his gaze was suffocating, stealing what remained of her breath. "I—I have not an inkling."

"No?"

She swallowed, her throat thick and dry. "No."

"Then I guess I'll have to remind you. I stopped by

your house last night. To retrieve my bag?" He made a squarish shape with his large hands. "A beaded bag about this big?"

He looked at her expectantly, one black brow higher than the other. She stiffened her spine—both figuratively and literally—drawing herself up until her corset cut into her sides.

"I am sorry," she said, employing her most aristocratic, lady-of-the-manor voice, "but I do not know *what* you are talking about."

Her patrician manner evidently failed to impress him, for he answered her with a scowl so menacing that the starch drained right out of her spine, settling like a loose jelly somewhere about her knees. Her reaction startled her, for throughout her life, Elizabeth had known many men—some truly evil, terrible men—but never had she come across one quite like this Indian incongruously named MacInnes. He was not evil; her instincts told her as much, despite his fierce demeanor. But he was most definitely dangerous.

And in some way, she sensed, he was especially dangerous to her.

Looping his ankles one over the other, he drew her attention to the long, muscled length of his breeches-clad legs. "Listen, we both know you took the bag and we both know why."

Elizabeth blinked, no longer focused on the fine sculpture of his thighs. Had she heard him correctly? *He knows why?*

"I'll admit you've got plenty to tempt a man," he said, his eyes going soft in the moonlight as they raked over her bodice. "Hmm-hmm, plenty nice *nunagan*," he added huskily. "Particularly in that dress."

She did not require a translation of the guttural and foreign-sounding word as an unwelcome warmth rushed into her chest and neck. *And woman's place.*

"But, tempting or not, it's my bag I want," he said, as if reminding himself of his purpose. "And I want it back. Now."

She swallowed again, unable to locate her voice. Was it her too tight corset or MacInnes's bold stare that had suddenly robbed her of speech?

"Come on, I don't want to play rough with you, but I will if I have to. Now, where is the bag?"

Elizabeth opened her mouth, but no sound emerged. MacInnes's ominous scowl resurfaced.

"I told you, woman, I'm not going to play games. Now either tell me when and where I can pick up my bandolier bag, or I'll have to tell your friend down there about your little tricks."

"F-friend?"

He wrenched his head in a downward motion, his inky hair flickering with sparks of vibrant blue. "Cresting, the *Ingelischman* you came with tonight."

With a tremulous hand, Elizabeth reached out and steadied herself on the bedpost. She could not believe it. She had to be dreaming or in the throes of a nightmare. Her greatest fears, the fears she'd been holding at bay a lifetime, were taking shape in that very instant.

A slow, calculating smile stretched across his sunbronzed features. "You don't much like the idea of me talking to Cresting, do you?"

No! Do not succumb to hysteria, Elizabeth told herself. *Do not lose your head.*

"I am . . . surprised that you know Lord Cresting." More a question than a statement, the evenness of her words was heartening to hear when measured against her damp palms and racing pulse.

"Let's just say I know a helluva lot more than you think I do."

"Oh?" She licked at her lips, her gaze darting in desperation around the four corners of the room. Could he know? Was it possible?

"I'll tell you what, Princess—"

"Countess," she corrected without thinking.

He smirked and folded his thick arms over his coat front, his shoulders bulging wide. "Yeah, all right, *Countess*. So I'll tell you what—I might be willing to make you a deal."

Hope seeped through her. "What . . . what sort of deal?"

She saw his eyes slowly shift lower, fixing to her décolletage with an intensity so potent her body—against her will—leaped in response. Then, to Elizabeth's complete and utter shame, she felt her nipples pucker beneath his heated gaze, drawing tight and full against her bodice, as if trying to reach out to him. Hurriedly she covered herself with her arms, hoping he had not taken notice.

He said nothing, but uncrossed his legs at the ankles, resetting his weight. His expression was unfathomable, closed and unrevealing. She felt as if she did not breathe a single drop of air while awaiting his reply.

"I will trade you my silence for the bag."

His . . . silence? But she had been under the impression he wanted—

Mortified by the direction of her thoughts, she dug her fingers into the flesh of her upper arms. She could not speak. She couldn't. Not if she hoped to hold on to what little remained of her dignity. She gave him a brief, quivering nod of assent.

"Then we have a deal." His eyes were silvery-blue slits as he shoved away from the door, his every movement inexplicably elegant, almost mesmerizing to see.

"I'll come by tomorrow for the bag. Oh, and this time, *Countess*—" He arched a mocking brow while reaching for the door latch. "Make sure that one-eyed lackey of yours knows that Wildcat MacInnes is 'fit to be received.' "

The hinges clicked closed, and for a long period afterward, Elizabeth remained where she stood, the room spinning around her in riotous shades of smoke and lilac.

"Now, there is no reason to fly into a panic, Lizzie," she whispered, twining her fingers in and out, back and forth as she struggled to compose herself. "There is nothing to worry about. Not really. Not yet."

Always in her deepest heart of hearts, she had feared that someday—some terrible, abominable day—she might be caught. It was almost inevitable, really; her own history demonstrated as much. But during these last months she had fallen into a state of false comfort, allowing herself to believe that her skill would protect her. She knew that she was good at what she did. Frightfully good, in fact. However, she was not perfect. She was fallible. As had now been so clearly proven by Mr. MacInnes.

But how? How in heaven's name had he found her out when no one else had? Did his Indian breeding somehow gift him with senses keener than those of the average man? After all, it did seem to her that he was extraordinarily keen and observant—really, how *had* he learned of Cresting? And, even worse, to realize that

MacInnes had followed her upstairs this evening without her having heard or seen him . . . She, who, after all these years, had never ceased to look over her shoulder.

But perhaps she gave the man too much credit. Perhaps it was she who was to blame, she who had slipped up. Was it not conceivable, probable even with the benefit of hindsight, that she had been distracted at the stationer's shop? She had been sliding her fingers along his hip when she'd paused for a second, thinking how wondrously firm the muscles were beneath those deerskin leggings—

"Oh, my."

Pressing her palms to her cheeks, she felt giggles threaten.

"You are the most pathetic of creatures, Elizabeth Pemsley," she whispered. "You've gone so long without a man that you've now taken to fondling your marks!"

The absurdity of it all helped to calm her. The room stopped spinning, the danger of succumbing to hysterical collapse abated. She'd had her moment of panic and now, by heavens, she had to turn her mind to resolving the predicament she'd created for herself. Elizabeth Pemsley was *not* a sniveler. She never had been. Never would be. In fact, if there was one element of her character Elizabeth took especial pride in, 'twas that she was not a whining, mewling, milk-and-water miss. Quite the contrary. She was a survivor, a scrapper. Granted, she had a tendency toward the nervous, but she knew how to carry on in the face of adversity.

If Jake had taught her nothing else—and he'd taught her a lot—he had shown her how to make the best of a bad situation. And frankly, once Elizabeth reconsidered the circumstances, her current difficulty with Mr. Mac-

Innes was not so awfully grievous as it had at first appeared.

Certainly, the man had frightened her by threatening to reveal her secret to Peter; indeed, the consequences of such a revelation were too dreadful even to contemplate. But, then again, she had no reason to contemplate them, did she? All she had to do was give MacInnes what he wanted and he would hold his tongue about her unfortunate little predilection.

His silence for the bag. Simple.

So tomorrow when Mr. MacInnes arrived, she would hand him the bag, and then—*poof!*—he would disappear from her life.

"He did promise to keep quiet," she reminded herself. Therefore she had nothing to fear, did she?

Nevertheless, as she let herself out of the quiet bedroom, her stays as wretchedly tight as ever, one question continued to turn in her mind: could one ever truly trust a man by the name of "Wildcat"?

Thankfully, the following morning, Elizabeth found herself far too involved with Oliver's departure to give Wildcat MacInnes a second thought.

The entire Bedford Square household had been bustling around since dawn in an effort to successfully launch the young Earl Pemsley into the world of public school. Trunks had been inspected not once, but twice, to ensure that enough woolens had been packed since Oliver, according to his mother, was unusually vulnerable to chill. And all manner of stomach-wrenching tonics had been bottled and labeled and packed in paper, in the event Oliver should fall victim to fever, gripe, fatigue, headache, or dog bite. The whole affair made for a circuslike atmosphere that had led Boyles to wonder aloud if they were sending his lordship a few miles away to school or rather off to a lengthy African junket.

"Now, Oliver, while I realize that you will be occupied with your new friends and with learning all sorts of wonderful facts and figures, I do hope to receive a letter from time to time, all right, darling?"

Elizabeth bent forward and smoothed a limp strand of wheat-colored hair from her son's forehead while, in front of the house, the horses snorted in irritation, questioning the many delays.

"You will remember to wear your muffler and—" With an abrupt frown, Elizabeth pressed her hand flat against Oliver's brow. "Boyles! Boyles, come quickly! Does Oliver feel warm to you?"

Her son's eyes rolled to the top of his head, as the butler obediently trotted forward.

"Mummy, I am fine."

"I'll be the judge of that," Elizabeth answered, watching with concern as the butler put Oliver's forehead to the test.

"I detect nothing unusual in his lordship's temperature, m'lady," Boyles announced, wiggling his fingers back into his glove.

"But that's impossible," Elizabeth argued. "I'm certain he's feverish." She reached out to lay her palm once more upon her son, but Oliver intercepted her, gently taking her hand in his much smaller one.

"I don't have a fever, Mummy."

"But, Oliver—"

He silenced her with a look. A sweet, little-boy look that made Elizabeth's heart flip sideways in her chest. A look, full of sympathy and understanding, that said he knew perfectly well what she was doing and loved her for it.

"I must do this," he said with a nine-year-old's stoicism. "And you must let me."

She squeezed his hand to keep her tears from slipping onto her cheeks. She knew that he, too, had fears about going away, but, like his father, Oliver possessed a quiet, steady courage Elizabeth could only admire.

Digging deep, she managed to muster that tight smile mothers reserve for painful moments such as these. "Goodness, aren't you wise? Of course, you must go. I am merely being silly, aren't I?"

He grinned. "I'll miss you, too," he said, just a hint of his old lisp audible in the "S."

He reached for his new hat, a miniature version of a gentleman's top hat that they'd purchased only last week. No more straw for her son. Her little boy was becoming a man.

"Oliver, if you need to come home for any reason . . ."

He shook his head, then stepped forward to hug her close, his thin little arms heartbreakingly fragile around her waist.

"The horses are getting restless," he whispered when she refused to release him.

"Yes, of course." Somehow, some way, she forced her arms to go slack and he stepped back, his gray eyes somber.

"Don't forget to take your tonic," she called as he strode toward the carriage. "And tell Mrs. Warring to order fresh milk at the inn."

He waved. She waved. He climbed into the coach. She cursed the beast who'd first decided children should be sent away for their education.

The coachman snapped the reins and Elizabeth bit hard into her lip, feeling as if the vicious lash had come down on her own back.

Many minutes later, Elizabeth still had her gaze trained to the empty roadway when from the opposite direction came hurtling another vehicle, its iron wheels screeching as if in pain. Even before the coachman's bright livery was visible, Elizabeth deduced by the breakneck speed, that the carriage's occupant could only be Valerie Ballatine.

With a noisy flourish, the landau pulled up alongside Pemsley House, and before the horses had quieted, Valerie was leaping from the carriage, exhibiting a shocking amount of ankle in the process.

"If you've come to say good-bye, you've just missed him," Elizabeth called, blinking away the moisture lingering in her vision.

"Lud, I am sorry! I completely forgot today was the day."

Valerie mashed her bonnet onto her coppery curls to keep it from flying off as she bolted up the stairs, looking about as graceful as a satin-clad water buffalo. Not, Elizabeth privately conceded, that she'd ever actually seen a water buffalo. In satin or any other fabric.

"I have to talk with you, Elizabeth," Valerie gasped, clutching at her friend's wrist. "I apologize. I know this must be a perfectly dreadful time for you, but I have no one else to turn to. No one else whom I trust. Elizabeth, my life is in ruins. Ruins!"

Although Valerie was notoriously prone to hyperbole, Elizabeth saw in her friend's tense features genuine emotion, genuine fear.

"Come in, come in." Elizabeth took Valerie's elbow

and led her inside, where freshly cut bouquets of flowers perfumed the front hall, their fragrance heightened in the advancing heat of morning. "Shall we go into the parlor?"

"As if it matters," Valerie moaned.

While making comforting, if meaningless, noises, Elizabeth guided her friend to a seat on the divan. Before she had a chance to utter a word, Valerie burst forth like a torrent.

"It is just as you warned, Elizabeth, just as you said! My reckless behavior has thoroughly cast me into the briars, and this time I fear there is no hope."

"There is always hope, dear. Always."

"Not this time." Valerie flattened the back of her palm to her forehead in a gesture just this side of melodramatic as she closed her eyes on a ragged sigh.

"Has this," Elizabeth asked, "any bearing on your . . . conduct last evening?"

Valerie's lips pinched with remorse. "I would imagine you refer to my public inebriation?"

"Well—"

"I was so distraught. I behaved terribly," Valerie admitted, thrusting her hand away from her brow. She lifted her lashes to reveal the carmine threads marking the whites of her eyes. "I know I made an absolute cake of myself—would you believe I arrived home without any slippers, my stockings in shreds? Honestly, I cannot bear to imagine what I might have done if Peter had failed to drag me away when he did."

"Yes," Elizabeth murmured, thinking that Cresting had handled the awkward situation exceedingly well. After arranging for Elizabeth to ride home with the Herndons, he had spirited Valerie away before she succeeded in embroiling herself in a bona fide scandal. "Have you had a chance to speak with Cresting? About the reason for your behavior last night?"

"Lud, Elizabeth, I couldn't possibly talk to Cresting about this. It would destroy him. And you know how he abhors anything the least bit personal. That's why I've come to you."

"Of course, darling, of course. What can I do to help?"

Valerie dragged a dejected hand down the side of her face. "I do not know if anyone can help me now."

A fist of fear gripped Elizabeth's heart. "Your plight cannot be as serious as all that."

"Oh, it is. It is," Valerie insisted. "Do you remember the Dutch artist I told you about? The one who was so comely and passionate?"

Elizabeth nodded, not caring for the direction of this conversation.

"And do you remember I had mentioned that we had been secretly meeting?"

Oh, no, Valerie. You didn't!

"Well." Valerie fixed a guilt-ridden gaze to her lap. "I cannot share with you the details—and kindly do not ask me to—but it is extremely important that I locate Hendrick. He has disappeared and now I must find him. Immediately. If I do not—" She buried her face in her hands. "Oh God, Elizabeth, my reputation will be left in tatters."

"Oh, Valerie."

The fingernail of Elizabeth's pinkie finger ended up between her teeth as she asked herself how she could have been so wretchedly careless. She ought to have foreseen this possibility; she ought to have counseled her young friend about the dangers of entering a romantic liaison with a less-than-upstanding gentleman. Admittedly, until now, she had steadfastly maintained a policy of noninterference when it came to Valerie's dalliances, but that was only because she had not believed Valerie would venture so far in her flirtations.

"Are you certain?" Elizabeth asked tentatively.

"Of course, I am certain. Do you think I would accuse him otherwise? The man is a scoundrel, a blackguard, a monster!"

"When you say 'monster' . . . You weren't—that is, he did not cause you *physical* harm, did he?" Elizabeth asked, horrified to think that her friend might have been forced.

"No, although—" Valerie glanced away, her discomfort evident in her reddening cheeks. "I am sorry, Elizabeth, but I cannot speak of it. It is too awful."

"Of course, dear, of course. But what do you plan to do?"

"Be humiliated, shamed, disgraced," Valerie answered with an incongruous flippancy. "As is only to be expected."

Elizabeth lay a comforting hand on Valerie's shoulder. "Perhaps if you were to go away for a while—"

" 'Twould do no good. Mother would find me. She'd hunt me down like the veriest bloodhound, and eat me alive. If only I had more time, but there is none."

Elizabeth's spine craned to a perfect vertical. "What do you mean 'there is no time'?"

"Oh, dear, I haven't told you, have I? We received a message last night prior to leaving for the soiree. Mother is expected this morning, Elizabeth. This morning! In fact, she might very well be taking tea with Peter when

I return. How, in God's name, can I ever hope to keep this a secret from her?"

Looking as if she were about to burst into tears, Valerie clutched a tasseled throw pillow to her chest, hugging it as a child would take solace from a blanket or favored toy.

"This morning," Elizabeth echoed under her breath.

"This morning," Valerie confirmed with a sniff. "And I warn you, Elizabeth: you ought to be prepared. Knowing Mother, she is likely to try to catch you off guard."

"Good heavens, you mustn't be thinking of me at a time like this."

The corners of Valerie's lips wobbled in weepy uncertainty. "I daresay you're right. Particularly since you might no longer wish to marry into the Ballatine name once my blunder becomes public."

"Nonsense. I am not such a fair-weather friend. We simply will put our heads together and determine how best to avoid any"—Elizabeth searched for the right word—"unpleasantness. Have you spoken to anyone other than me about your predicament?"

"Well . . ." Valerie's nose wrinkled as she sent Elizabeth a measuring glance. "I did approach someone. A man whom I recently met. I cannot be sure, but it is possible that he might be able to solve my particular problem."

"Oh, I see." Although she did not condone the practice, Elizabeth accepted that sometimes women in Valerie's circumstances had to marry any gentleman willing to have them. The man might be no more than a stranger, his motives suspect, his character questionable, but if he agreed to take on a wife already of a delicate condition . . .

"Does he know the nature of your plight?"

"Yes, but please don't think it was easy to speak of it. I had no choice but to tell him everything."

"I understand," Elizabeth said. It had to be devastating for a woman as proud as Valerie to find herself in such dire straits.

"At any rate"—Valerie gave a disheartened shrug—"I offered to pay him whatever he wants."

Masking a wince, Elizabeth asked herself what kind of man Valerie was dealing with. "And what did he say to your offer?"

"He said he would consider it and contact me if he decides to help. I explained to him that I've not much time, so I hope to hear from him soon."

"Is there no one else? Another gentleman who might serve as well?"

Valerie sighed. "I would not even know where to start looking."

Elizabeth bit into the side of her cheek. "I wish there was more that I could do."

"You have listened without judgment, without condemning my foolishness," Valerie said, with a small, sad smile, "and that is worth a very great deal." She tossed the pillow aside and stood, wavering slightly as she rose.

"Would you like to stay with me for a while?" Elizabeth offered. "Now that Oliver is away, I should love the company."

Valerie shook her head, her freckles unusually vivid against her ashen complexion. "How kind of you to ask, but I do not wish to drag you too deeply into this unsavory affair. Let us first wait and see if my dark knight comes to my rescue."

Elizabeth did not know the reason, but even after she

had walked Valerie to the door and bid her good-bye, the description "dark knight" lingered in her thoughts. The words haunted her up the staircase and pursued her into her bedroom, begetting images shadowy and indistinct and forbidding.

"What could it mean?" Elizabeth asked as she walked to her open window to glance to the rose-studded garden below, where weaker blooms were wilting beneath the heat of an unusually potent May sun.

Suddenly her vision shifted, as her mind's eye brought into focus the image of a man with broad shoulders, lean hips, and a mane of jet-black hair.

"Dark knight," she whispered.

And there, standing in the warm wash of sunshine, Elizabeth felt goose bumps dance over her flesh.

Six
❦

Wildcat was in a bad mood. A *real* bad mood.

He stood on the stoop of Pemsley House, staring at the shiny brass door knocker before him while, at his back, an undersized, overscruffed mutt barked from the sidewalk in piercing staccato bursts.

His collar damp with sweat, Wildcat stood in the midday sun, gently cradling the hilt of his knife. Already this day, he had been obliged to take one life. He sure as hell hoped he wouldn't have to end another.

His day had begun at sunrise when he'd been wakened by an odd, rasping sound in his room. Still half-asleep, he had snatched his hunting knife from the bedside table in the same instant he located the source of the noise. On the floor under the unshuttered window, a rat, the size of a baby elk, had been busily gnawing away at the edges of his traveling case. With an angry scowl and a snap of his wrist, he soon dispatched the rat to rodent heaven.

Then, following a cold, nearly inedible breakfast at the Scabbard, he had gone to the shipping office to inquire about the casks he was awaiting from Spain. Unfortunately, the half-wits in charge had been unable to supply him with any useful information about the casks' arrival date, other than to warn him that shipments were running late due to the military activities on the seas. As if Wildcat had not figured that much out on his own.

Then, to make his morning perfectly complete, while on his way to Pemsley House, a vendor of spring mackerel lost control of his cart and spilled his fishy goods onto the street, well dousing Wildcat's boots in the process. As he owned only one pair of footwear, Wildcat had no choice but to walk through town, commanding the attention of every hungry feline from Haymarket to Bedford Square.

Therefore, when it came time to strike the knocker upon the door, Wildcat did so with more force than was required. He was determined to retrieve his *pindachsenakan* as quickly and easily as possible, then to find himself some new, vermin-free lodgings for the remainder of his London stay.

The front door swung halfway open, allowing him a brief glimpse of a black eye patch before abruptly the door started to swing shut again.

"Now, wait a minute," Wildcat said tersely, thrusting his smelly boot into the opening to keep the door from fully closing. "Before you get any ideas about slamming that door in my face, *allogagan,* you better go talk to the countess. She and I have some business to take care of."

Through the crack, the eye patch studied him. Murmurs droned from within. Wildcat thought he heard someone pad away, even as the one-eyed butler held securely to his post. Wildcat waited, his foot pinned against the jamb, his shoulder pushed hard into the wood. He was *not* leaving without his bag, dammit.

After a moment, a spattering of whispers could again be heard. At last, the butler stepped aside and Wildcat was grudgingly ushered into the foyer. He gave the servant a thin, triumphant smile.

"This way," the man said, his welcome a few degrees shy of frigid.

Wildcat followed him from the front hall to a spacious study, its lead-paned windows looking out onto the peaceful, tree-lined Bedford Square.

"Her ladyship will be down shortly," the butler said stiffly. "Pray, do not . . . disturb anything."

He shut the door and Wildcat smirked. *Disturb anything?*

After helping himself to a tall glass of hock from the sideboard, he sat down behind the massive Chinese desk that dominated the room like a mahogany Buddha. Its surface, free of paperwork, gleamed with lemony polish. Wildcat kicked his feet up onto the desk, and leaned back in the chair, his gaze drawn immediately to the portrait of Elizabeth Pemsley hanging above the fireplace mantel.

Young—maybe fifteen or sixteen at the time of the sitting—she had been painted standing beside a potted palm, her disgruntled, almost embarrassed, expression suggesting that she'd rather have been hiding behind the tree than posing beside it. With her head tilted to one shoulder, not in a coy gesture, but rather one of youthful impatience, she looked thinner, more gangly. There was also an impudence to her, a surprising brashness visible in the tilt of her chin and bold set of her shoulders. She did not seem at all like a young woman who was destined someday to be a countess; instead she looked like a little girl who had waded through creeks and scraped elbows and knees and rolled around in the mud. She looked scrappy and stubborn and—this he could not quite understand—a little frightened.

He took a long swig of his drink, noticing how deftly the artist had managed to capture her distinctive skittishness, a trait she must have possessed, he assumed, from a young age. Beneath her skirts, her ankle was rolled outward as if she'd been rocking back and forth on her foot; and, in her fingers, a frond of the palm tree was being shredded to pieces.

Wildcat let the cool crystal of the tumbler linger on his lips as he fell deeper and deeper into the painting. There was something in her gaze that spoke to him. He couldn't exactly put his finger on it, but he felt a connection to the girl that had once been and the woman she'd become. Perhaps it was the change he saw in her, the maturation. Or perhaps it was the sense that there was more below the surface than just diamonds and lace. Perhaps it was that small hint of fear—

With a muffled cry, the subject of his contemplation materialized on the threshold in what appeared to be mid-trip. Listing forward unnaturally, her expression alarmed, she was in the act of lunging for the door latch to prevent herself from falling. At the very last second, as her nose looked in peril of being flattened by the floor, she managed to right herself.

"Those slippers still giving you trouble?" Wildcat

asked unkindly, in sarcastic reference to the excuse she'd used for grabbing him at the stationer's shop.

Instinct caused her to glance at her feet as though to blame them for her near fall. "I, um . . ." Her gaze skittered from him to his feathered braid to the dirty boots propped on the desk while she smoothed her skirts with an unsteady hand, the hair at her temple with the other.

Dressed today in a gown of pinkish orange, her cheeks high with embarrassed color, she reminded Wildcat of something ripe and round and succulent that would send juice dripping down a man's chin at the very first bite. *Oh, yeah, I wouldn't mind a taste of that,* he thought. *Maybe even two tastes.*

Assuming a patrician aloofness, undoubtedly meant to put him in his place, she made a visible effort to reclaim her composure. "I see you have made yourself at home, Mr. MacInnes."

"I have," he agreed, hoisting the tumbler in an insincere salute. "Though I should be fair and tell you, Countess, that the mud-and-grass hut *I* called home doesn't quite match up to . . . this."

With a swirl of his wrist, he indicated the luxurious appointments surrounding them: the plush Eastern carpets, the Belgian tapestries, the French brocades.

For a moment, she seemed taken aback, at a loss how to answer him. Her brows furrowing into a pale yellow vee, she glanced from the marble-encrusted fireplace to the Italian statuary, looking as if she did not understand how the pieces might have come to be in her study.

Then, with a shake of her head, she turned her attention back to him, saying in her peculiar, precise way, "I confess, Mr. MacInnes, that I completely forgot about our appointment—I apologize. It has been an unsettling morning and I've only now begun to put my day to rights. I am sure you want to conclude our business as swiftly as possible, so if you will give me a moment?"

He tipped his chin in a gesture that might have been insolent. Or maybe just lazy.

She frowned again and started to turn away, but the sudden appearance of the butler in the doorway drew her up short.

"What is it, Boyles?" Her tone suggested that she, like Wildcat, recognized a certain tension in the butler—a tension the man was trying unsuccessfully to hide.

"M'lady," Boyles whispered, though not low enough to thwart Wildcat's keen hearing. "The Marchioness of Cresting has come to call."

"The Mar—" Blue eyes widened to the size of soup plates. "Here? Now?"

The butler bobbed his hairless pate. "I have put her in the parlor."

"I—oh, God!" The sapphire saucers swung around to Wildcat. He merely took another long, thoughtful swallow of hock, pretending he had not overheard the exchange.

"Very well," she whispered, taking hold of Boyles's elbow. "Have tea brought around to the parlor. I will attend to Mr. MacInnes and be in shortly."

The butler retreated as his mistress had directed while she lingered on the threshold, gnawing fretfully at her lower lip, her fingers curling open and closed at her sides, as if she had completely forgotten both Wildcat's presence and purpose.

When it began to appear that the woman would never awaken from her torpor, Wildcat prompted in a bored drawl, "The bag?"

She gave a start so violent that her blond curls quivered and bounced. "Y-yes, the bag," she stammered. "As I said, if you will give me but a moment."

With an agitated twitch of her shoulders, she left, but only after ensuring that the study's double doors were shut behind her. Slowly, Wildcat drained his glass, his curiosity stoked. *Cresting . . . Oh, yeah.* The caller had to be related to the old starched shirt he'd seen the other night at the party.

Interesting. What was it about the Marchioness of Cresting that had nearly sent Elizabeth Pemsley into a dead faint just now? And, even more peculiar, why did he find himself determined to learn the reason?

Elizabeth flew upstairs to her room, as fast as her corset would allow.

"Such rotten luck," she muttered. "Such blasted rotten luck."

Why could Lady Cresting not have arrived a mere half hour later? Even twenty minutes more should have been enough to see Wildcat MacInnes gone from Pemsley House. But now . . . Now her future mother-in-law sat less than two rooms away from a feather-wearing, tattoo-bearing, knife-toting Indian!

Good heavens, how could she ever hope to explain MacInnes's presence to the dowager? She, a young widow, receiving gentlemen callers without the benefit of a chaperon was a serious breach of protocol in and of itself; but, for the man in question to be someone so obviously and thoroughly unsuitable as Wildcat MacInnes . . .

Elizabeth tore a nail to the quick as she scrambled to open her bedroom door. Within seconds, she had the secret compartment unlocked and the chest lying open on her bedroom floor.

"Beaded bag," she mumbled, "beaded bag. It should be here on top."

Gold watch fobs, silky pillow tassels, and a small sugar box all went flying as Elizabeth rummaged through the chest's contents. She shoved aside scarves and books and buttons; she dug through saltcellars and fans and brushes. She emptied the chest of every single item . . . but could not find a beaded bag.

In utter bafflement, she surveyed the scattered pile of goods. "But 'tis impossible. I am certain I placed it in the chest. Quite certain."

Then where could it have gone?

She peered into the darkness of the secret compartment. There was nothing within but the smell of old air. She ran her hand around all five sides of the nook, but came away with nothing more than a dusty handprint. She grabbed hold of the empty chest and lifted it over her head, shaking furiously until her arms ached and burned. But for naught. All that fell from the chest was a spider the size of a freckle and a loose sequin the color of blood.

The bag had disappeared.

From the fireplace mantel the clock chimed the hour in cheerful, melodic tones that mocked Elizabeth, mocked her plight. Already she had left Lady Cresting waiting for longer than was seemly. She had to return downstairs posthaste and offer the marchioness a proper welcome—but what to do with Mr. MacInnes?

Elizabeth's stomach growled with frustration. Caught between the proverbial rock and a hard place, she knew she had to choose when, in truth, there was no choice.

She had to be rid of that stubborn man MacInnes immediately. If not sooner.

As she sped down the staircase, Elizabeth reminded herself of the enormous significance of her upcoming interview. For months, she had been awaiting this opportunity, had been anticipating the chance to finally secure her place at Peter's side. Her future was at stake—her future and that of her son, as well. Oliver needed Peter Cresting; he needed a man who could be father, mentor, and friend. Protector.

What then did it signify if "the Dragon of Devonshire" proved to be somewhat cantankerous, as Valerie claimed? Very well, so the woman was eccentric, idiosyncratic, perhaps even to the point of being disagreeable. So be it. Elizabeth had experience at rubbing along with people of all sorts, from all walks of life. She would manage. She had to. She would don the role of St. George and slay her dragon, not with a sword, but with charm, wit, and a gentle temperament.

Her spirits thus fortified, Elizabeth marched into the parlor head high, to find the marchioness, not awaiting her on the sofa, but standing at the near wall beside a gilt-framed Gainsborough. She was trailing a gloved finger down the side of the frame.

A large woman, particularly in the posterior region, Lady Cresting was garbed in a satiny puce ensemble that, when coupled with a florid complexion, forced an unfortunate and distinct resemblance to an eggplant. An eggplant adorned in an abundant display of amethysts and diamonds.

It took less than a heartbeat for Elizabeth to recognize that the eggplant-dragon dowager would not be an adversary easily conquered. The light of battle shone in the marchioness's hooded brown eyes as she turned away from the painting, heavily rouged lips pursed disapprovingly.

"Lady Cresting, what a pleasant surprise. I am honored you have come to call."

As Elizabeth rose from her curtsy, she nearly lost an eye as the marchioness thrust the sooty tip of a white glove into her face.

"Disgraceful," the dowager trumpeted. "I have never witnessed the like. You absolutely must see about acquiring better help, Lady Pemsley, for this type of filth is unbefitting the home of a peeress."

Elizabeth's eyes crossed as she tried to gauge the amount of dirt soiling the marchioness's glove.

"And that butler of yours," Lady Cresting huffed, moving away to cast an accusing glare in the direction of the front hall. "I vow I fairly swooned in terror when he admitted me. That cyclopean aspect may serve you well in keeping ruffians from your door, but I should think you ought to employ someone who does not frighten your callers into apoplexy, don't you, Lady Pemsley?"

Elizabeth blinked. She'd not been prepared for such a head-on attack. "I apologize. I have never considered Boyles to be—"

"Of course, you haven't." The marchioness sniffed loudly, drawing Elizabeth's gaze to the globs of magenta rouge ringing the older woman's mouth.

"And can you not see that I am fair to expiring of thirst?" Lady Cresting demanded. "Do you or do you not plan to ring for tea?"

"Tea?" Elizabeth echoed in a flustered daze, feeling as if her ears had just been thoroughly boxed. Until today, she had generally taken Valerie's descriptions of the dowager with a grain of salt, believing the strained relationship between mother and daughter to be at fault. Now, however, Elizabeth was beginning to believe that Valerie had been rather circumspect in her portrayal of the Ballatine matriarch.

Although she had already ordered Boyles to bring in refreshment, Elizabeth went ahead and groped for the bellpull, if only to escape the marchioness's direct line of fire. As she yanked at the braided cord with the force of desperation, the marchioness crossed the room and began to examine the seamwork on the crewel window hangings.

"Abominable," the dowager muttered, tsking beneath her breath at regular five-second intervals. "Why, at ten years of age, I made neater stitches than these."

"I am sure you must have been an excellent seamstress," Elizabeth offered, hoping somehow to divert the woman from her systematic scrutiny of the entire house and its contents.

"Did you say 'must have been'?" The marchioness whirled from the window, an outraged blur of violet satin. "Are you suggesting, Lady Pemsley, that due to my advanced years, I am no longer proficient with a needle?"

"Goodness, no, your ladyship, I did not mean to suggest anything of the sort!" Elizabeth argued, horrified at how the woman had twisted her words. "In fact, Lady Cresting, I would sincerely appreciate any help you'd be willing to offer, as I am hopeless with a needle. Truly hopeless."

"Hmmph, girls aren't taught anything useful these days, are they?" Lady Cresting muttered balefully.

She let the curtains fall from her hand as the maid entered the room with the tea tray. Elizabeth quickly began to pour out, though her hands trembled with nerves. After successfully passing the marchioness a sugar-laden cup of Bohea and two almond cakes, she carefully poured out her own cup. Alas, when she glanced up from her pouring, Elizabeth nearly ruined the moment, coming dangerously close to letting her refreshment plummet to the floor.

Perhaps it was due to steam from the tea or perhaps from the action of sipping at the cup's edge, but the marchioness's generous application of rouge had spread, now surrounding a wide swath of skin around her mouth . . . and venturing even farther afield. Elizabeth did her utmost not to stare, but it was nearly impossible for her to ignore the dowager's oily red lip salve glinting off a few, rather lengthy nose hairs.

Elizabeth gave a subtle dab to her own nose with her kerchief.

The dowager ignored her and took a bite of cookie, adding a smattering of crumbs to the nose-hair crisis.

Elizabeth then attempted a more forceful signal—pat, pat, rub, rub with the kerchief.

The marchioness glared at her beneath her purple-plumed turban. "Is something ailing you, Lady Pemsley?"

Before Elizabeth could produce an answer, a muffled crash sounded from the other end of the house. Elizabeth's spine abruptly stiffened to the point of pain. *MacInnes!*

"I say, what is all that ruckus?"

Elizabeth bolted from her seat. "If you will excuse me a moment, Lady Cresting?"

"Hmmph, I do not know if I should—"

The marchioness was still grumbling and sputtering as Elizabeth closed the parlor door. Halfway down the corridor, she ran into Boyles, who was hurrying from the opposite direction, his cravat askew.

"I apologize, m'lady, but he insisted on searching for you, so I had no choice but to try and restrain him."

"Oh, heavens." Elizabeth pressed her palm to her forehead. "Did he cause you injury, Boyles?"

The butler adjusted his neckcloth. "No, m'lady, for once I was dispossessed of the fireplace poker, I prudently decided to seek reinforcements. Shall I call for the watch?"

"No, no, Boyles, I will take care of this. Where did you leave Mr. MacInnes?"

"In the front hall, m'lady, but—"

Gathering her skirts in both hands, Elizabeth half ran the dozen yards to the cupola-topped foyer, her mind spinning crazily as she wondered what on earth could have happened to the missing bag. She was certain she had placed it in the niche . . .

As she entered the front hall, her peripheral vision spotted Wildcat sitting on the bottom riser of the marble staircase, serenely picking his teeth with the pointed end of a very large knife. He did not appear to have recently been involved in a fray with her butler. In fact, he looked perfectly composed.

"Would you kindly put that *thing* away?" she asked, casting an anxious glance to the corridor behind her.

Calmly he sheathed the knife, its sleek curve catching the sunlight in dazzling flashes of silver.

Elizabeth licked at her lips, searching for the appropriate, and least agitating way, to phrase what she needed to say. "Now, Mr. MacInnes, I want you to know that I fully plan to cooperate with you—fully. However, as it happens, I am entertaining a most important guest at the moment—"

"More important than me?" he drawled, the merest hint of a grin softening the hard planes of cheek and jaw.

Elizabeth feared that her next pronouncement was bound to result in an unfortunate shift of the handsome Indian's mood.

"No, of course not," she lied, tacking on a bright smile. "I certainly didn't mean to measure the degree of anyone's importance. Nonetheless, if you might consider returning later this evening . . ."

As anticipated, the grin swiftly faded from his features, suspicion making his pale blue eyes appear glassy and cold.

"Why would I want to come back later? Just give me the bag and we're done."

A prolonged breath swelled Elizabeth's bosom. This was even more taxing than she'd anticipated. "I am sorry, Mr. MacInnes, but I do not seem to have your bag."

His chin cocked, his silky, dark hair swaying. "I'm sure I didn't hear you right."

"I said . . . I do not have it."

"Uh-huh." He stood, one hand resting very near the site where seconds earlier he'd stowed the knife. "And just what the hell do you think you're trying to pull here, huh, Countess?"

"Please, I would ask you to keep your voice down," she urged, darting another glance to the hallway. "I am sorry. I thought I had the bag, but I do not."

"What do you mean 'thought'?"

An impatient sigh caught near her ribs. This was taking too long. Couldn't the impossible man simply leave well enough alone? Couldn't he understand that she would give him the bag if she were able to find it? And honestly, how much could the silly thing be worth?

"Please, Mr. MacInnes, let us both try to be reasonable about this. After all, it was only some leather and beads." She gave him a flirtatious little smile intended to placate. "Surely I can recompense you somehow?"

His brows dipped low over his eyes, his jaw grew taut, and inexplicably, or perhaps taken from some adventure story she'd once read Oliver, Elizabeth had a sudden vision of this man riding bare-chested into the wind, his midnight hair flowing wild and free, his bloodstained knife clenched tightly between his teeth. It was an exhilarating image. Exhilarating and disturbing.

"Here." She hurriedly unclasped a sapphire bracelet from her wrist and thrust it toward him. "Take this instead."

His eyes fierce and focused, he studied the jeweled piece coiled in her palm, as if trying to assess its value.

"I want my bag."

Blast.

"Lady Pemsley? Lady Pemsley? Where have you gone off to?" an indignant voice cried.

As dragon-y footsteps clomped down the hall, Elizabeth tasted panic, chalky and sour, at the back of her throat. She seized Wildcat's hand, trying to force the bracelet into his fingers as she tugged him toward the door.

"Please," she begged. "Please take it and go."

She fumbled for the door latch.

"Where is everyone? Where have all the servants disappeared to, for heaven's sake?" the marchioness called again, sounding as if she was nearly on top of them now.

Elizabeth's stomach churned as she held Wildcat MacInnes's gaze. He was scowling. Scowling as if he alone understood the true meaning of fury.

"Please," she whispered, the warm breeze taking up her plaint as it whined through the partially open doorway.

To her surprise, he let loose with one of the foulest curses known to man, but she did not even flinch.

"All right," he murmured, leaning so far over her that she felt his breath stir her eyelashes. "I'll go now, but I warn you, Elizabeth Pemsley, I *will* be back for that bag."

Then he stormed out the door. Without the sapphire bracelet.

Seven

~~~

Wildcat had a healthy respect for the power of alcohol, having witnessed time and time again the extraordinary control it wielded over men both red and white. Throughout the years, he had seen friends killed in quarrels over matters as insignificant as the lint on a coat sleeve, if only because a man's sanity and innate sense of self-preservation had been ravaged by the deadly force of the bottle. Therefore, when it came to drink, Wildcat's policy was one of moderation. He enjoyed spirits, but did not enjoy them to excess. Not ordinarily, that is.

Sitting at the corner table of a Cheapside pub later that evening, however, he had to ask himself if on this occasion he might not have exceeded his allowance. He was feeling just a little too loose in his limbs, just a shade too fuzzy in his thinking. And damned if he wasn't halfway to involving himself in a situation that was none of his affair and likely to end in bloodshed.

"C'mon, lad, 'ave a tankard," the burly Irishman insisted again, pushing a mug at the frail-boned youth who had twice already rejected the offer of drink.

"No. Not thirsty," the boy said hoarsely, shaking his head beneath a woolen cap that had to be baking his brain in the oppressive heat of the unusually warm spring evening.

"Wot?" the man asked, glancing around to draw support from the onlookers. "Do ye think with yer fancy accent and shiny boots that ye're too good to drink with the likes of an O'Malley?"

The boy flinched and hunkered down under his coat, as Wildcat tried to gauge just how foolhardy it would be to get up from his seat. He was fairly sure, after watching the Irishman these past few hours, that the man peddled in flesh—either for purposes of prostitution or for those who impressed young men into slavery on the seas. In either case, the lad's future would be taking an unfortunate turn if he fell into the Irishman's hands—an occurrence which, under normal circumstances, Wildcat would let pass with a vague sense of fatalistic regret. After all, he didn't know the boy and it sure as hell wasn't his life's mission to go around saving every *wuskilenno* who didn't have enough common sense to stay out of establishments such as this.

Nonetheless, for whatever reason, be it the quantity of max he'd imbibed or the fact that the lad's gray eyes reminded him of Oliver Pemsley, Wildcat kicked back from his chair with a low sigh.

"Come on, lad, ye've gone and hurt me feelin's now," O'Malley said, swaddling the boy's shoulders with a beefy arm. "And I sure don't much care for that."

"Please." The boy hunched forward. "I'd like to go home now."

"Home? Ach, ye must think yerself quite the—"

"Let him go," Wildcat interrupted.

Though the words were pitched low, they resounded through the room with the impact of a rifle shot. Conversation ceased, tankards stilled in midair. Even the blind man whistling near the doorway fell silent. The proprietor started to reach for a stout cane at the end of the bar, but then appeared to reconsider after sizing up first Wildcat, then the thickset O'Malley. He ultimately chose to beat a hasty retreat to the back of the pub.

"Why don't you go home to your tepee, Indian?" the Irishman said, dismissing Wildcat with an inattentive sneer. "This doesn't concern ye none."

"Maybe not," Wildcat agreed, his shrug dispassionate as he withdrew his knife from its leather sheath. Immediately chairs started scraping over the stone floor as the bar's occupants scurried for cover. "But"—he smoothed the pad of his thumb over the razor-sharp tip— "I've decided to make it my concern."

Indecision rippled through O'Malley's close-set eyes. Then he reached into his coat front and pulled out a stilettolike dagger. "Well, wot do ye know? Ye aren't the only one with a blade, red man."

"No?" Wildcat studied the blade in his hand and smiled thinly. "Even so, I'm willing to bet I'm the only one who can do . . . this."

And with an unpretentious flick of his wrist, he sent the knife sailing through the air to pierce O'Malley's coat sleeve and anchor it, his hand, and the dagger, to the nearby tabletop.

"Blimey," someone murmured.

"Did ye see that? Why, he 'as to be standing a good twenty feet 'way," another man added as people craned forward to better view Wildcat's handiwork.

Ignoring their measuring stares and not-so-quiet whispers, Wildcat headed toward the boy, who looked to be teetering on the verge of a faint.

O'Malley hastily removed his free hand from the younger man's shoulders. "Go ahead, take the lad," he said in a shaky burr. "I don't want no trouble."

Wildcat extracted his knife from the scarred tabletop. "Neither do I," he muttered. But it seemed he'd just acquired some. He glanced to the boy, whose quivering chin was resting on his chest, his angular face nearly obscured by his coat collar.

"Ready to go?" he asked, hoping the youngster wouldn't collapse before they made it out the door.

The lad gave a brief nod, then followed him from the bar, his steps shuffling and swift. He continued to dog Wildcat's heels until they had walked a good dozen yards down the dark, quiet street fronting the tavern. Then the boy stopped. Wildcat might have continued on his way but, as he turned to bid the lad good night, he noticed how, beneath the milky moonlight, the boy looked even younger than he had inside the saloon. How old was the young fool anyway? Twelve? Thirteen?

Hell, the pup doesn't even have any whiskers coming up yet—

"Oh, God, thank you!"

Before Wildcat could jump aside, the lad launched himself forward and wrapped his arms around Wildcat in a fierce hug. A hug with . . . breasts.

What the—

"How did you know where to find me?" a woman's

voice breathed in his ear. "I'd almost given up hope and then when that horrid Irishman tried to force ale on me, I didn't know how on earth I would ever manage to be saved."

Wildcat's stomach sank as the voice tickled at the edges of his memory. Gripping the woman by her bony shoulders, he wrenched her arms from around his neck.

"Damn." It *was* her. It was the intoxicated redhead from the party. Fercrissake, just how unlucky could he be? Or was there more than luck at play here? Was it possible, he wondered, for Watching Leaves' father to have been angry enough to set an evil spirit upon him in the form of this woman?

"I didn't believe you when you said that you'd find me," she said, pulling the cap from her fire-red curls with a nervous laugh.

"Jeez, woman, what are you doing?" Wildcat quickly checked out the empty street. "Do you have no sense at all?" he hissed. "Put that back on!"

As he jammed the cap back onto her head, he dragged her by the arm—none too gently—into the shadows.

Her gray eyes grew round. "What is the matter?"

"What is the matter?" Wildcat echoed in disbelief. The matter was that he had obviously been cursed. First he'd had his bandolier bag stolen by the sexiest bit of woman he'd laid eyes on in decades, then the shipment he was awaiting had been delayed for an indeterminate period, and now this brainless scarecrow of a female kept popping up all over the place. Dammit, it *had* to be a curse.

"Don't you know what would have happened to you in there if that dumb Irishman had figured out you were a woman? Do you have any idea? Hell, it wasn't looking all that good for you when he thought you were a boy!"

A faint grimace wrinkled her overly pointy nose. "Yes, I know it was somewhat risky," she admitted with an irritating lack of concern, "but a friend of Hendrick's had mentioned that he'd frequented that tavern, so I thought—"

"You thought?" Wildcat spat onto the cobbled street, making plain his opinion of her judgment. "Well, let me tell you, lady, going to a place like that is about as far from thinking as you can get. It's stupid is what it is. *Matta wochkwat.*"

Wildcat was angry now as he realized that not only had he been duped into believing her a boy, but he'd also managed to hook himself up again with this crazy-ass woman.

"I—I don't understand. Why then didn't you stop me from going into the tavern? Weren't you following me?"

"Following you?"

She gave a confused rub to the elbow he'd manhandled. "I—I assumed you had to be, or how else would you have known where to find me?"

Holy *muitschi*. She actually thought he'd been looking for her. Admittedly, he had told her he'd contact her if he decided to join the search for her missing jewelry. But that was hardly the case.

"Look, lady, I gotta go. But do yourself a favor and, in the future, stay out of places like that, all right?" He started to turn away, but she seized the frayed fringe of his deerskin vest.

"But don't you understand? I can't stay out of those places! If it means searching every tavern and brothel in London, I *will* find Hendrick. I must."

Wildcat was about to tell her that it was only a piece

of jewelry, hardly worth risking her life over . . . Then he remembered similar words being tossed at him that morning by Elizabeth Pemsley.

"Please, you have to help me," the redhead entreated, falling to her knees in a theatrical stunt that nearly had Wildcat laughing out loud. "I can tell that you must be a man of honor to have come to my rescue as you did—I ask you, how in good conscience can you walk away, knowing that without your assistance, I will have no choice but to endanger myself yet again? Perhaps even meet my death?"

Wildcat eyed her evenly. The woman was maneuvering him into a corner with her dramatics, and he didn't much enjoy being played for a fool. However, at the same time, he knew that a few hours hunting for this jewel thief would not inconvenience him to any great extent. After all, the cask shipment still hadn't arrived and he sure as blazes wasn't going to leave London until he'd reclaimed his *pindachsenakan* from the lovely Lady Pemsley. Hell, the hunt for her thief might even provide a diversion.

"Is the brooch really that important?"

"Oh, yes! Terribly important. My entire future depends on it."

Wildcat glanced down the alley and swore under his breath. If the woman was, in fact, an evil spirit sent by Moonface, surely she would leave him in peace once he performed this labor for her.

"Look here, I've got some business of my own to take care of—"

Hope lit her dusky gaze as she heard capitulation threading his voice.

He sighed and jammed his hands under his arms. "So tell me what you know about this Hendrick."

But a few hours later, Elizabeth and Peter were bidding each other good night, following an excruciating and interminable dinner in which the marchioness had found fault with everything from the squeaky dumbwaiter to the angle at which the beans had been sliced. Fortunately, however, since they had dined at the Ballatines' home, Elizabeth had come to realize that Lady Cresting's criticisms were not reserved for her and her alone. Even the oft-lauded Peter had been soundly chastised for his choice of cravat pin, which had eventually led to him going upstairs between removes to replace the offensive clip.

Valerie had left a note, claiming a previous dinner engagement, thereby leaving at table only the marchioness, Peter, Elizabeth, and the marchioness's hard-of-hearing cousin and companion, Lady Fillig. At least a dozen times throughout the never-ending meal, Elizabeth had cast a wistful glance to the Lady Fillig, whose serene smile never seemed to waver, no matter how stridently Lady Cresting decried the deplorable state of the Regency, the church, the institution of marriage, and so on and so forth.

"Mother is a woman of strong opinions," Peter acknowledged as he escorted Elizabeth to her carriage under a warm, nearly moonless, sky. "As you may have noticed, she is not afraid to share those opinions."

Elizabeth murmured her accord, thinking that Peter Ballatine had to be the uncrowned master of understatement.

"She can be difficult," he went on. "At times, very

difficult, as Valerie has surely informed you. But I would ask, Elizabeth, that you try to be patient with her if you can. She is not called the Dragon of Devonshire for nothing, I know," he said on a quiet, self-conscious laugh. "Yet when I recollect how strong she had to be in the years after Father's death . . ."

Remorse stabbed at Elizabeth. "Oh, Peter, you are so very good. Always you seek the finest in people whom the rest of us are too quick to judge. You shame me."

He shook his head, his thinning strawberry-blond hair reflecting the light of the gas street lamps. "Kindly do not make me out a saint, Elizabeth dear. I am merely a man who is fond of his willful old mother."

"And I can think of little else to more highly recommend a gentleman. Why, I may only hope that when I am aged and opinionated, Oliver is as fine a son to me as you are to the marchioness."

Peter bowed and bent over her hand to brush it with his dry lips. Elizabeth had to assume that the footman's presence thwarted any greater show of affection.

The carriage door stood open and waiting, but Elizabeth lingered at Peter's side, eager for one tiny morsel of reassurance. She had been a mass of nerves all evening, desperate to learn if she had thoroughly bungled matters that afternoon.

"Peter, I am not certain I made as splendid a first impression as I might have earlier today," she said, her palms starting to itch. "Did Lady Cresting happen to say anything to you about her visit to Pemsley House?"

Peter smiled and patted her hand with a fatherlylike regard. "There is no need to fret, Elizabeth. I am convinced Mother will come to admire you as much as Valerie and I both do."

"Come" to admire? Oh dear, had Lady Cresting spoken ill of her? Had the marchioness perhaps seen Wildcat MacInnes taking his leave?

She wanted to question Peter at greater length, but he handed her up into the carriage, cutting off any chance for further conversation. Elizabeth wished that she felt more comfortable in pressing the issue. For although Peter was the most amiable of men, he was not easy to get close to, holding himself in reserve, uneasy with intimacy.

As Elizabeth craned her neck to glance back at the Ballatine home—and Peter standing at the curb—she noticed that she was once again gnawing at her nails. Through her silk gloves. *No, no, no,* she scolded herself, glaring at the ragged fingertips. *I hereby make a conscious decision to stop this!*

For months now, she had been slowly slipping deeper and deeper into a whirlpool of anxiety as she fretted over her prolonged courtship with Peter, the difficulties of raising Oliver alone, and now, the final straw, the horrific crisis in which her dearest friend presently found herself. And as the tension continued to mount, not only did Elizabeth's waistline continue to expand, but there was also that other rather unpleasant manifestation of her nervous condition that she simply had not been able to get under control—

"Oh, my goodness!"

Elizabeth's gaze shot to the reticule lying on the seat beside her as a sudden and dreadful realization struck.

"Oh, no, I couldn't have!" she murmured, her breath fast. "I couldn't have!"

Yet . . . had she?

With mounting trepidation, she lifted the purse from

the red velvet bench, cautiously measuring its weight in her palm. The reticule *did* feel heavier than it had when she'd left home that evening.

She nibbled at the corner of her lip for a long moment, afraid to learn the truth. Then, with slow, deliberate tugs, she pulled at the silken strings . . .

A small, sharp-edged object tumbled into her lap.

"Blast."

Tilting her head back, she gazed in defeat at the carriage ceiling above. She did not need to hold the object up to the coach lantern to know what it was she held—it was a very distinctive, ivory-inlaid snuffbox that she'd seen Lady Fillig use earlier in the evening.

She had done it again.

"Why?" she asked the empty carriage. "Why? What manner of person steals a snuffbox from such a sweet little old lady?"

From the depths of Elizabeth's conscience, a reproachful voice questioned: *And you believe yourself worthy of a man like Peter Ballatine?* She, who pickpocketed articles from his godmother!

Yet, did she not believe Peter to be precisely the antidote she needed to cure her of her ills? Peter Ballatine, the most honorable, upstanding gentleman she'd met since her late husband passed from this earth? Surely he, if anyone, would make a better woman of her just by the fine example he set. After all, while Oscar—wonderful, caring Oscar—was alive, Elizabeth had not suffered from this nasty little habit of hers. In fact, it had only surfaced in the months following the Earl Pemsley's death.

Therefore, was it not natural to assume that the habit would disappear once she was securely settled again?

Truly, just the knowledge that Oliver had such a man as the Marquess Cresting for a role model would go far to relieving her of her anxieties. And as her worries abated, so would her predilection for pinching.

Surely.

Elizabeth knew she ought to be able to curb these impulses on her own, if for no other reason than to safeguard the Pemsley name for Oliver. Why, if she were ever to be found out, the scandal would be devastating, haunting the family for decades to come. It would mean social ruin, perhaps complete ostracism from the *ton*. It would mean the worst sort of disgrace for both her and her son—a disgrace for which she would never be able to forgive herself. Never.

Unfortunately, however, the fear of discovery did not serve as an incentive to stop stealing, Elizabeth had come to realize; rather, the fear acted as yet another reason to pickpocket. Worrying about discovery was actually feeding her need to pinch things. The more she fretted about being found out, the more she stole. It was like the tales she'd heard about the dangers of quicksand: the harder one struggled to free oneself, the more deeply one sank into the mire.

And Elizabeth was sinking. Sinking fast.

She blew out a long, shallow breath, casting a glance of resignation at the evidence in her lap. What was done was done. Of course, she regretted her slipup, but she saw no reason to continue to fret when the fretting would only exacerbate her condition.

Upon returning home, she was headed upstairs to "dispose" of the snuffbox, when Boyles intercepted her in the foyer.

"M'lady, might I have a word?"

"What is it, Boyles?" Already overwrought, Elizabeth heard her shrill tone, suspecting that she must sound positively mad to those around her.

"It concerns the upstairs maid we discharged last week. Hattie Sparks?"

Elizabeth's fingers clenched on the balustrade. "What about her?"

"The girl's mother came by today." Boyles adjusted his eye patch. "She was rather distraught."

"Why should she be? We gave the girl a month's severance pay and a glowing reference, did we not?"

"Yes, ma'am. But she has not yet found another position, and the mother wanted to know why we had let her go."

The muscles in Elizabeth's throat spasmed. The girl had been dismissed because, while chattering away in Elizabeth's bedroom one day, she'd mentioned that she had a brother Billy who'd run afoul of the law during his youth. Now, logically, Elizabeth realized that London was an enormous city; there might have been literally dozens upon dozens of Billy Sparkses running around town. But that name was a name from her past. And it mattered not to her whether Hattie's Billy was the same Billy Elizabeth had known or not. The threat of exposure had been too great.

"As I said last week, Boyles, 'twas no fault of Hattie's. I simply was not comfortable with her. Pay the girl another month's salary and then see if Lady Hollister has need of a chambermaid, will you, please?"

"Very good, ma'am."

But it *wasn't* very good, Elizabeth decided as she continued upstairs. It wasn't good at all that her secrets had cost the young chambermaid her position.

Tomorrow, she promised, *I'll ask Boyles to make it three months' salary.*

After regretfully adding Lady Fillig's snuffbox to her ignominious collection, Elizabeth resolved that this night's sleep would be a restful one. No worrying over marriage proposals or dismissed chambermaids or little boys away at school. No fretting over reckless friends, impossible marchionesses, or captivating Indians. Tonight she would corral all of her concerns into one corner of her mind, then close the door upon them.

This fretting had to stop.

With that determination, she clambered into bed and doused the lamp. And then she tossed. And she turned. And she kicked at the bedsheets. London's unseasonable heat had yet to run its course and this night was as unbearably hot as the three that had gone before it.

Finally, after many long, uncomfortable minutes, Elizabeth sat up and pulled off her nightrail. The gown's absence provided just enough relief to allow her to fall asleep. She was hovering on the very threshold of sweet slumber . . .

Eight

ᴖᴖ

Terror jolted her awake. A movement. A shadow.

Elizabeth opened her mouth to scream, when a large, strong hand clapped over the bottom half of her face. She jerked her head to the side, attempting to dig her teeth into the intruder's fingers, as she struggled up from the pillows, arms thrashing out every which direction.

"Be still," the man hissed, his flat, American accent causing her eyes to dilate with sudden recognition.

She did as Wildcat asked, and went still.

"I'm going to remove my hand," he whispered at her ear. "I don't want any yelling, understand?"

She nodded, vaguely aware of the smell of raw leather that clung to his hair and the scent of spirits on his breath. Very slowly, he pulled his palm from her mouth. In the ensuing silence, Elizabeth could hear her heart hammering like the sound of a thousand drums.

"You were expecting me, I see?"

The question hinted of amusement, an amusement that seemed jarring and out of place compared with the fright Elizabeth had just experienced. It was not until her eyes adjusted to the dimness that she perceived the reason: his gaze was trained directly on her exposed bosom.

She gasped and scrabbled for the bedsheet, drawing it up to her chin so tightly her knuckles ached. To her utter mortification, when she finally mustered the courage to look back at him, he was smiling a luminescent, white smile, as if vastly entertained by her show of modesty.

"A-are you mad?" she asked, taking refuge in outraged indignation. "What can you be thinking to trespass here?"

"I'm thinkin' I like the view," he drawled, his smile widening to wolfish proportions.

A chill shimmied up Elizabeth's spine. This man— this wholly dangerous man—had broken into her chamber and was now sitting upon her bed, his knee pressed close to the side of her thigh, with only a gossamer layer of cotton lying between them.

"But this is outrageous! Do you not realize that you could be hanged for this?"

"Oh? You mean like they hang folks for stealing?"

Her fingers convulsed on the border of the sheet. In the darkness, he was all shadows and planes and a man's musky heat.

"Wh-what do you want?" she asked, although she knew perfectly well the answer.

"I want what's owed me, Elizabeth."

She drew in her breath, shocked by his use of her given name and equally shocked by how pleasant it sounded on his lips. She might have objected to the familiarity if not for the vulnerable position in which she found herself at the moment.

"I told you," she said, drawing her braid over her shoulder with a nervous tug. "I do not have the bag."

"You had it two days ago," he answered, leaning closer, so that his long, inky hair caressed the dark stubble at his jaw. "Do you really expect me to believe you don't know where it is now?"

Suffocated by his nearness, Elizabeth wanted to scoot back and away, but her sheet was trapped beneath him, stretched as far as it would go.

"Please, believe me. I would gladly give you the bag if I could. But I cannot."

"You cannot," he repeated flatly, his hand snaking out to flick the thick braid back over her shoulder. She fought a shiver as his callus-rough fingers wandered across the sensitive flesh of her upper arm.

"Do you know what it is you stole from me, Elizabeth Pemsley?"

"I—" She licked at her lips. His hand traveled lower to the soft spot inside her elbow.

"Did you know that I am half Lenape Indian?"

Oh, God. She was having trouble breathing.

"I assumed—that is, your hair and . . ." Elizabeth lost her train of thought when he shifted even farther forward, the motion uncanny in its lightness and ease.

"Where I come from," he said, "a debt cannot be left unpaid."

"But I offered you the bracelet," she rushed to point out, although her voice sounded weak and unsure. "And I do have other jewelry. Diamonds, opals, sapphires, whatever you would like."

He made a show of appearing to consider. "Trinkets don't really interest me."

Panic flitted along Elizabeth's nerves. She ought to shove him away. She ought to push his hand from her elbow and scream until her lungs bled. "You do appreciate," she said, with a confidence she did not feel, "that I could call for help, and a half-dozen people would be here in the blink of an eye?"

"Yes. I know."

And he was not in the least frightened by the fact, she realized. Could it be because of that knife he wore so brazenly on his hip? Yet his confidence, his self-possession, was due to more than merely a weapon—that much was clear. Wildcat MacInnes was quite comfortable being Wildcat MacInnes.

"Wh-what do you want?" she repeated.

His hand dropped from her arm to rest on the mattress near her bent knees. "You have taken something of mine. Now I must take something of yours."

She made a muffled noise that he mistook as a question.

"You know what I want, Elizabeth."

"I cannot possibly!"

He shrugged, rolling his muscled shoulder in a slow, fluid arc. "Very well. However, in my experience, I've learned that a woman who is trying to keep secrets doesn't usually have a lot to bargain with." His gaze fell conspicuously to her barely concealed breasts. "But then again you've got more to bargain with than most."

She splayed a hand at the base of her throat. "You would blackmail me?" she asked brokenly, thinking of Peter-the-Perfect-Gentleman and knowing that this man

MacInnes was no gentleman. And never, ever would he be.

"Not blackmail—such an ugly word, isn't it? I prefer 'restitution.' But if you would rather, you could hand over my bandolier bag right now, and I will go. Never to be seen again." He stretched his arm outward, inviting her to search her bedroom one last time. As he did so, she noticed the bizarre geometric pattern of tattoos decorating his wrist and forearm.

"You know I do not have it. I have told you so over and over again."

"Then"—he brought his nose almost to hers, his ebony braid swaying like something alive and sinister—"I shall have to claim my repayment."

A hundred images flashed through Elizabeth's mind then, a hundred images both past and present, joyous and sad. She saw a young towheaded girl, lost and uncertain. She saw a new mother, weeping in wonderment as she cradled her firstborn child in her arms. She revisited her son's first, faltering steps, and the memory of two lone figures standing beside a freshly covered grave . . .

The pictures ran together like watercolors, blurry around the edges, yet somehow stunningly vivid in her mind's eye. And in that instant, Elizabeth knew that she stood at the crossroads of a very important decision. A decision that would forever mark her life as it had been before that moment and afterward.

She *could* end the charade. She could end it here and now. She could call out for help, knowing that she would then be exposed and forced to face the consequences of her thievery.

But Oliver . . . My hopes for his future . . . The consequences were not hers and hers alone to face, now, were they? She had to think of her son. Could she bear for him to be marked by her weakness?

And, an insidious voice asked from within, would it be so terribly difficult to surrender? To give herself up to this man who was unlike any other she'd ever known? In all her years, she had known intimacy with only one man, lain only with her husband, kind, gentle—apologetic. What would it be like to be with someone else? Someone whose eyes plundered her soul and secrets?

Slowly, purposefully, Elizabeth allowed her lashes to flutter closed. In those few, interminable seconds that followed, her senses felt tuned to their highest pitch, keener than she could ever remember them being before. She heard the velvety swish of deerskin fringe brushing across the satin trim of her counterpane. She smelled not only the lingering scent of leather in his unbound hair, but also the hint of cheap lye soap underlying the leather. She tasted on her tongue the first whiff of his breath, faint and warm and whiskeyed, as it drew close enough to stir the fine hairs at her temple.

Elizabeth squeezed her eyes more tightly shut.

Lips, surprisingly soft, winged across the curve of her upper cheek. She gasped, astonished to recognize that the tension shooting through her did not arise from fear, but from some other emotion long dormant. Some other emotion she was too terrified to name.

Staggered by that realization, Elizabeth nearly forgot to breathe as his lips drifted lower and pressed a moist, lingering kiss to the corner of her mouth. She clenched the sheet in desperation, her fingers shaking uncontrollably. Shaking with the need to clutch his shoulders and draw him closer.

What am I doing, what am I thinking? she asked herself.

She ought to be repulsed by this stranger's advances. She ought to be paralyzed with dread, fearing, if not for her life, for her reputation, her virtue. Yet, she was not.

Why not?

Perhaps because none of this felt real to her—it was like a dream. A dark, misty dream. With her eyes closed, she could pretend that this man was merely a fantasy, a product of her overheated imagination, a mirage she'd concocted during too many long, lonely nights.

She knew it was wrong, but the knowledge made the dream only sweeter and more intoxicating.

He pressed kisses to either corner of her mouth, before fully taking possession of her lips, pushing her back onto the pillows as his tongue pushed into her warmth. She jerked with shock—and pleasure—when his palm greedily molded her breast.

This is wrong, her conscience cried.

Yet, God help her, it felt so right. So damnably right.

She let her body go pliant beneath him, let his tongue ravish her mouth, let his fingers knead her softness. She abandoned herself to sensation, telling herself she was safe here in the shadows.

Then . . . there was a coolness, a loss of body heat, an absence of touch. She lay there, her breathing labored, her thoughts in chaos. Cautiously, she opened her eyes, her gaze searching the darkness. The window hangings undulated as if they were waving a good-bye.

She did not at first believe it, but as the minutes passed, she had to accept that he had gone. He had left as quickly and silently as he had come.

Releasing her grip on the bedsheet, Elizabeth brought

her trembling fingers to her lips, feeling the blood pulse beneath their throbbing surface.

Was her debt now paid?

In the alley behind the Pemsley town house, Wildcat leaned back against a brick wall and closed his eyes to the sweltering spring night. His brow and nape were sticky with perspiration, his lungs tight and constricted.

"*Mitsui*. What the hell is the matter with me?"

Already this evening, he was guilty three times over of committing acts of utter and complete madness. Granted, the first offense—the overindulgence in whiskey—might have contributed to the other two lapses of judgment, he decided. Because, if not for the whiskey, he probably never would have agreed to help that crazy redhead, and he surely would not have done the damn-fool thing he'd just done.

After all, he had not gone to Elizabeth Pemsley's room with the intention of making love to her. *Hell, no*. His goal had been to give the little snow princess a scare, to frighten her a bit, in the hopes she might then "remember" where she'd hidden his bag. But something had gone wrong with his plan. Distracted by her breasts, as full and round and smooth as a harvest moon, he'd forgotten his purpose. Forgotten everything, in fact.

He wiped the back of his hand across his damp forehead, savoring the memory. His breath released in a long, shallow *whoosh*, and a tomcat on the other side of the alley answered with an unfriendly hiss.

Yes, indeed, finding Lady Pemsley in her "natural" state had been a most pleasant surprise. Or . . . had it been a surprise? Could it be that this was all part and parcel of the lady's game?

"First, she steals my bag, then pretends to have lost it," he explained to the disinterested cat. "Then, when I come for the bag in the middle of the night, I discover my charming pickpocket conveniently unclothed."

Why, even her threat to scream for help had proved to be false. For, as soon as he'd kissed her, she'd stopped struggling, her resistance melting away to nothing but soft moans and hushed whimpers. In truth, she had begun to respond to him, hadn't she? Her sweet tongue tangling around his, her breast swelling in his palm . . .

"But wait a minute—"

How could the woman possibly have known that he was planning to sneak into her room tonight? She couldn't have known. Yet might she have suspected? Hoped?

"Ah, jeez, who knows?" he muttered to himself. "I've no idea how the upper class thinks." Particularly the *females* of the upper class.

It could be that Elizabeth Pemsley really had lost his bandolier bag. But then again maybe she hadn't. Maybe she was keeping the bag as bait to force a liaison, an affair for which she wouldn't have to feel responsible if he were to "push" his attentions on her.

But did he think her that cunning, that calculated? Not really. Nonetheless his instincts told him that there was more to Elizabeth Pemsley than met the eye. She was a mystery, his countess. A mystery to be plumbed.

And whatever the mystery, Wildcat sensed that solving it would involve his treading into dangerous waters. A tempting morsel of a countess who was involved with a powerful and wealthy marquess who just happened to be related to the foreign minister of England . . . Yeah, perhaps the safest course was simply to forget the bag and to forget Elizabeth Pemsley.

Yet, as Wildcat lifted his gaze to the countess's bedroom window, her lily-of-the-valley scent seemed to rise up again to haunt him.

Oh, what the hell, he thought as he shoved away from the wall. Since when had he ever been smart enough to choose the safe course?

Nine

༩

"*M'lady, shall I* ask Allen to send the horses back 'round to the stables?"

Seated in her husband's chair, Elizabeth gave a startled jump as she glanced to the study doorway. She had been so thoroughly mired in her own chaotic musings that she'd completely failed to hear the butler enter the room.

"I am sorry, Boyles. What was that? About the stables, you say?"

"Your visit to the sanitarium, Lady Pemsley. Will you not be going this week?"

Goodness. Could it be Thursday already? How could she have forgotten? Then again, in light of all that had happened this turbulent week, how could she possibly have hoped to remember?

"No, I mean—yes. Yes, I am coming." She rose with

a flustered shake of her head. "I need only to fetch a parcel from my sitting room and—"

"This parcel, m'lady?"

The butler indicated the large, banded hatbox he was holding in his hands.

"Oh, yes. Thank you." Elizabeth flushed to the roots of her hair, convinced that the servants were bound to believe her an exquisite nodcock if she continued to go about as if in a mesmerist's trance. "Have I kept the horses waiting long?"

"No longer than is customary, m'lady. I don't anticipate you'll have any difficulty arriving at your normally appointed hour."

Elizabeth looked around somewhat helplessly. "Now if I could only recall what I did with my gloves and bonnet—"

She bit her tongue when she realized that both articles were prominently displayed atop the hatbox Boyles was holding out to her.

"You'll have to excuse me, Boyles," she mumbled as she donned her veiled bonnet with more haste than grace. "I don't seem to be myself of late."

"You need not apologize, your ladyship. We've all of us felt the absence of the young earl."

The absence— Elizabeth thought shame might shrivel her up to the size of a dried pea. Here her staff believed her to be pining away for her son's company when, in fact, she'd spent the entire morning in the study thinking of nothing but a certain pale-eyed, dark-haired stranger. A stranger who, last night, had awakened in her sensations that were as foreign to her as he was. Sensations she had found at once intriguing, stirring . . . and terrifying.

Even as the Pemsley carriage conveyed her across town to Mr. Morgan's exclusive, privately funded sanitarium, Elizabeth could not stop questioning what had passed between her and Wildcat MacInnes the previous night. She wanted to blame the strain of recent events. She wanted to believe that her response was singular, a result of too many emotions coming to play in too short a period. For, really, how else might she explain such intensity of feeling? How else to explain the ease with which she'd thrown away propriety, caution, and virtue?

Granted, in recent weeks, she had secretly begun to worry that life was passing her by. After dedicating the last dozen years of her existence to husband and son, Elizabeth did not know what to do with herself now that the two were gone. Oliver, of course, was not gone forever. He would return from school during vacation and holidays and such. But someday—someday sooner rather than later—she would wake up and discover that her little boy was a man. A grown man who had no need of a mother hovering over him like a fidgety hen. And then what would be left for Elizabeth?

Although Valerie had advised her any number of times to cast aside the proverbial widow's weeds and have an adventure or two before it was too late, Elizabeth paid no heed to her friend's counsel. After all, Valerie Ballatine, though eminently endearing, was far from Elizabeth's idea of an exemplar of ladylike comportment. Never would she, the Countess Pemsley, dare dabble in the sort of reckless, mindless adventures Valerie engaged in. *Heavens, no.* Never.

But what, she asked herself, of a teeny tiny adventure?

The danger of entertaining such thoughts, Elizabeth realized, came not from the threat presented by Wildcat

MacInnes, but from within herself. At one time, she had known adventures aplenty, had been infamous in certain circles for her daring and impetuosity. But those days were long gone and Elizabeth was afraid to let down the barriers that separated now and then, afraid to open that door to the past. Vigilance was her watchword. She had to guard against her own nature, to be forever aware of the fact that she was more than simply Elizabeth, a young, lonely widow—she was also a lady, a countess, and mother to the fourth Earl Pemsley.

Already her unfortunate pinching habit evidenced a breakdown of those barriers, a weakening of her self-control. If she could not curb the impulse to steal, what made her think she could contend with a force as formidable as Wildcat MacInnes?

No. Whatever inappropriate fascination she felt for the man could not, and should not, be indulged. If he was appealing in that moth-to-flame fashion, he was also coarse and rough and ungentlemanly. He was uncivilized and uncouth. He was at the very extreme end of the social spectrum, the absolute antithesis of all she'd worked to achieve for herself and for Oliver. And, worse yet, Wildcat knew about her pickpocketing. He knew of her secret and thereby possessed the power to destroy her.

If she did not destroy herself first.

As the carriage pulled up outside Mr. Morgan's hospital, she strove to put aside all thought of Wildcat Mac-Innes. Jake, despite his memory loss and confusion, was still surprisingly sensitive to her mood. He could not always remember Oliver's name, but he could sense if she was worried or preoccupied or tired. And, when it came time for her visit to end, Elizabeth wanted, above all else, for Jake to be comfortable in the knowledge that his "Lizzie" had not a care in the world.

"Lady Pemsley, good day, good day."

Mr. Morgan, the sanitarium's physician, hurried from his office to greet her, his round face and puckish features wreathed in smiles.

"Mr. Morgan, how are you this afternoon?"

"Never better, your ladyship, never better."

The doctor had a delightful custom of repeating himself, which might have proved annoying in a person less affable.

"And Jake?"

"Ah, today is an especially good day for our patient. He asked earlier about your visit, and even made reference to the story you read him last week."

"Did he? That is wonderful."

Jake's memory had begun to fade in and out from day to day, so that Elizabeth could never be sure how much he remembered of their time together.

"And the Messieurs Black, Listman, and Meeker?"

"All well, thanks to your ladyship's benevolence. Who is to say what might have become of any one of them if not for your kindness, Lady Pemsley? We are blessed to have you for a benefactress. Blessed, blessed, blessed."

Elizabeth inclined her head, abashed by the physician's excessive praise. Although she sometimes questioned her right to subsidize the hospital at the expense of Oliver's inheritance, she rationalized her decision by reminding herself of the late earl's passion for philanthropy. When she had first approached Oscar about founding the sanitarium, he had been nothing short of thrilled, gratified that she had taken an interest in charitable works. After establishing a line of credit on her behalf, the earl had then given her free rein to proceed as she saw fit, and soon thereafter, Mr. Morgan's modest facility had been born.

Whereas Elizabeth's initial intention had been to establish a proper home for Jake, she was nonetheless pleased once it became evident that the hospital could benefit others as well.

"And you've brought another hatbox," the physician commented with a jovial wink. "Our friend is amassing quite a collection."

Elizabeth smiled wistfully at the box. "He does so enjoy them."

"But I daresay not half as well as he enjoys your visits, m'lady," Mr. Morgan said as he escorted her up the stairs to Jake's room. "Shall I have tea brought up?"

"No, thank you. Not today."

"Give a ring if you need me."

As Mr. Morgan turned and scampered down the hall, looking for all the world like a sprightly leprechaun, Elizabeth acknowledged how fortunate she was to have found such a caretaker for Jake. Not only was the good doctor compassionate and gentle, but he was also, thank heavens, discreet. And discretion was an attribute that grew increasingly more important as Jake's memory deteriorated and his conversations grew more far-reaching.

Taking a moment to check her appearance, Elizabeth fluffed the puffy satin bow at her bodice, then straightened the gold-rimmed ruby pendant encircling her throat. Although she did not normally like to wear a great deal of jewelry during the day, Jake insisted on it. He said he liked to see his Lizzie all fancied up in her fine "gingambobs" and "rum rigging."

She tapped at the door.

"Is 'at you, Lizzie?" a craggy voice called.

"Aye, it's me, Jake." She smiled as she entered to find her friend buttressed by a half-dozen tasseled pillows in the bed she'd commissioned for him nearly ten years earlier. The contrast between the frail old man of eighty and the chubby-cheeked cherubs decorating the gilded bed canopy would have been comical, if Elizabeth had not been so disturbed by her friend's pallor.

"Gor, and ain't ye lookin' the rum mort today?" Jake said, chuckling gleefully as he held out his gnarled hand to her.

She took his fingers in hers, and seated herself in an Egyptian-style armchair drawn close to the bed, its front legs fashioned as two bare-breasted sphinxes. Jake was inordinately fond of that chair and its carvings. He called the pair of sphinxes his sweethearts.

On closer inspection, Elizabeth was relieved to note that Jake's complexion was not as anemic as it had appeared from the doorway and, in fact, there shone a brightness and lucidity to his gaze that dispelled her initial impression of diminishing health. He still appeared too thin, his long, narrow face punctuated by two elephantine ears, but his grip on hers was firm, his gap-toothed smile wide.

"Just look at ye," Jake said admiringly. "Take me for a cod's 'ead if that ain't Italian silk ye're wearing, Lizzie girl."

"It is."

He grinned wider and nodded, his feathery white hairs drifting over his head like dandelion fluff. "Naught but the best for my Lizzie. Ye're never purse-proud though, and that's a credit to ye, lass. A credit to yer character."

"Why, Jake, I should be a very silly woman to take any consequence from money when it is Oliver to whom the Pemsley fortune rightly belongs," she said, giving him a teasing wink and a squeeze of the hand.

"All the same, in rags or king's robes, anyone could ken ye're gentry from your toes to your top," he argued loyally. "Yes, ma'am, ye're a gen-u-ine lady, Lizzie Moore."

Genuine? *Hah.* And she didn't bother to correct Jake's use of her maiden name, since his memory was such that he'd just as likely call her Lady Pemsley in the very next breath.

"Speaking of top . . ." She handed Jake the hatbox she'd placed on the floor.

"Ah, ye shouldn't 'ave." But he rubbed his hands together in anticipation as he carefully balanced the package on his lap.

As long as Elizabeth could remember, Jake had claimed that the mark of a gentleman was what he wore on his head, so even in the worst of circumstances, he had managed to sport either a peruke or a well-turned cap. When Elizabeth had become the Countess Pemsley, she had taken her first month's pin money to the famed hatter Lock and bought her friend the finest high-crowned beaver to be had in all of London. The day she'd presented him with the gift, Jake had wept like a child, nearly breaking her heart.

"Well, lend me a polt in the muns if this ain't the most elegant nob topper I've seen yet!" he exclaimed as he pulled the beaver from its case. " 'Ow do I look, luv?" He settled the headpiece at a rakish angle over his liver-spotted forehead.

"Devilish handsome. A real jemmy fellow."

" 'Ey now, watch yer tongue," Jake admonished with a counterfeit glower. "None of that St. Giles's Greek for ye, girl. Ye're a countess, don't forget. Or . . ." He tilted a sparse white brow. "Are ye soon to be a marchioness?"

Elizabeth sighed, studying the ragged tips of her gloves. "As a matter of fact, Cresting's mother arrived from Devonshire only the day before yesterday."

"And?" Jake prodded.

"She has not yet pronounced judgment."

"Is she as crabbed as ye'd been told?"

"A hundred times more so, I fear. Nothing seems to please her."

"Eh, now, I wouldn't worry none, lass. I know my idea pot ain't what it used to be, but somethin' tells me it'll all work out."

Elizabeth smiled and reached over to tweak the brim of Jake's new chapeau. "That's right. It always does, doesn't it?"

Sitting back, she glanced around the room, as opulent and ostentatious as a pasha's palace. For his own reasons, Jake couldn't seem to surround himself with enough gold leaf or purple velvet.

"Do you need anything?"

The old man chortled and spread open his bony arms. "What more could an old bloke like me need, lass? 'Cept maybe a few more teeth. Why, the new cook is such a fair dab in the kitchen"—he patted his ribs—"that I'm gettin' as round and roly-poly as old Prinny hisself."

"You're not bored? Lonely?"

"Pshaw, far from it. Me and that bloke Listman play at cards—when we've got our wits 'bout us, that is. And Mr. Morgan's brung in a sweet li'l miss who reads to me three mornin's a week."

"The doctor has hired an apprentice?"

In the past, Elizabeth had always interviewed any prospective employees to ensure that waggling tongues did not carry tales outside the sanitarium. Although there'd been as yet no cause for alarm, she worried that Jake, in one of his less lucid moments, might prattle on about matters better left unprattled. She had to assume that in this case, Mr. Morgan simply hadn't thought to consult her about filling such a lowly position.

"What are you reading?" Elizabeth asked.

Jake gave a sheepish tug at his neckcloth. "Well, I weren't too keen on it at first, it bein' a love story and all . . ." He waved to a copy of *Louisa* sitting on an Egyptian tripod table.

Elizabeth's lips twitched. "Would you like me to read you the next chapter?"

She guessed that Jake, sentimental darling that he was, was most likely losing sleep over the unknown fate of the lovelorn heroine.

"Oh, it don' mind to me," he answered unconvincingly, hefting a shoulder. "If ye like, it's a decent 'nough way to pass the time, I s'pose." He then proceeded to prop himself up into an expectant pose.

With a knowing smile, Elizabeth picked up the novel and opened to the page marked by the sterling-silver bookmark. She then began to read.

Across the street from a sedate and nondescript, three-story brick house, Wildcat waited beneath a shadowed porch overhang for Elizabeth to reappear.

She'd entered the house over an hour earlier, her manner secretive as she mounted the shallow steps, a beribboned box clutched to her chest, a beaded parasol pulled low across her face. Evidently her coachman had not been instructed to wait, for as soon as she'd been admitted, the Pemsley carriage had driven away. Almost, Wildcat thought, as if she did not want her carriage to be identified on the quiet north London street.

As time passed, Wildcat's imagination took hold, until he was of the belief that Elizabeth had smuggled his bandolier bag into the house by way of the hatbox. Unfortunately, try as he might, he couldn't establish a *reason* for her to have done so, since the bag was of no real value to anyone but him. Unless, he mused, she feared he would discover it when next he visited her bedroom? But why, then, hide it here?

Still pondering, he watched as a man, small and scruffily attired, appeared from around the corner to take up a post along the alley side of the house. He, too, appeared to be waiting for someone within.

Wildcat crossed the street. The younger man stiffened as he saw him approach.

"I could use some help," Wildcat said by way of an introduction. With his right hand, he deftly rolled a gold guinea over the ridges of his knuckles.

"Wot d'ye need?" the man asked suspiciously, even as his covetous gaze followed the trail of the coin.

"Information," Wildcat answered, coming to a quick conclusion about the shifty-eyed *lennos*. If the man was not a felon, he surely knew those who were.

"I'm looking for a man by the name of Hendrick," Wildcat said. "He recently came into possession of some jewelry. Heard of him?"

"I may 'ave."

"Do you know where I could find him?"

The man scratched behind his ear, and deliberated a

long moment. "There's a Dutchman who's livin' next door to me cousin John."

"And where's that?"

"Above the coffeehouse in St. Michael's Alley."

The man reached for the coin, but with a swift toss, Wildcat caught it in the air before it could be seized.

"Not so fast," Wildcat said. "Who lives here?" He jerked his chin to the left.

The man snickered and ran a hand under his drippy nose. "Gor, no story there, guv. It's a bunch of loony old codgers. Like a 'ospital, ye see."

"A private hospital?"

"Uh-huh. Some rich duchess or somethin' pays to keep 'em here in grand style. Me sister just got a plummy job 'elping the caretaker."

The man's eyes were glazing over with greed as he watched Wildcat play with the coin.

"This duchess—is there someone in particular she sees here?"

"Aye," the man grudgingly confessed, his expression growing truculent. Apparently he was of the belief he'd already earned his golden guinea. "Every week like clockwork, she's supposed to call on a bloke name of Jake. He's a real cagey rascal that 'un, a legend up in St. Giles. They say he escaped the hangman's noose near to a dozen times."

Wildcat's brows spiked together. "Are you sure she's not visiting someone else?"

The man's thick lips turned down at the corners in an admission of ignorance. "That's just wot me sister tells me."

"Huh." Wildcat sent a thoughtful look to the building's moss-blanketed brick wall before asking, "Do you have any idea why the duchess visits Jake?"

"Blimey, I dunno. Me sister thinks the old fellow's the woman's bloody father."

Ten

"*Frankly, I do* not see what all the fuss is about," the Marchioness Cresting huffed. "The marble is corroded and lacking luster, and nearly all of these pieces are missing limbs of some sort."

Behind Lady Cresting's back, Elizabeth sent a helpless glance to Valerie. It was she who had suggested the outing to view the marbles—an outing which the dowager did not appear to be enjoying overmuch.

"Mother, I think we ought to consider ourselves fortunate to have been granted an appointment at all," Valerie said. "As I understand it, Lord Elgin plans to relocate the exhibit as early as next month. Who knows when next the marbles will be available for viewing?"

The marchioness sniffed, clearly unimpressed, and Valerie tried again.

"What of this torso of Hermes, Mother? Is it not magnificent? Granted, I am no expert, but I understand that from an artistic perspective, it is considered rare and admirable the degree to which the marbles so closely resemble nature."

"Oh, poppycock," Lady Cresting answered acidly, fluttering the orange feathers in her cap. "I do not believe it resembles nature one whit for people to go about without their heads!"

Elizabeth pressed her fingertips against her lips, suppressing a desire to giggle. Humor, she had learned, was not a quality that the dowager appreciated in people, much less in a prospective daughter-in-law.

"Nevertheless," Valerie retorted, evidently refusing to concede the argument, "the marbles must be of significant historical and artistic value for the British Museum to be negotiating their purchase, wouldn't you agree?"

"I would not," the marchioness snapped. " 'Tis a waste of England's money. As far as I am concerned, the man ought to march all these pieces right back to Greece. Why, look at this! I should never dream of furnishing my home with a piece of statuary as dirtied as this."

Valerie's eyes narrowed to irritated slits. "I am quite convinced that Lord Elgin did not plan for you to decorate—"

"Perhaps you'll find this frieze along the wall more to your liking, Lady Cresting," Elizabeth interrupted, gently steering the dowager away before Valerie could launch into a full-scale battle with her mother.

"And why is there no air in this place?" the marchioness added. "It is stifling, intolerable! I should think that if the statues are so terribly important, Elgin could find a better place to display them than a penthouse in his back garden."

Elizabeth murmured something agreeable then, once the dowager was out of hearing, retreated a few steps to speak privately with Valerie, which she'd not been able to do for a number of days.

"By Jove, Elizabeth, the woman is driving me to complete distraction," Valerie hissed, clutching her parasol handle with white-knuckled fists. "She finds fault in everything and everyone. Constantly. It never stops and, in fact, I think it grows worse with her advancing years. Did Peter tell you that she spends interminable hours praying aloud in the parlor?"

Elizabeth nodded crookedly.

"Well, even in prayer, all the woman does is complain to God!"

Unspoken sympathy shone in Elizabeth's gaze as she observed the dowager fix her monocle to her eye. The appearance of the eyeglass never boded well.

"I vow, nothing is good enough for her," Valerie grumbled. "Nothing is good enough for a *Ballatine,* you know."

Elizabeth did know, but held her counsel, comforting her friend with a pat on the shoulder. "Yes, dear, I understand. But apart from your frustrations, have you been faring well . . . otherwise?"

Strawberry-colored freckles bunched together in confusion. "Oh, that! Gracious, Elizabeth, I've not had a chance to tell you. It has all been settled. The man I spoke to you about? He has agreed to help, after all."

Elizabeth blinked, taken aback by her friend's facile acceptance of her circumstances and her complete disregard for Elizabeth's concern. Did Valerie not realize that she had spent many long hours worrying for her during these last days? That she'd been racking her brain, trying to produce a solution? But, then again, Valerie was Valerie. She had always tended toward the self-involved.

Setting aside her own feelings of pique, Elizabeth focused on her friend's good news. "Heavens, Valerie, I am glad to hear you have found a resolution—I suppose. You are satisfied?"

"Yes, yes," Valerie said, with a breezy toss of her curls, as she turned her attention to the caryatid at the center of the room. "I have every confidence in him."

"Why, that's wonderful." From under her bonnet's brim, Elizabeth snuck a curious peek at Valerie's profile, marveling at her extraordinary sangfroid. Though she hoped her friend would feel comfortable enough to confide in her, Valerie had chosen to remain silent, leaving Elizabeth to conclude she ought not pry.

All the same, she had to wonder: did the couple hope to flee to Gretna Green without the family's knowledge? If so, when? And how?

"At the risk of repeating myself, if there is anything at all that I can do . . ."

"La, I should imagine there is nothing, but you're a dear to offer," Valerie said, dismissing the subject once and for all with a good-natured wink.

As Elizabeth chewed fretfully at the inside of her cheek, questioning her friend's incongruously light-hearted manner, the marchioness turned back to them from her inspection of the frieze.

"Actually, there is something," Valerie exclaimed in a rushed whisper, as if she'd suddenly remembered. "I am supposed to meet with my, ahem, gentleman friend this afternoon, and I have not yet decided how to rid myself of Mother. Would you be the dearest of darlings and take her off my hands?"

Elizabeth's toes curled. As favors went, Valerie might as well have asked for her head on a platter, for it would have been less painful to give. Yet her friend *was* in trouble—

"Certainly. Did the marchioness not mention she needed new gloves for the Regent's fete? Perhaps I can coerce Peter into escorting us around the shops this afternoon."

"Splendid," Valerie said. "I am in your debt."

Despite the heat, Elizabeth felt a shudder work up her spine as she wished Valerie had used any other word but "debt."

Three hours later, Elizabeth's fingernails were digging crescents so deep into the palms of her hands that she feared she was about to draw blood. As difficult as it was to suffer blithely the marchioness's criticisms, it was doubly so when in Peter's company. His courtesy and patience made Elizabeth feel as if she were the veriest shrew, incapable of showing any forbearance for the woman she hoped to someday be her mother-in-law.

"Lady Pemsley, what is your opinion of these?" the marchioness demanded, pointing to a pair of lavender silk gloves.

"Very pretty—"

"Hmmph." The dowager sent her son a tart look. "The workmanship is obviously inferior."

Elizabeth swallowed a scream that would have shattered crystal. She did not know how much more of this she could take. Without a respite from the marchioness's incessant haranguing, she was likely to do something rash like shove those "inferior" lavender gloves straight down the dowager's gullet!

"I say," Elizabeth blurted out, craning toward the shop's window. "Was that Mrs. Pollock who just passed by? I have been meaning to share a word with her since her son Jeremy is away at school with Oliver, but I've not yet had the opportunity. Will you both excuse me a moment?"

Before Cresting or his mother could point out that not a living soul had passed the shop's window for a good five minutes, Elizabeth was out the door like a streak of lightning.

"Sanctuary," she gasped, turning the corner into a sleepy watchmaker's workshop that wasn't much larger than the Pemsley House linen closet.

"May I help you?" a silver-pated gentleman asked as he peeked out from behind a curtained doorway.

Elizabeth smoothed the tension from her forehead with quaking fingers, already beginning to grow calmer thanks to the soothing *tick-tick* of the surrounding clocks and timepieces. "Might I beg a kindness, sir? If I could simply rest here a minute or two?"

The man's gaze marked her pearl-encrusted headband and the delicate lace of her vandyked collar.

"Make yourself at home," he invited, then disappeared into the back room.

Elizabeth sighed and reached for her handkerchief to dab at her brow—

No. Her heart plummeted to the stone floor. *Good heavens, no!*

Wrapped in her linen kerchief was the Marchioness Cresting's small, gold crucifix, easily identified by its uncommon Baroque design.

"Her crucifix?" Elizabeth gasped. "Her crucifix?"

Lord-a-mercy, what would come next? The bustle off the dowager's bum?

"I am going to have to sequester myself," Elizabeth decided breathlessly. "It is not safe for me to go out in public."

But, if she refused to go out, how then could she hope to finally bring Peter to his knees? And what of the dowager marchioness, who would only be in London another fortnight or so?

Despite all evidence to the contrary, Valerie insisted that Lady Cresting was leaning toward a favorable verdict on Elizabeth's behalf, a revelation that Elizabeth did not know whether to celebrate or mourn. While she remained convinced that Peter Cresting was the ideal gentleman to take the place of the irreplaceable Oscar Pemsley, questions had arisen in her mind regarding the dowager's role in their future family life.

These last days, she had noticed that though Peter treated his mother with considerable and, at times, awe-inspiring patience, he neither deferred to the dowager on matters of importance nor allowed her to force unwelcome decisions upon him. Diplomacy being the foundation of his disposition, he handled his mother with an iron hand inside a kid glove.

Thusly, Elizabeth had no reservations about Cresting's ability to manage the dowager; instead she worried about Oliver. Even should his contact with the marchioness prove to be fairly limited, would it nonetheless be harmful? A quiet, sensitive child, Oliver's poor health and reticent manner would scarcely go unremarked by the dowager. Might she be cruel in her comments? Unfeeling in her appraisal?

It was a source of substantial concern for Elizabeth, enough so that she had determined to speak with Peter should he ever actually come up to scratch. For as much as she admired Cresting, her primary allegiance was to Oliver, her son. In truth, had she not singled out Peter because of his impeccable qualifications as mentor to a nine-year-old earl?

With a prolonged sigh, and knowing that she could not hide forever, Elizabeth tucked away the dowager's crucifix and left the safe confines of the watchmaker's shop, the bell tinkling behind her. Upon rounding the corner to the milliner's, she paused to slip the kerchief and its contents back into her pocket when she saw the man and woman in conversation down the street.

She stopped so suddenly that a young buck strolling behind her walked up onto her heels.

"I say, I *am* sorry."

He tried to offer a more lengthy apology, but she waved him off without even a glance, her attention fixed to the unlikely duo of Wildcat MacInnes and Valerie Ballatine.

Coincidence, Elizabeth told herself, feeling a peculiar weight descend into her lungs. It had to be nothing more than a ghastly, bizarre coincidence. Surely Valerie could not be planning to elope with Wildcat? A man who wore animal hides and carried foot-long knives? A man who crept into women's beds in the dead of night and made them feel things a decent woman was never intended to feel? Surely not.

But Valerie had said that she was to meet her gentleman friend this afternoon. The man she had called her . . . dark knight.

But how? How could it be?

When Wildcat had failed to come to her room the previous evening, Elizabeth had assumed that her "debt" had been paid, that never again would she have to encounter the oddly compelling stranger who had so tormented her thoughts in recent days. She had felt relief. Tremendous relief. Relief so intense that she'd been unable to sleep the balance of the night.

Yet, she had been wrong. For in this city of thousands, the man she had begun to believe a ghost, a shadow, now stood less than a hundred yards away, his broad shoulders curved protectively over Valerie's slight figure.

"There you are, Elizabeth." Peter loomed before her in his staid charcoal coat, cutting off her view of the street. "Mother feared that we had lost you in the crowds."

"N-no, not lost," Elizabeth stammered, staring numbly into Peter's kind, green eyes. "I, um—" She attempted to peer around him, but he followed her movement, bending sideways at the waist.

"You, um?" he prompted, his smile gently curious.

"I—" She gnawed rabidly at her thumbnail.

Oh, dear God, have they disappeared? What if they were planning to leave for Scotland this very day? What if her best friend were to become that man's wife?

"Are you unwell, Elizabeth?" Peter took a solicitous step forward, providing her a clear perspective all the way down the street.

"Oh. They've gone."

A groove formed in Peter's brow. "Who has gone? Mrs. Pollock?"

"Mrs. Pol—" With effort, Elizabeth dragged herself

out of her daze before Peter believed her as profoundly queer as old King George.

"Yes," she said, looking him straight in the eye with what composure she could muster. "I was unable to find Mrs. Pollock and spent all that time searching. Is that not silly?"

"No, not silly," he said, tucking her ice-cold hand into the crook of his elbow. "Rather a sign of perseverance. A laudable quality, I'd say."

Elizabeth glanced in dismay at her hand cradled in Peter's arm. Did he see nothing in her but the good?

Eleven

༒

There was an ancient Algonquin legend that told of the Great Manito, who, after defeating giants and sorcerers and monsters and evil spirits, one day encountered a babe in his path. Unfamiliar with the ways of children, Manito instructed the babe to move. Since the infant could not understand Manito's words, the child only smiled and babbled. Then Manito yelled and stomped his feet, which caused the baby to cry—but still not move. Manito then used his magic to bring fire into the sky, which impressed the baby, but did not induce him to budge even an inch. Frustrated, Manito flopped down on the ground in defeat, reduced to echoing the infant's nonsensical noises.

Perched on the railing outside Elizabeth's chambers, Wildcat wondered if he was not like Manito, reduced to the nonsensical games of his seemingly ingenuous adversary. Over the course of the last week, he had cajoled, bullied, and flustered Elizabeth Pemsley in a continuous and concerted effort to force her to turn over his bag. Yet without success.

Instead, he had been drawn in to the point where he now dangled from a shaky, wrought-iron bar twenty feet above a particularly thorny rose garden. And why? So that he could court the hangman's noose by again sneaking into the bedroom of a princess. Or a duchess. Or whatever the hell title it was she bore.

Rolling his tense shoulders on his equally tense neck, Wildcat tried to convince himself to turn back. He had managed to stay away the previous night only because he'd wandered halfway across London in his hunt for the redhead's Dutchman, ultimately finding himself in a whorehouse somewhere south of Lincoln's Inn Fields. His quarry had already vacated the lodgings above the St. Michael's Alley coffeehouse, but not without leaving a goodly number of clues. Enough clues that Wildcat felt certain that Hendrick would be found if not tomorrow, then the following day, which left him this evening to take another stab at recovering his *pindachsenakan*.

His desire for the bag notwithstanding, Wildcat had doubts about again confronting Elizabeth Pemsley. He could not help but believe that the other night had been a warning, a sign that he was far too vulnerable to this woman, that his attraction for her ran too deep. Absurd though it was, he could not escape the sense that there existed between the two of them a bond, a commonality that defied all reasonable, logical explanation.

After all, what in the blazes could he possibly have in common with a pampered and wealthy aristocrat? A woman whose very existence made a mockery of his? While his people starved, forced from their land by the ever-encroaching white man, the English nobility spent tens of thousands of pounds on galas that were nothing more than reflections of their own wasteful egotism.

Honestly, what could he have in common with a woman of that world? Lust?

But if it was merely lust, Wildcat did not think his instincts would be urging caution. And, if it was merely lust, he would not fear finding Elizabeth soft and naked in her bed once more. He would wait until the lamps were extinguished, instead of risking so much by sneaking into her room while she was still awake.

If it was merely lust . . .

Silently he cradled the sash in his fingers and pushed. The window was unlocked. With one cautious hand, he shoved aside the curtains and leaned forward to peer inside. Elizabeth was kneeling on the carpet next to the wall, her pale skirts billowing about her waist like the froth on freshly churned cream. She was drawing her palm across the paneling—

Wildcat grunted softly in surprise as a hidden door sprang open, revealing a niche in the wall. He brought his breath to a controlled, noiseless cadence, grateful that Elizabeth sat with her back to him, her position low to the floor, so that he could follow her movements.

Of course, the bag had to be in the wall. But why, he asked himself, had she hidden it from him? What could have been her motive in concealing it? Had she hoped to string him along with the goal of initiating a romantic intrigue? Yet, somehow, that reasoning did not ring true any longer . . .

From the opening in the wall, she withdrew a small trunk, struggling as if its weight made it unwieldy. After setting the trunk upon the floor, she then took from her pocket an ivory handkerchief and began to unwrap it.

Wildcat twisted forward in an attempt to see what the handkerchief concealed, but as he did so, his leather knife sheath lightly scraped against the building's stone facade. Quickly he lunged back from the window, nearly losing his balance.

"Wh-who goes there?" He heard Elizabeth scramble to her feet. "Reveal yourself," she demanded in a shrill, tremulous voice.

With a sigh and a shrug of resignation, he drew aside the curtain and slid over the window jamb.

She uttered a strangled sound and pressed the back of her hand to her mouth.

"What? Were you expecting someone else?" he asked dryly, trying not to notice how her soft curves spilled over the top of her bodice and how her lips glimmered pink and moist.

"You should not have come."

Hell, he'd been telling himself that all evening.

"I still have not found your bag," she said, sidestepping a pace in an obvious attempt to conceal the wall opening from him.

"No?" He made straight for her, his stride long and determined. "Then you wouldn't object to my taking a look, would you?"

She scooted backward to flatten herself against the silk Chinese wallpaper. At the same time, he saw her gaze swerve to the trunk on the carpet.

"You really ought to go!"

He wagged his head with contained amusement. "Not without my bandolier bag, princess."

As he watched her pupils dilate to twice their normal size, black almost overtaking the blue, he identified her perfume again. The haunting lily of the valley. She suppressed a cry behind her hand when he bent down and picked up the miniature trunk. It *was* heavy. Unexpectedly so. With no small measure of curiosity, he flipped back the lid to reveal what looked to be a gypsy's assortment of trinkets and gewgaws.

"What's this?"

Elizabeth did not answer. Wildcat unceremoniously turned the trunk upside down and let its treasures tumble onto the carpet as a tangled mass of glass, beads, and fringe. A quick yet thorough scan confirmed that his bandolier bag was not among the loot.

"Step aside," he ordered.

She hesitated. Then, with little, mincing steps, she shuffled away from the hidden niche, inching her way toward the door.

"That's far enough."

She froze, her movements reminding him of a startled rabbit. A *sexy,* startled rabbit.

Wildcat hunkered down on his heels and squinted into the opening. "It's empty."

"I told you."

He leveled a disgruntled scowl at Elizabeth, who was now fidgeting furiously with her lace collar. His regard shifted back to the fantastic assortment of pillboxes, ribands, and buttons.

"Just what the hell is going on here?"

Blond brows arched high into her forehead. "I do not know what—"

Abruptly she cut short her denial, glancing down to her dress front. Her nervous fidgeting had torn a hole in the delicate lace. She stared at the damage, her chin beginning to quiver. Then, to Wildcat's complete amazement, her lovely face suddenly crumpled like fine tissue as she slid to the floor in tears.

"This is all your fault, you know," she accused on a broken sob. "I was getting by perfectly well until you had to come along. I knew what I wanted. I knew where my future was headed. You've ruined everything. Everything!"

Mutely Wildcat rose from his crouch and walked to where she sat curled up against the wall.

"Don't," he said gruffly.

She covered her face with her hands.

"Goddammit, Elizabeth, I mean it! Don't do this," he said, dropping down to kneel beside her.

"I cannot seem to stop," she wailed through the cracks between her fingers.

"Hell, of course, you can. Dry your face and be done with it."

Her hands fell away from her cheeks and she glared at him through pink-edged eyes. "I can stop crying. What I cannot seem to stop is *stealing*," she clarified in succinct syllables.

He reared back, his heel connecting with a saltcellar that had rolled away from the cache. Glancing over his shoulder, he finally understood what she was saying.

"You . . . stole all that?" There had to be close to a hundred trinkets mounded on the bedroom floor.

She nodded disconsolately, blotting her eyes with the hem of her skirt. "All within the last year. The majority within these last few months."

"Fercrissakes, why?" It was evident she sure as heck didn't need the money, and only a handful of the items appeared to be of any real value.

"I do not know," she said, sniffling. "I simply become

nervous, and before I know it, I have a hat pin in my reticule."

Her lips trembled. Lush, pink lips that needed to be kissed. Kissed until they were rosy and swollen . . .

"Honestly, I truly do not plan to steal. It just happens. Without even realizing what I am doing, I pickpocket something like this." From the folds of her linen handkerchief, she sadly unveiled a gold cross on a chain. "Would you believe I pinched this off the Marchioness Cresting today?"

Cresting. Wildcat's back teeth clenched. He'd developed an instinctive aversion to the name. Specifically, the marquess who claimed it.

"A compulsion is what it is," Elizabeth said, trying to explain the unexplainable. "I'm scarcely aware of what I've done until it is too late."

Wildcat stroked the beads in his braid, remembering hearing of a blacksmith with a similar affliction. But instead of thievery, the blacksmith had suffered from an ungovernable propensity to bellow profanities at the top of his lungs.

"When did you, uh, start noticing this problem?"

She tilted her head back in a reflective pose, baring the succulent length of her plump, white neck. At first, she did not answer, then she said in a very quiet voice, as if talking to herself, "I believe it began shortly after Oscar passed away."

"Oscar?"

"My late husband."

Wildcat rubbed at his jaw, uncomfortable with the reverential tones she used to speak of the man. As another would speak of a priest.

"You have to understand that no one knows. Absolutely no one." Her gaze filled with uncertainty as she looked him squarely in the eye, her voice rising an octave. "If my secret were to be revealed, my reputation would be ruined, devastated. My son's future imperiled. You must swear to me on all that you hold holy to never speak of this, to tell no one what I have just confided. Do you give me your word?"

His eyes narrowed. "Where is my bandolier bag?"

"Oh, God." She pinched the bridge of her nose between thumb and forefinger. "You will never believe me, will you? Very well, I admit to stealing the bag. I admit to placing it in the trunk. But I swear to you, I have no idea what happened to it afterward. The bag simply disappeared, as if a ghost or some unseen entity plucked it from the wall." She threw her hands into the air, plainly frustrated.

Wildcat was feeling pretty damned frustrated himself. And he didn't much care for her joke about ghosts, when he had yet to vanquish all the many superstitions with which he'd been raised.

The question was: did he believe her? A part of him wanted to, while another part of him found it impossible to accept her claim. How could he walk away without his bandolier bag? Or, he wondered uneasily, was it the thought of walking away from Elizabeth he found so unpalatable?

"What must I do," she asked, "to convince you?"

Wildcat eyed her dubiously.

"Very well, then." Her tongue darted out to wet her lips. "If I cannot convince you, what must I do to guarantee your silence?"

He bit back a sardonic laugh. "What are you offering, princess?"

Instantly, he regretted his words as the mood subtly shifted between them. The single lamp on the mantel flickered and hissed as if it, too, recognized the growing tension, the increasing heat. It was a moment that felt measureless, endless, limitless.

"Tell me why."

"Wh-why?"

"Why did you steal my bag?"

He saw her struggle with an answer, her lowered lids switching back and forth, as she sought the truth—perhaps a truth she had not asked of herself until now.

"I am sorry," she answered in a guilty whisper. "I could not help myself."

His jaw hardened as he gazed down at the silvery sheen of her bent head. "You don't have to be sorry, *tschimammus*. I know the feeling."

And without further ado, he drew her by the shoulders onto the floor until she lay beneath him, sandwiched between his body and the plush Oriental carpet. As he dragged her hands up and over her head, her breasts pressed stubbornly against his chest in a jerky rhythm that mimicked her breathing.

Deliberately he wedged a firm thigh between her legs, pushing against her woman's softness. She made a sound at the base of her throat, but did not attempt to free herself.

"Look at me, Elizabeth."

She lifted her head one tiny degree a minute. Her eyes were like crystal-blue mountain pools, begging him to take the plunge.

"Is this what you offer?"

He gave her the chance to deny him. He gave her the chance to curse him to hell and back again.

"I shouldn't."

But that denial was meant for herself, not him.

He waited, his manhood swelling against her hip, her perfume an intoxicant in his mouth and nose. Against the wall, the candlelight continued to sway.

Elizabeth sighed and wriggled slightly, sliding along the hard length of his thigh. Her breath caught and she closed her eyes.

"I shouldn't," she repeated in a whisper. And then, with her eyes squeezed shut, she lifted her head. Her lips were unerring, targeting his mouth with wet, warm precision. His tongue answered with force, sweeping boldly to claim her softness.

"Open for me," he begged. She did, moaning delicately when he showed her the mating dance of tongues.

As they kissed—kisses both hard and soft—Wildcat stroked his thigh between her legs, slipping easily along the creamy, silk fabric. But the fabric was only a substitute. A substitute for the creamy, silken skin he craved.

Releasing her hands, he rolled onto his side. She gasped as he unapologetically shoved both dress and chemise to her waist, tearing at the fragile fabric while raining hot kisses along her neck and shoulders.

"Oh, God, Elizabeth," he said as he gazed down upon her. "Oh, God, you are so beautiful."

He cupped her breast in his large palm, his fingers spreading wide to take all of her fullness. Then he bent over her, burying his face in the valley between her breasts. She smelled as he would have imagined heaven must smell.

His tongue snaked out, licking a joyful path up her

cleavage, savoring the sugary-salty taste of her. Her breath was fast and ragged near his ear. Gently he squeezed her breast in his palm, pushing her pink, taut nipple up toward him.

"Beautiful," he whispered again before latching on greedily. She cried out. He suckled and licked, his teeth gently scoring the sensitive nub. All the while, his thigh pushed insistently into her softness, rocking against her heat.

Up and down his back, her hands moved in a frantic cadence, either keeping time with her gasps or with the pull of his mouth. He continued to feast on her, his shaft painfully stiff and swollen.

"I . . . I—" she cried, her back arching up from the rug.

Suddenly she was tugging at his shirt, and he had to draw back on his knees to help pull the garment free.

"Oh, my." Bosom heaving, eyes wide, she skimmed her palms across his smooth chest. Her gaze traveled over his shoulders and down his arms, before she trailed a curious finger along his tattoos.

He stilled, hoping she would not be offended by the markings.

"You are not afraid, are you?" she asked in breathless wonder.

He watched her trace a pattern near his wrist, his heart hammering. "Afraid of what?" he asked huskily.

"Afraid to be who you are. Afraid to reveal who you truly are."

"And who do you think I am, Elizabeth?"

She peered up at him from beneath the screen of her lashes, shrugging self-consciously. "Well, of course, I do not know. Not really. Although you have seemed to me to be unusually honest about yourself. With no need to hide or to play false."

Wildcat leaned back, his desire slowly waning. "Do you mean about being an Indian?"

She nodded, drawing a curly, blond lock to the upper swell of her bosom.

"Did you know that I'm also part Scots?"

Her pale brows lifted.

Gazing down at her, half-naked and heartbreakingly lovely against the vivid golds of the carpet, Wildcat suddenly felt forced to answer his own question: Who *did* he believe himself to be? Could he see this thing through and not hate himself later? Could he be comfortable making love to Elizabeth under the pretense of a "debt" being paid, or did he want her to come to him without strings attached? To make love to her free and clear?

"You know," he said, his voice raspy, "just because I do not hide who I am does not mean I don't doubt myself. There isn't a man on God's green earth who doesn't wake up some mornings wondering who the hell he is, and what the hell he's doing here. Not a man on earth who doesn't grapple with right and wrong."

Her blue eyes flickered in bewilderment.

With a small, regretful smile, Wildcat leaned over and placed a soft kiss upon her mouth.

"Your debt is paid."

Then he left as he had come.

Twelve

❦

Elizabeth jabbed her needle through the tautly stretched linen, determined to keep her hands occupied the duration of Cresting's visit. As long as she did not allow her fingers to roam farther than the embroidery frame, she couldn't possibly get herself into any trouble, now, could she?

"Mother's preference is to keep the guest list fairly modest—I believe she is planning on no more than twenty to table," Peter said. "I know it is rather short notice, but would you pose any objections to Wednesday evening?"

"Goodness, no," Elizabeth answered, smiling until the muscles in her cheeks ached. "I think it perfectly lovely that the marchioness wishes to host a dinner."

And, really, why should I have any objections? she asked with a panicky sort of self-mockery. *'Twill, no*

*doubt, be a wonderful opportunity to pick up a new vin-
aigrette bottle or opera fan!*

She took an agitated stab at the embroidery hoop,
missing the material altogether, then blushed when she
saw Peter's thoughtful gaze follow the path of her wayward needle. Thankfully, the selection of a new thread
color offered a welcome diversion as she vaulted virtually headfirst into the large quilted basket at her feet.

Peter cleared his throat on a gentlemanly harrumph.
Elizabeth dove yet deeper, rummaging through her embroidery supplies as if the fate of the world hung on
finding a skein of persimmon-hued silk.

"Elizabeth, I"—Peter cleared his throat again—"owe
you my thanks."

Elizabeth's head came up like a shot, trailing a wad
of green floss by the ear. *Oh, God, Cresting claims to
owe* me *thanks?* She flapped both hands about her ear,
swatting the green silk to the floor. *He owes me thanks
for what, in heaven's name? For nearly giving myself to
his sister's intended last night?*

She felt her cheeks grow hot again as she met Peter's
steady, comforting gaze.

"It has not escaped my attention that Mother has been
exceptionally, shall we say, outspoken, of late—"

Elizabeth feigned astonishment with batted lashes and
an O-shaped mouth.

"Yes." Peter nodded. "She has been relentlessly can-
did, often to the point of discourtesy—even I have remarked on it."

"Oh, I don't know . . ." she demurred.

"But I have further remarked on your patient forbearance, Elizabeth, and I must say it reflects well upon you.
Very well, indeed."

She swallowed, certain that her cheeks must be ablaze. Although flattered by Cresting's praise—as it was rare and therefore much prized—she doubted that the marquess would think as highly of her if he knew of her behavior last night.

No, I don't think he'd care to learn of it, she thought wryly. *Not one little bit.*

For last night, she had behaved like a veritable wanton, a woman completely lacking in restraint, virtue, or breeding.

Elizabeth, many years ago, had been taught that it was the duty of a lady, once married, to politely endure her husband's amorous attentions. Yet, last night, in the arms of Wildcat MacInnes—a man most assuredly *not* her husband—she had chosen to toss aside the standard of "politeness" for something else altogether. She had moaned and panted and writhed about with no consideration of duty. She had touched and tasted and sighed with no thought to courtesy.

In short, she had responded to Wildcat with such unseemly, unladylike abandon that, this morning, she had scarcely been able to convince herself that she had not dreamed the entire sinful episode. Alas, the faint whisker rash upon her breasts had settled any debate.

The first flash of guilt Elizabeth experienced, arriving approximately twenty seconds after awakening, had been on account of Valerie. Valerie, her dearest friend in the whole world besides Jake. Fortunately, however, Elizabeth had swiftly cast aside her guilt by consoling herself with the knowledge that Valerie had no emotional attachment to Wildcat whatsoever and was, in fact, compensating him to exchange vows with her. From that point, Elizabeth chose not to look further, to consider that someday she and Wildcat MacInnes might possibly, through marriage, be brother and sister. The prospect had been too distasteful to ponder.

Then, riding briskly on the heels of the first flash of guilt had come the second, hitting Elizabeth before she'd even pulled her head from the pillow. Granted, she and Cresting had no agreement or understanding between them. And admittedly, no one in society would fault her one whit should she up and wed another man this very day. Still, Elizabeth did feel as if she owed Cresting something. An implied fidelity—a fidelity that she had not merely broken last night, but one she'd shattered to pieces. Just as she'd been shattered to pieces.

By the time her breakfast tray had arrived, Elizabeth had determined Wildcat MacInnes to be as dangerous and uncontrollable a compulsion as her pickpocketing. And both he and the pinching simply had to be stopped.

Fixing her gaze to her lap, Elizabeth took heart in the fact that the solution to her problems was standing just a few feet away. A wealthy and kind solution smartly dressed in a striped ivory waistcoat, immaculate neckcloth, and polished boots. *Cresting will set it all right again,* she assured herself. Just as Oscar had set it all right.

Once she was no longer burdened with the myriad responsibilities of managing the monies and overseeing the estate and raising her son to be an earl, then those nasty habits of hers would all fall by the wayside. There would be no reason for her to overindulge in tarts, or to foray into strangers' pockets, or to—

Or to make wild, passionate love to a man completely and utterly wrong for her.

"Elizabeth?" Her solution spoke.

"Yes?"

Standing at the window in the harsh light of late afternoon, Cresting looked somehow older than he had even the previous week, the sun underscoring his graying temples and drooping jowls.

Elizabeth rose and drew the sheers across the window. "Has Mother's visit placed an undue strain upon you?"

She turned to him, blinking. He quickly tucked his chin into his cravat, as if regretting the personal nature of the question.

"I only ask," he said, his words rushed, "because Valerie has found the situation so intolerable that she has, to all intents and purposes"—he gave a low, embarrassed chuckle—"fled the house."

"What?" Elizabeth's heart slammed into her chest as she braced a hand against the wall. "Never say she has gone missing? That's not possible. She had to be at home this morning, surely?"

Cresting's intelligent brow wrinkled into fine lines. "No, no," he hurried to assure. "I did not wish to imply she's run off. I only meant that Valerie has avoided Mother with a dizzying round of social engagements that have kept her away from home."

"Oh." Elizabeth felt her way to a chair, her knees suddenly weak.

"Are you quite well?"

"No—yes!"

She laughed at the enormity of her stupidity as Peter dropped to one knee before her chair.

"Are you sure, Elizabeth? Pardon my saying so, but you've not seemed yourself of late. Distracted . . . distant."

"Oliver," she blurted out, digging her fingers into the arms of the chair.

"Of course." He shook his head. "How beastly insensitive of me," he said, urging her to say no more with a contrite, upraised hand. "Will you kindly accept my apologies?"

Her answering smile overlaid a grimace of shame.

"I have an idea," Peter said brightly. "Shall we drive out to see him tomorrow?"

Elizabeth drew in an eager breath as she sat forward. "Do you think we should? He has barely been gone a week and it's such a long drive."

"On the contrary, it's a lovely drive. We'll make a day of it. In fact, Aunt Lillian said only yesterday how she'd love to escape to the cool of the country. We can invite her to join us as chaperon."

Chaperon? Leave it to Peter not to overlook the proprieties.

"Well, I would feel better if I knew Oliver was getting on," Elizabeth admitted. And secretly she had to believe that seeing her son again would help anchor her priorities, and serve as a much-needed reminder of the consequence of her position. Her position as it related to Oliver's future.

"It is settled, then," Peter said, rising. "I will send 'round a footman with a note once I speak to Aunt Lillian."

And, Elizabeth added as a mental postscript, *please ask your godmother to leave her valuables safely at home.*

Valerie drew her bonnet's veil down almost to her nose, and sent a small prayer of thanks to the stars above. In keeping with her recent turn of luck, the park was quiet, with no familiar faces to be seen walking the paths or riding of a late afternoon. If only her luck would hold and "Cat" might recover the brooch sooner rather than later . . .

He appeared at her side as if summoned by a magician—one moment the bench sat vacant, and the next, he was there smoking a cheroot. Today he wore a cap similar to those favored by the Scots.

"How *do* you manage that?" she demanded in a low voice. "At the very least, I ought to have detected the scent of tobacco as you approached."

He merely shrugged and tossed aside the smoke, his attention fixed directly ahead to a gimpy pigeon pecking at rocks.

"Well? Have you found Hendrick?"

"More or less."

Valerie pursed her lips, rolling her eyes heavenward. It hadn't taken her long to learn that 'twas easier to draw blood from the proverbial turnip than information from this man named "Cat."

"Would you care to elaborate?" she said in a voice like syrup.

He smiled, but not with pleasure. "I know where he is lodging. Now I only need wait until he decides to return. Five days ago, he had a tooth drawn that laid him up with fever, but he's getting around pretty good now. Heard he dropped a few coins last night rolling dice."

"You discovered all that since yesterday?" Valerie was impressed. Impressed and relieved. "Have you any idea what the scoundrel has done with my jewelry?"

"I've asked some questions, but my guess is that he still has it. Like I said, the fever slowed him down."

"Thank God."

Valerie made a surreptitious count on her fingers, calculating that less than three weeks remained until the Regent's grand fete. So far fortune had smiled on her, since her mother had not yet checked the vault for the brooch. Oftentimes, the marchioness liked to have the settings inspected prior to wearing pieces from the collection, which meant that any day now, tomorrow or the next, she might discover the loss. Since the brooch had not been worn in many years—her mother thought it too valuable to wear but for special events—the dowager would undoubtedly want the jeweler to examine the piece.

"What will you do when you recover the brooch?" Valerie asked.

"What do you want me to do, Mockwasaka?"

"Blast it, *must* you call me that?" Valerie asked peevishly. "It sounds so ugly and harsh in that language."

"If you do not wish to tell me your real name . . ."

Valerie jerked at the sash on her gown. "As I told you, I would prefer not to divulge it. Gossip being what it is in this town, I dare not take the risk."

She thought she saw his lip quirk to one side.

"I know, I know," she said on a sigh. "It would probably take you all of half a minute to learn my name, if you have not already chosen to do so."

"There is no need." His disinterest, she felt, fell just shy of insulting.

Studying his profile through the translucent veil, Valerie questioned the fairness of the world in which she lived—why should a man have been blessed with those irresistibly thick lashes when her own were so thin as to be invisible? And his eyes were not merely blue, or a drab gray as were hers, but they were the angry color of the sky before a summer storm. His eyes frightened her a little.

His gaze was still fixed on the other side of the path, where the underfed pigeon was hobbling through the grass in search of its dinner. When Wildcat addressed the bird in a soft, rumbling, cooing sound, she nearly laughed out loud with surprise. She was less surprised, however, when the pigeon actually halted and turned to regard him with its flat, black eyes.

Valerie shooed away the bird with an impatient wave of her closed parasol. "Now, if we might return to my earlier question—what will you do once you recover the brooch?"

"I will bring it to you."

She knew better than to ask how he expected to find her.

"And what will you do with Hendrick? You will not harm him—will you?"

He sidled her a look that made her want to squirm. "Would you like me to?"

By Jove, he knows. But how could he? How could he understand the humiliation she'd felt awakening alone in Christian Morse's bed? How could this complete stranger appreciate the fury that had fairly suffocated her when she'd realized how she'd been duped and deceived? Drugged by a man who'd feigned affection for her.

Like a bucket of icy water cast upon her head, the truth had left her gasping with shock and outrage. She'd been cozened by Hendrick's false kisses and flattery. She'd been played the fool. And, by God, she wanted vengeance.

"How do you do it?" she demanded in amazement. "Are you some manner of clairvoyant?"

He didn't pretend to not understand her. "You reveal more than you realize, Mockwasaka."

Frowning, Valerie glanced aside, ill at ease with her mysterious ally. Although she'd initially been attracted to his dark good looks and devil-may-care attitude, she could no longer envision him from a romantic perspective. When she was with this man "Cat," it was as if she peered into a looking glass, which reflected back on her the Valerie she did not wish to see.

"You will only hurt yourself by seeking revenge," he said, his tone aloof, indifferent.

Her mouth tightened as she plucked at the buttons on her pelisse. "But Hendrick must be punished."

Wildcat stood then, forcing her to shield her eyes with her hand as she gazed up into the too bright sunshine.

"You and I both know that I was not speaking of Hendrick."

Before Valerie could catch her breath, he had turned away, disappearing into the trees.

Thirteen

❧

"*Do you need* anything?" Elizabeth asked, clinging to her son's hand with all her might. "Licorice for your cough or a warmer nightcap?"

At Oliver's back, dusk was streaking the verdant landscape crimson and orange, signaling the lateness of the hour. Soon the Ballatine coach needed to begin its long return trip to London.

"No, Mother," Oliver answered, whisking the hair from his brow with a boyish disregard for neatness or style. "I am doing well. Truly. The other boys are jolly, and Mr. Frazer treats us as gentlemen."

Elizabeth smiled, resisting the urge to smooth the pale blond cowlick sticking up at his temple. In spite of her fears, her son did look hale and hearty and happy. More so than she could ever remember him being. In fact, according to the school's director, Oliver had actually assumed a leadership role among his peers, which was remarkable considering the brief time in which he'd been at the school—doubly so, when one factored in his history of illness and timidity.

"You do look splendid, dear," Elizabeth conceded. "Perhaps I should sojourn to the country to put roses in my cheeks, as well."

Oliver grinned and, for the first time in a long time, his face was round enough for a dimple to appear. "To tell you the truth, Mother, I believe it's more than the country air that has improved my health."

"Oh?" Elizabeth swung their joined hands together in a playful arc. "Will you share your secret?"

Oliver's smile broadened, but before he could answer, Peter joined them from where he'd been waiting beside the carriage.

"I do so hate to tear you away, Lady Pemsley, but we should be taking our leave. Aunt Lillian has an engagement later this evening."

Peter always addressed her as Lady Pemsley in front of Oliver.

Oliver released his grip on her to shake Cresting's hand. "It's been a pleasure, m'lord."

"Yes, good to see you again, Oliver."

With a keen eye, Elizabeth studied the interaction between suitor and son, looking for a warmth or affinity on which to base a future father-son relationship. Although neither Cresting nor Oliver had spoken of it, there did seem to be a feeling of reserve between the two, which she believed would be overcome once they were joined together as a family. After all, both were eminently likable and shared a common love of literature and history. Surely a bond would develop in time.

After another desperate hug, Elizabeth allowed herself

to be dragged away to the carriage. Lady Fillig was already snoring lightly in her corner, no doubt taxed by the day's exertions. While Elizabeth had enjoyed her brief visit with Oliver, Cresting and his aunt had toured a local church famous for its tapestries.

Elizabeth was feeling out of sorts for some reason, so when Peter produced a book a few minutes into the ride, asking her if she'd mind, she indicated no. There was much to think about following her afternoon with her son—one particular exchange lingering in her thoughts.

While questioning Oliver about the difficulties of adjusting to new environs, she had suddenly felt his small hand come down on her shoulder. Then, his gaze so amazingly wise for his age, he had said to her in a solemn, quiet voice, "I must learn to stand on my own two feet, don't you think, Mother?"

Taken aback, Elizabeth had rushed to agree, without taking the time to reflect on his statement. But, really, what could he have meant, a nine-year-old child standing on his own two feet? What nonsense was that? Why, the boy had only moved out of short coats two summers past!

Yet, the longer she deliberated beneath the wavering light of the coach lamp, the closer Elizabeth came to understanding—or, at least, believing she understood—Oliver's curious statement. It was not physical independence he had been referring to, the fact that he'd recently been "liberated" from his mother's home. And it was not financial independence, which would be his once he reached his majority and gained access to his father's wealth. No, what Elizabeth believed Oliver had referred to was the emotional freedom that neither of them had yet achieved in the wake of the earl's death.

The passing of Oscar Pemsley did not draw the attention of many, as her husband had lived a quiet, almost reclusive, existence in their Bedford Square home. But for the two surviving members of the Pemsley family, the earl's loss came as a terrible blow; it was a truly devastating event in the peaceful and tightly knit home life Elizabeth had crafted for them all. As would be expected, Elizabeth and Oliver had grown even closer after Oscar's death, forging an emotional interdependence that, while initially healing, had eventually developed into something else. Something more harmful than curative.

Although Elizabeth had felt its effects when she'd sent Oliver away to Mr. Frazer's Academy, she had not understood it. She had not appreciated how, through their emotional dependence on each other, she and her son had become weak. Emotionally weak. Yet, apparently, Oliver *had* understood, for even though she had procrastinated at every point along the way, Oliver had been subtly pushing her to make the decision about his schooling. His instincts had told him that it was time "to stand on his own two feet."

But what of me? Elizabeth asked herself. *Have I learned to stand on my own or am I leaning on those around me?* During Elizabeth's marriage, Valerie had frequently intimated that she had relied too greatly on Oscar. Was she likely to continue in the same pattern? She cast a pensive glance across the cabin to Peter, who had drawn his book almost to the tip of his nose in order to read under the meager light. He looked so solid and dependable in his bottle-green coat and simple cravat.

Was it wrong for her to want to depend on someone like Cresting? She did not think so. After all, it was perfectly natural that she would seek stability for both herself and her son.

But is life no more than feeling safe? a secret voice questioned. Would she be content choosing safety over excitement? Security over passion? Stability over . . . true love?

Elizabeth picked at a loose thread on her cuff, her brows knit in sober deliberation. Why had she, months after setting her cap for Peter, now begun to be plagued by second thoughts, to distrust her choices? Less than a fortnight ago, she was convinced that she would be the Marchioness Cresting before the year was out. And she was furthermore convinced that nothing could have delighted her more.

With a frustrated sigh, Elizabeth yanked at the loose thread, then watched in dismay as her cuff's stitching swiftly unraveled like a perfect metaphor to her current situation. If she'd only had the good sense to leave well enough alone, the cuff would not have suffered so much damage. And if she had only had the good sense to leave Wildcat MacInnes well enough alone, she would not now be doubting the course she'd set for herself.

She was so caught up in her musings that when Peter snapped closed his book prior to calling instructions to the driver, she could scarcely believe that they were already back in London.

"Aunt Lillian?" Peter said, before leaning over to gently nudge his godmother's knee.

She came awake with a smile and a snuffle.

"Since the route to Pemsley House takes us directly past the town house," Peter said in a terrifically loud voice, "I have instructed John Coachman to stop briefly before I see Elizabeth home. Mother was most concerned that you not be late for the opera this evening and the hour has got away from us, I fear."

The elderly lady nodded affably, though Elizabeth did not believe she had understood a word of it. Just as she was unlikely to hear a single note of tonight's performance.

In front of the Ballatine home, Elizabeth waited in the coach while Peter dutifully saw his godmother inside. Still thinking of Oliver and their earlier conversation, Elizabeth scarcely took note of the hooded figure exiting the house via the servants' entrance. Her black cape screening her well in the darkness, the woman would not have drawn Elizabeth's notice at all if not for the unusual buoyancy of her gait.

In Elizabeth's experience, servant girls who passed the day in arduous, backbreaking labor did not move with the same vivacity as this particular woman. And the ladylike slope of her shoulders did not indicate hours spent at scrubbing floors or—

Elizabeth sprang forward, nearly catapulting herself through the carriage's open door.

"Ma'am?" she heard the footman question as he steadied her at the elbow.

By Jove, it is. It is her! The proud Ballatine posture coupled with the confident Ballatine stride left little room for doubt. But, goodness, what in heaven's name was Valerie Ballatine doing, skulking through the night like some agent of espionage?

Impulse seized Elizabeth, and she pulled her cloak closed at the throat.

"Kindly inform Lord Cresting that I will no longer be in need of a ride."

"Ma'am?" the footman repeated, concern making his voice wobble.

"Tell the marquess that I will manage my own return home, thank you," Elizabeth said firmly as she drew her cape's hood over her head. "Yes, and please extend to him my appreciation for a perfectly wonderful afternoon."

Then, with the young footman gawking, she set off at a brisk pace, determined not to lose sight of Valerie in the advancing fog.

After no more than one hundred yards, Elizabeth was cursing her stays to perdition. "Blast these rotten things," she panted. "Blast, blast, blast."

As her whalebone supports bit into her side, she vowed that someday soon the day would come when she would bask before a lovely bonfire composed entirely of corsets.

Fortunately, Valerie did not act at all concerned about being followed, for she strolled along at a sedate speed straight down the middle of the walk. Elizabeth was thus able to keep pace with her, despite her stays and the drifting fog, although, unlike Valerie, she was careful to stick to the shadowy side of the footpath. Even in this fashionable quarter, the city streets were most assuredly unsafe for a young woman walking alone at night.

So why then was Valerie out roaming London at this dangerous hour? And why had Elizabeth felt compelled to follow her? Common sense would demand that she overtake Valerie right this minute, and urge her friend to find safer transport through the streets. That would be the prudent course of action. That would be the sensible thing to do.

Yet, Elizabeth hesitated. What if Valerie was on her

way to meet Wildcat? What if the pair intended this very
night to make a dash for the Scottish border? Valerie
had said that the two of them had reached an agreement,
so it seemed only logical that they would move to for-
malize their plans before Valerie's condition revealed
itself.

Elizabeth's stomach gave a sudden sharp twist. Perhaps she had followed Valerie, hoping to prove with her
own two eyes that it truly was Wildcat MacInnes whom
her friend planned to wed. Or rather not prove, but . . .
disprove. After all, did she not secretly hope that it had
been a misunderstanding, that it was not Wildcat, but
some other man, whom Valerie had found to marry her?

Beneath her cloak, Elizabeth clamped a hand to her
roiling middle. She did not want to conjecture as to why
her innards were churning with anxiety. As to why she'd
silently begun to pray that Wildcat would not be waiting
at the end of this chase.

Approximately thirty minutes later, and after successfully dodging a growling mutt, a drunk mendicant, and
a pair of sedan chairs traveling far too fast, Valerie began to slow. They had been weaving in and out of the
smaller streets, Clifford and Vine, moving southeast into
a neighborhood that, while not dangerous, was nonetheless disreputable, at least as compared with Berkeley
Square. It was a working-class neighborhood, an area
that served as a buffer between the elegant houses bor-
dering Hyde and St. James's parks and the less agreeable
Haymarket district.

Here, caution appeared to take hold of Valerie as she
now crept along, ducking in and out of doorways and
the sheltered alcoves of shuttered shops. Elizabeth, trailing her by some distance, almost lost sight of her when

she veered suddenly into a dark, dirty lane running alongside a ramshackle inn.

Elizabeth hurried around the corner just as Valerie slipped through a door halfway down the alley. She paused, questioning the wisdom of following her friend into the building. For, truly, what difference would it make if it were Wildcat or some other man awaiting Valerie? Since Elizabeth had no plans to impede the elopement, what was to be gained?

Peace of mind?

The door latch was sticky, but not locked, the air stale and smelling of decaying food as she entered the building. A back entrance to some sort of lodgings, the hall led to a lopsided, wooden staircase that only the bravest of souls would have dared try to climb. From above, a light shone down into the well, and Elizabeth thought she might have heard voices. After casting a wary glance over her shoulder, she slowly mounted the stairs. The steps creaked and groaned, noises comically similar to those old Jake made when hauling himself from his bed.

At the top of the stairs, a rusty sconce illuminated the narrow corridor. To the left, a door stood open, it, too, spilling light into the hallway. Carefully Elizabeth tiptoed forward to peek between the hinges.

The room was windowless, boasting only a bed, clothespress, and washstand. Without even so much as a rag carpet covering the warped and rough-hewn floorboards, the sounds from within the room were amplified, echoing into the rafters of the slant-roofed ceiling. Those sounds, Elizabeth soon realized, were coming from Valerie. Angry sounds. Irritated sounds. Unladylike sounds. All of which must have muffled Elizabeth's noisy ascent up the stairs.

Sitting on the bed, her hood pushed back from her orange curls, Valerie was rifling through a heap of men's clothing, muttering under her breath.

"Dammit," Elizabeth heard her grumble as she shook out a man's coat that was much too large and much too "poetic" in its cut to have belonged to Wildcat MacInnes. It was in the style favored by the young musicians and painters of the day—not at all what she had seen Wildcat wear.

"Damn," Valerie repeated, tossing aside the coat to examine a violet-striped waistcoat. "Dammit to hell."

Mildly shocked by her friend's language—Valerie *was* a Ballatine, remember—Elizabeth concluded that an elopement was apparently not the objective of this night's work. Valerie was quite obviously searching for something. But for what?

Prior to entering the room, Elizabeth first took a moment to size up their surroundings. Only two doors opened from the smoke-stained hallway and the other had been boarded shut, so she did not think it likely that she and Valerie would be taken by surprise by any unsavory characters. Especially since she knew to listen for the squeaky staircase.

She rapped lightly at the door—

Valerie vaulted from the bed so fast one would have thought her skirts were afire.

"By Jove, Elizabeth, you frightened the very wits from me!" she cried, pressing a hand to her stomach. "What on earth are you doing here?"

"I was prepared to ask the same of you."

Valerie huffed out a breath and plopped back down on the mattress. "However did you find me?" she asked, without answering Elizabeth's question.

"By coincidence, Cresting and I had just returned from visiting Oliver when I happened to see you sneak away from the town house. Valerie, you must know that it is dreadfully unsafe for you to roam the streets unescorted."

"Lud, Elizabeth," Valerie said, with a dismissive purse of her lips, "why, that 'twas a Sunday stroll through the park compared to some of my more ill-advised adventures."

Somehow it always struck Elizabeth as sad the manner in which Valerie gloated about her exploits.

"What *are* you looking for?" Elizabeth nodded to the clothing strewn about the room.

"Oh, fudge, I suppose since you're here . . ." Valerie tossed her a satchel, which Elizabeth caught against the front of her cloak.

"Would you care to tell me what we're hoping to find?" Elizabeth asked archly.

She saw indecision streak across Valerie's freckled features. "Jewelry."

Elizabeth's hands went still on the satchel. "Are we stealing some?"

"Oh, God, Elizabeth," Valerie said, raking her fingers over her crown, and making a terrific muddle of her coiffure. "I implore you not to play Mrs. Princum Prancum just now, hmm?"

Elizabeth's jaw set. In the past, she'd not objected to Valerie's teasing. In fact, she had been pleased to know that she was viewed by the world in general as a proper, genteel lady. But, on this occasion, Valerie's barb had stung.

"Valerie, until now, I have aimed not to interfere in your affairs, providing only a shoulder to cry on or an ear to bend when you so desired. But, here, I must draw the line," Elizabeth said, raising her chin. "You cannot hint to me of dreadful crises, and then go gadding about the streets in the dead of night, and *then* ask me to join you in a jewel heist without offering some explanation."

Valerie's mouth pushed into a pout. "What do you want to know?"

"Well, let us begin with: whose rooms are these?"

"Hendrick's." Her nose wrinkled as she added weakly, "I believe."

"And how did you get in? Had he given you a key?"

"No."

Elizabeth frowned suspiciously. She could tell by Valerie's quasi-guilty expression that something was amiss. "Was the door unlocked?"

"No," Val said again. Reluctantly. "In fact, it was ajar."

"Ajar?" Alarm shot through Elizabeth, setting goose bumps to spiking along her flesh. "Goodness, Valerie, did you not find that odd?"

Her friend shrugged both shoulders. "To be honest, I did not think about it."

"Well, we should jolly well think about it now," Elizabeth said hotly. "Whoever left that door open was most likely intending to return. And soon. We must leave here immediately."

"But—"

"No, Valerie, we have to go!"

Elizabeth pivoted toward the door—

Wham! Her face plowed into a chest. A man's rock-hard chest. And before she could retreat, powerful fingers dug into her arms, holding her in place.

Fourteen

The man smelled of rawhide and lye soap, his scent triggering in Elizabeth a feeling of inexplicable calm.

The scream forming in her lungs receded as her brain made the intuitive connection. *Wildcat.* Swiftly she pushed away from him, even as his arms moved to encircle her for balance.

She staggered back, confused. Was there to be an elopement this night, after all?

His penetrating blue gaze shuttled from Elizabeth to Valerie. Though he hid it well, Elizabeth sensed that he was as puzzled as she. Angry and puzzled.

"There's no time to figure out what the hell's going on here," he said gruffly. "I'm afraid that we are about to have company—"

Suddenly he went perfectly still, lifting his forefinger in a bid for silence, his black brows dipping low over his nose. Then Elizabeth heard it. The telltale creak of the first riser.

"Omigod, we're trapped," she mouthed to Wildcat, gesturing frantically to the boarded-up room across the corridor.

He nodded, signaling again with an assertive wave of his hand to keep silent. When he reached over and pulled closed the door, shutting them inside, Elizabeth wondered if he had employed some Indian sorcery to prevent the aged hinges from squeaking. He then withdrew from inside his coat a penknife, which he wedged into the lock's opening.

It was difficult for Elizabeth to follow his actions the way he moved with such purpose, such decision. Next she realized he had padded on his silent cat feet across the room and, in an instant, the lantern was extinguished, throwing them into a complete and profound darkness.

Never could Elizabeth remember a darkness so complete. In the confined quarters, the air was close and heavy, almost unbearable. She wished she might remove her cloak, but knew she should not chance even that faint rustling, as the ominous footsteps continued to groan ever higher toward the head of the staircase.

The footsteps came to a halt on the other side of the door. A key jangled in the lock. Valerie gasped and Elizabeth kicked out, connecting lightly with a bony shin. The key clanked again.

"Bloody—" a man's scratchy voice cursed.

Then the door rattled in its frame, suggesting that a shoulder or fist had been put to the wood. Twice more, the door shook as if possessed by demons, both times accompanied by the most offensive of oaths.

How unreal this is, Elizabeth thought. *Only a few*

hours earlier, I was eating strawberries with my son in a bucolic paradise. She had just begun to shiver, when a large, comforting hand unexpectedly wrapped around hers. Surprise drew her up stiff for the space of a second. Then she relented and allowed her fingers to lace through his. At once, the tension started to leach from her spine and, in the secrecy of the shadow-filled room, she leaned into Wildcat's shoulder.

Outside the door, the man ceased his cursing and pounding. The ensuing silence was such that Elizabeth could almost picture the foulmouthed stranger pressing his ear to the wood, listening. After what seemed like an eternity of holding her breath, he grunted and stepped away from the door. Then from the bed where Valerie had been sitting there came a muffled *thump.* The man's footstep arrested. Again, a silence.

Elizabeth tightened her grip on Wildcat's fingers, the warmth of his hand radiating up into her arm. *How peculiar,* she thought. For the first time, in as long as she could remember, she felt genuinely calm. Calm, despite the fact that an anonymous danger lurked outside the doorway, intent on who knew what evil purpose. Yet, she felt at ease. Not at ease with the situation, but at ease with herself. Her palms were not itching, her stomach did not growl.

Finally, after what seemed hours, the stranger turned once again for the stairs. *Clomp, clomp, clomp,* followed by the slap of a closing door.

Elizabeth swung around blindly in the direction of the bed. "Val—"

Her words were cut off by lips firm and smooth. Before Elizabeth could react, the lips were replaced by a finger pressing against her mouth.

"Shhh."

Vaguely Elizabeth wondered how his kiss had landed with such accuracy when the room was as black as pitch. She could not even find her own hand in front of her face, she realized, spreading her fingers before her eyes—fingers still warm from Wildcat's grip.

Movement at her back preceded his whisper, "I've got the redhead. She's fainted."

The redhead?

"Just keep quiet for a bit," he said.

She nodded, realizing that she was oddly exhilarated. Exhilarated, yet also obsessed with the thought that Valerie and Wildcat had been planning to run away together. But how did Valerie's search for jewelry tie into this? Had she gifted Hendrick a ring or some item of value, which she'd hoped to recover? Perhaps to finance her and Wildcat's flight to Scotland?

"All right," Wildcat whispered directly into her ear. "I want you to hold on to my coat and follow me."

She nodded again and reached out—

Oh, my. She had grabbed a handful of something, but it sure as the dickens was not coat. Wildcat made a low sound deep in his throat, and Elizabeth snatched her hand away, mortified beyond words.

"I—I am sorry," she whispered.

"Don't be."

She heard the laughter in his voice, which only made her cheeks burn brighter. Her second grab was more prudently placed. She drifted behind him, four shuffling strides bringing them to the door, then listened as he quietly wiggled the penknife free.

He pulled the door open, and Elizabeth blinked, for having passed the last minutes in utter darkness, even the meager light from the hall sconce seemed too bright. Valerie, as limp as a child's rag doll, was hanging over Wildcat's left shoulder.

"Stay close," Wildcat said.

She planned to.

As they descended the stairs, she marveled at his ability to negotiate the warped wooden risers without so much as creating a squeak. She did her best to descend quietly, but could not match Wildcat's noiseless tread.

In the alley, he paused just outside the door to the building, his piercing blue eyes narrowing into the distance.

"I wonder where our friend has gone."

Elizabeth did not wish to speculate.

"Here." Wildcat reached beneath his coat, withdrawing his long, silvery knife. "Take this. I don't think I could do much with it," he said, resettling Valerie's weight on his shoulder.

Her mouth dry, Elizabeth took the weapon, holding it at her side under her wrap.

"And, Elizabeth—"

"Yes?"

"For God's sake, don't be afraid to use it if you have to."

"I won't," she promised.

They started down the alley, Elizabeth forced into a half run in order to keep up with Wildcat's long-legged gait. As they reached the corner, Wildcat glanced up and down the seemingly deserted street.

"Damn."

"We might have better luck finding a hackney on Picadilly," she pointed out. "It should be but a few blocks to the north."

His small smile was admiring. "Lead the way, then."

Although he'd asked her to lead, it was soon a case of Elizabeth being dragged along by the wrist as she labored to stay by his side.

"There," she gasped, two blocks later. "There's one."

Wildcat followed her gaze and waved down the approaching hackney. "Let's hope he stops," he muttered.

From where she hung halfway down Wildcat's back, Valerie gave a light moan.

"It's London," Elizabeth said derisively. "I'm sure he's seen worse."

And the coachman did stop, pretending not to see the unconscious woman slung over Wildcat's shoulder.

Elizabeth provided the driver her direction and they were off, Valerie sprawled like a heap of bones on the opposite banquette.

"She'll come to in a minute," Wildcat said, as if he'd read Elizabeth's mind.

Elizabeth swallowed and, with a shaky sigh, sank against the tattered upholstery, closing her eyes. Never could she have imagined her day would have ended like this.

When she considered what fate might have awaited her and Valerie if Wildcat had not come to their rescue . . .

She turned to him, wondering how best to express the full measure of her gratitude, when, for the first time that evening, she noticed the broad stain on his shirt-front. A vibrant red—

"Oh, dear God!" she cried, at the exact moment Wildcat fell forward onto his face.

Fifteen

Valerie awoke with a man's face buried in her lap, his breath hot and slow between her thighs. It was a singular sensation, a—

"Here," a woman cried, "help me lift him."

Valerie shook her head, blinking. As her vision cleared, adjusting to the surrounding gloom, she saw that it was Elizabeth yelling, Elizabeth who was tugging with all her might at a man's broad shoulders. The man in her lap.

"Valerie, please! Wildcat has been injured."

Wildcat? Of a sudden, her memory came rushing back and she remembered the terror that had gripped her as she waited for the stranger to break down the door of Hendrick's room. Had the stranger succeeded? Is that how Wildcat had become wounded? But then how would she and Elizabeth have managed to—

"Valerie!"

Wedging her hands under Wildcat's chest, Valerie shoved until, between the two of them, they were finally able to push him into an upright position.

"My, he's heavier than he looks," Valerie commented, massaging her wrist.

But Elizabeth was not listening, as she was in the process of ripping her petticoat to shreds.

"Have you lost your wits? That is the finest silk to be had—"

"Valerie, he is bleeding!"

Oh, God. She glanced across the coach to where Wildcat was propped up against the wall, his dark head lolling drunkenly to one side. Across his white shirtfront stretched an ugly, red blotch. *Oh, dear. Blood.* And lots of it. She felt the tips of her ears grow hot, and her stomach start to churn—

"Oh, no, you don't!" Elizabeth said in a frightfully fierce tone, her eyes sparking in the murky light. "You may not faint on me again."

"I, um—" She opened her mouth wide, taking in a large gulp of air. "Wh-what happened?"

"I haven't any idea." Elizabeth, exhibiting a remarkable degree of composure, swiftly folded her scrap of petticoat into a thick square pad. She then dragged aside Wildcat's deerskin vest and pressed the makeshift bandage to the center of the burgundy stain.

He groaned and tossed his head to the side but, thankfully, did not fall over.

"I can only assume," Elizabeth said, her features tight, "that he was already injured when he found us in Hendrick's chambers."

"But how could we not have noticed?"

Elizabeth loosened Wildcat's shabby cravat, answering in a distracted manner, "Sometimes a knife wound will be slow to start bleeding."

"Oh." Valerie frowned and scratched at her head. Since when did the Countess Pemsley know the first thing about knife wounds? *And furthermore . . .*

"Now, see here, Elizabeth, this is an awful botheration. I cannot make heads nor tails of it. Do you know who this man is?"

Elizabeth flung her an odd, guarded look before returning to her ministrations. "I met Mr. MacInnes not too long ago. While shopping."

"By Jove, how exceedingly queer." Valerie fell back onto the banquette. "Do you know that I am acquainted with him, as well? That he is the 'dark knight' to whom I have referred?"

"Hmm-mm."

"You do? But, how? Why, I am simply astonished by the coincidence. Astonished."

"I should think instead of being astonished," Elizabeth said in a testy tone, "you might try to be more solicitous of your future husband's health."

"H-husband?" Valerie huffed a laugh of utter disbelief. "My dear girl, are you all about in the head? I am not planning to marry this man! Good Lord, Peter would have a conniption. Why, he's—" She cast an incredulous glance to Wildcat's long, black hair and the brightly beaded and feathered braid swinging with every jolt of the coach. "Why, he's not even English, for heaven's sake."

"But what of your predicament?" Elizabeth asked through a confused scowl.

"What of it? Hendrick stole from me a rather valuable

article and I have enlisted Wildcat's help in recovering it. It's very simple."

"Oh." Elizabeth's cheeks turned pink. "I see."

"What would lead you to believe that I wanted to marry him?"

"I—I misunderstood. I, um—" Elizabeth winced as the hackney coach came to an abrupt and jerky stop, forcing her to pin Wildcat back with both hands to prevent his tumbling to the floor.

Valerie looked outside and nearly squawked. "You cannot be thinking to bring him into your house!"

"What should we then do with him?" Elizabeth rejoined. "Take him to yours?"

"No!" *Goodness, no.*

"Very well, then, Valerie, why don't you make yourself of use? Run to the door and fetch Boyles."

Valerie drew in a startled breath. Elizabeth had never spoken to her so harshly before. In fact, no one had, excepting her mother.

"Yes, yes, of course," she mumbled. And, for once, she did as she was told.

Wildcat regained consciousness as he was being toted up a flight of stairs by two liveried servants.

"Hey—" he growled, struggling to gain his feet.

"Do not drop him," a voice cried.

He followed that voice directly overhead. Elizabeth Pemsley was gazing down upon him, her lower lip caught between her little, white teeth.

"You're awake," she said.

"Uh-huh. And wishing I was dead."

Maybe that was an exaggeration, but his side *did* hurt like hell, and he sure didn't much appreciate the way the two footmen were lugging him up the staircase like a sack of flour.

"Careful now," Elizabeth instructed as the servants carried him through a doorway into a bedroom draped all around from ceiling to floor in panels of ivory silk.

They laid him on the bed, and he let out a low hiss. He felt weak and sore and he didn't like it.

"Valerie," Elizabeth said, speaking to the redhead, who had just walked in. "Did you ask Boyles to bring up a tray of tea?"

In spite of the burning in his ribs, Wildcat felt his chest rumble with laughter. These English believed that anything could be cured with a cup of Bohea.

"Yes," Valerie-the-redhead answered, sidling cautiously into the room. "Do you think he'll live?" she added in a low whisper.

"Thanks for the concern, Mockwasaka," he said from the bed, "but I'll be just fine."

His eyes slitted as he saw her give a guilty start.

"Mind telling me," he asked, "what you were doing in a place you sure as hell had no business being?"

Her back went arrow stiff. "Not that I need to explain myself to you. But after our conversation of the other day, I was impatient to see"—she arched a suggestive glance in Elizabeth's direction—"our *business* concluded."

So evidently Valerie had not confided in Elizabeth about the missing brooch . . .

"Well," he drawled, "your impatience cost me a hole in my side, since your darling Hendrick has fallen in with some dangerous friends. They got hold of the message you sent, asking to meet with him."

"Oh." Valerie gasped and pressed both hands to her mouth.

"You didn't trust me, did you, Mockwasaka?"

"No, it wasn't that—"

"Sure, it wasn't."

She couldn't know that he had read the note. Read it only moments before he had been ambushed by a group of ruffians hoping to take the Ballatine brooch off of old Hendrick's hands.

"So is it lost forever?" Valerie asked tremulously, her gray eyes assuming a watery sheen.

He let her sweat it out a good thirty seconds or so, waiting until her chin started to quiver. After all, the stupid woman was the reason he'd lost a pint of blood this evening.

"No. I know where to find it."

"Oh, thank goodness," she answered, before realization dawned. Thrusting her fists onto her hips, she said, "You scoundrel, why didn't you say so immediately? How could you have allowed me to believe that it was gone—"

"Please, please," Elizabeth interrupted, her palms outstretched in a bid for calm. "Mr. MacInnes ought not to be wasting his breath in senseless argument, Valerie. He ought to be conserving his strength."

With a waggle of her finger, she indicated his blood-soaked shirt. He had to admit it had definitely seen better days.

"So what is *your* excuse?" Wildcat asked, turning his displeasure on Elizabeth.

Her lashes fluttered. "I beg your pardon?"

"Beg all you want, princess, but that was a damn-fool thing to do, venturing into that part of town. Do you have any idea how close you and your redheaded friend came to getting your throats slashed tonight?"

Elizabeth folded her arms across her chest, her eyes flashing with indignation.

Just then, the butler appeared in the doorway, bearing a tray. "Mr. Anderson has arrived, m'lady. Shall I have him sent up?"

"Yes, please," Elizabeth answered, clearly still peeved by Wildcat's attack. "And, Boyles, I believe that Lady Valerie and I will take our refreshment in my sitting room."

As she proceeded to the door, the redhead two paces ahead, Wildcat started to get a bad feeling in his gut. One to accompany the even worse feeling in his side.

"Wait a second. Who's this Anderson?" he asked as he struggled to sit up.

Elizabeth did not even turn around, but sailed from the room, leaving it to the butler to explain, "Mr. Anderson is the doctor, sir."

Ah, hell. Wildcat grit his teeth as he collapsed back onto the pillows. Given the choice, he'd have preferred to go a few rounds with Hendrick's associates rather than be sewed up by a ham-handed English leech who'd probably not bothered to wash in a monthful of Sundays.

Not, of course, that he had that choice.

"Hey, Boyles, before you go—"

"Yes, sir?"

"Got any whiskey in this place?"

"Elizabeth, I simply do not know what to say. I admit I initially found him attractive in a primitive fashion, but the man does forget himself, doesn't he?"

"Tea?"

"You know I never take tea after sunset." Valerie spread her skirts in a neat semicircle. "His manner is altogether too familiar, don't you think? Why, I could scarcely believe how he reprimanded you, when you were only trying to help me."

"How much have you paid him, Valerie?"

She cocked her chin in a funny chickenlike gesture. "Why, nothing yet."

"And how much have you promised to pay him?"

"Well, we hadn't yet discussed an actual figure."

"Therefore, one could argue that, without having received any payment, Mr. MacInnes has also only been 'trying to help'?"

"Goodness, I did not mean to imply—"

"Down the hall, Valerie, there lies a man," Elizabeth said, her voice shaking as severely as her hand on the saucer, "who took a knife in the ribs tonight because of you. A man who risked his life for both of us, when 'twould have been far easier for him to save his own skin and not bother. A man who, instead of running when he had the chance, carried you on his back halfway across London."

Valerie splayed a hand at her throat, tears welling in her eyes. "I say, you needn't read me a scold."

Elizabeth's lips thinned. Perhaps she had been a bit severe.

"Surely it cannot be the first time he's been cut with a knife," Valerie rationalized, pouting as her tears dried on her lashes. "I mean, only think what kind of life he has led. As if you and I are even capable of imagining such an existence."

Elizabeth took a long drink of her tea, glad of the hot

liquid burning her tongue. It prevented her from saying what she should not.

"And I appreciate that you must be grateful, Elizabeth. 'Tis only to be expected after he came to our rescue. However, you do realize, don't you, that he cannot possibly remain here? Why, you'll be fortunate indeed if the physician doesn't spread tales of being called to your home at midnight to tend some feathered savage."

Savage?

Elizabeth drained her cup and set it down on the tray, hopeful that if she could control that small movement, she could control her reaction to Valerie's shockingly cavalier attitude. Doubtless, some of this posturing on her friend's part arose from guilt. At heart, Valerie had to be feeling responsible for the night's misadventures; she had to be conscience-stricken with the knowledge that she'd led so many into a situation fraught with danger.

Nonetheless, whether or not Valerie was attempting to shield herself from her own conscience, one element of her discourse strongly affected Elizabeth. An element that she had deliberately overlooked. An element that she could no longer ignore.

Wildcat MacInnes was not of their world.

Over the course of the last few days, she had ceased to view him as an outsider, as a man who came from a society a thousand leagues removed from the society of Pemsleys and Ballatines. Caught up in the passion he had introduced to her, she had regarded him only as a man. No less, no more. A man detached from the distinctions of class or race or social standing. An honest man with whom she could be honest. At least, partially.

By perceiving him this way, however, she had failed

to acknowledge the reality of their relationship—the reality that there could never be anything between them. Nothing. Not ever.

I am the Countess Pemsley. My son is the fourth earl in the succession. The man I hope to marry is an influential and powerful marquess.

She could hardly overlook those truths, for they were the truths she'd battled a lifetime to establish. The truths she would die to protect.

"Oh, let us not fuss, Elizabeth. He's hardly worth it, now, is he?" Valerie asked. "Let us talk instead of the Dragon's dinner party tomorrow evening. What do you plan to wear? That lovely new gold-spangled crepe?"

Elizabeth stared fixedly at the silver tea set, a wedding gift from the Duke of York, monogrammed with an intricate, flowing "P."

Tea sets and evening dresses. Yes, this is what I know, and all that I should.

"The crepe," she answered slowly. "I suppose that would be a sound choice."

"Splendid. I wish I could tell you that Mother will adore it, but the woman is as unpredictable as the weather. I would have wagered my back teeth that she was leaning toward giving you her blessing, but, these last days, she has been especially disagreeable."

Elizabeth labored to bring her thoughts around to tomorrow's dinner. "Is it a test, you think?"

"Indubitably. Cresting told me in confidence that he believes it to be the final hurdle, so to speak. Therefore, should you acquit yourself favorably, Elizabeth, as you no doubt will, your goal will have finally been met."

"My goal . . ."

"Yes." Valerie sighed and, coincidentally or not, turned her gaze in the direction of Wildcat's room. "I would wish you luck but, as a friend, I honestly wonder whether I should."

Sixteen

To say that Elizabeth was nervous was to say that Prinny was portly. Both facts were patently obvious to anyone with two good eyes in his head.

The day leading up to the dowager's party was supposed to have been a restful one for her, filled only with such entertaining details as choosing slippers, selecting hair ribbons, and soaking in perfumed baths. Instead, Elizabeth had spent the entire afternoon conducting a quiet, yet frantic, search for Wildcat MacInnes.

The previous evening, while she and Valerie had been chatting over midnight tea and cakes, Wildcat had disappeared from his sickroom.

"What do you mean 'missing'?" Elizabeth had asked.

The weary Boyles had appeared taken aback by the sharpness of her tone.

"Ah, well . . . He is gone, m'lady. According to Mr. Anderson, he had just finished stitching Mr. MacInnes's wound, when he walked out to the hall to call for fresh water. Evidently when he returned to the room, his patient had vanished."

"But, that is impossible, Boyles. Only a half hour earlier, the man was unconscious! Where could he have gone at this hour? And how?"

Dissatisfied with her butler's account, Elizabeth had insisted on interviewing the doctor himself, only to be granted the same bewildering tale. One minute Wildcat was resting in bed with a dozen fresh stitches, the next he'd vanished into thin air.

Convinced that he had to be lying somewhere in a pool of his own blood, Elizabeth, after sending Valerie home with her coachman, had called for a search of the house from cellar to attic. All the servants had been roused from their beds, every nook and cranny explored. A small crew had even been sent to patrol the surrounding streets and alleys, yet Wildcat was simply not to be found.

At this point, Elizabeth could have resigned herself to the fact that he had left of his own free will. For whatever reason, he had preferred to chance the streets in his weakened condition rather than to remain in her home.

She could not, however, accept that. How would she ever be able to forgive herself if Wildcat did not survive his injuries, after having saved her life that night? How would she ever again pass a decent night's sleep if he were to perish in some vermin-infested alley while she slept among her cool linen sheets?

Therefore, in the morning, instead of arranging for her modiste to make last-minute alterations to her gold crepe gown, she had met with an investigator whom Oscar had once employed many years ago. As might be presumed, she had not divulged the full scope of her relationship with Wildcat. It had not seemed relevant. She had merely engaged the agent to ascertain that he was alive and well. Nothing more.

For as she saw it, Wildcat must have had his reasons for sneaking away in the dead of night, without so much as a "how do you do" or "enjoy the rest of your life." And, if he chose not to have further contact with her, it was all for the good, really, and to her benefit.

For the good, Elizabeth kept telling herself.

Certain that his beaded bag was never going to resurface, she was equally as certain that Wildcat MacInnes was a hazardous influence, a threat to her hopes and plans, a menace to her future. Like the pickpocketing, he was a compulsion she was determined to master, and it did not take a great intellect to determine that mastering that compulsion would be far easier if she did not lay eyes on Wildcat again.

So, once she could rest easy in the knowledge that he was well, she would then wipe him from her mind like chalk from a slate. *Whoosh.* Clean forgotten.

Of course, with all the tumult of hiring the investigator, and worrying about Wildcat half-dead somewhere, and stewing over yesterday's conversations with Oliver and Valerie, Elizabeth had scarcely had time even to think about the Marchioness of Cresting's party. Until it was too late, that is.

"My stars, Marjorie, I have done it again!"

"Ye're not doin' so bad," her abigail replied. "In fact, measured against most nights, why, I'd say ye're ahead of schedule."

Elizabeth scrunched up her nose as she glanced to the clock. "Actually, I was referring to the fact that I've chewed through another pair of gloves. And before I'd even put them on."

She tossed the mangled glove onto the floor, thinking that its condition did not bode well for the rest of the evening. The more nervous she became, the more likely she was to pinch something.

"You know, Marjorie, on second thought, perhaps I *will* wear that sapphire bracelet."

"As you like, m'lady."

"And the ring, as well."

Her maid lifted a sandy eyebrow, but said nothing.

It was unusual for Elizabeth to adorn herself so liberally, but she was hopeful that by weighing down her hands with jewelry, she might find it more difficult to pickpocket.

"No, not that bracelet," Elizabeth said. "The dangly one with the pearls. And pour me another glass of sherry, will you?"

Again, the abigail questioned her with a quizzical look, which Elizabeth pretended not to see. Just as she did not normally wear much jewelry, neither was it her custom to drink away from the table. Tonight, however, she was desperate; if she did not calm down, she was going to make an absolute cake of herself at the dowager's dinner.

After checking the hour, Elizabeth groaned, and drained in a single gulp the glass Marjorie had just topped off.

"My," she murmured as a sizzling warmth poured into her stomach. "That is potent sherry."

"It's only the third glass that feels potent, m'lady. The first ye hardly noticed."

The third? Elizabeth questioned as she hurried downstairs to the waiting carriage. Surely Marjorie had miscounted.

However, if the maid had confused her numbers, the dowager certainly had not, Elizabeth realized, a quarter of an hour later as she was admitted to the Ballatines' salon.

Instead of the traditional hostess's greeting, the marchioness asked loudly enough for the entire room to hear, "Lady Pemsley, do you have any idea what time it is?"

Shamed beyond words, Elizabeth could only think that the dowager's choice of gown this evening, a shiny, bottle-green silk taffeta, was particularly dragonlike, wanting only for scales and a forked tail.

"Oh, dear," she answered as innocently as she could, "am I late?"

"By twenty-two minutes," the dowager answered crisply, her red lip salve spread, as usual, from chin to cheek.

"Twenty-two?" Elizabeth produced a credible expression of contrition. "My apologies, Lady Cresting. I do hope I've not kept you waiting."

"Of course you've kept us waiting," the marchioness replied, tugging imperiously at the hem of her short evening jacket. "What else were we to do?"

"I could have offered to sing," Valerie piped in, walking up to stand behind her mother. "But I feared Cresting's French chef would skewer me onto the spit if my warbling soured the guests' appetites."

"Nonsense," Peter said as he, too, joined them, accompanied by the war hero Christian Morse. "You have a lovely voice, Valerie. Perhaps you will consent to honor us after dinner."

He then turned to Elizabeth and bowed, his warm smile apologizing for his mother's rudeness. "You are looking particularly well this evening, Elizabeth."

"Thank you."

"Do you also sing, Lady Pemsley?" Mr. Morse asked. "Perhaps we could have a duet?"

Before Elizabeth could explain that her last attempt at song had resulted in a horse bolting from its gig, Peter said, "How curious, Morse. I, myself, do not know whether the countess sings."

"I fear there's much you don't know about me, Cresting," Elizabeth answered, on a saucy burst of laughter.

Alas, the instant the words left her mouth, Elizabeth regretted them, blaming the effects of the sherry. Her pronouncement had brought a sudden pall upon the conversation as she and Cresting both appeared to sense its validity. They had been acquainted for years, but did they honestly know each other? Did he truly know her at all or did he see only what he wanted in her? Only what she permitted him to see?

Valerie leaped in to fill the awkward void. "Indeed, Elizabeth is quite the lady of mystery," she said, her playful tone precisely what was needed to mask Elizabeth's gaffe. "You do understand that I cannot reveal my sources, but rumor has it she's secretly been masterminding Wellington's military maneuvers."

This produced an appreciative chuckle from all but the marchioness.

"Poppycock! I do not believe Lady Pemsley knows the first thing about strategies of war."

Mr. Morse smiled and gently offered, "I believe Lady Valerie spoke in jest, ma'am."

The glacial stare the dowager subsequently leveled on

young Morse would have sent a less confident man crying for his nanny.

"I say," Valerie said, once again trying to rescue the moment. "Did you know, Elizabeth, that Mr. Morse's dearest friend from school hails from Lincoln Wolds? Is that not a remarkable coincidence?"

"Yes," Mr. Morse agreed. "You must be acquainted with the Jamison family, Lady Pemsley. Parker Jamison and I were at Eton together."

"Jamison?" Elizabeth echoed. She glanced around the circle of faces, noting that Peter had turned away to speak with Sir Wilding. "I, um—"

"Oh, surely, you must know them," Mr. Morse pressed smilingly. "Parker is scarcely the sort of fellow you're likely to forget. And his older sister would have been of your age, I believe. Clarissa? Clarissa Jamison?"

The dowager bestowed on her an expectant, piercing look that made Elizabeth want to run screaming from the room.

"I am sorry," she said haltingly, "but my memory is deplorable."

"Oh, but the family is one of the—" Mr. Morse abruptly silenced as he must have recognized Elizabeth's discomfort. "At any rate, Jamison is a good sort. Perhaps you'll get to meet him sometime," he finished weakly.

Elizabeth felt as if the smile pinned to her face were as brittle as glass.

"Come, Elizabeth," Valerie said, reaching for her hand. "Let us take you around to greet our guests."

"There is no time for that," the marchioness trumpeted. "We go in to dinner now."

Valerie made a face. "Mother, but it is still early and Elizabeth hasn't had—"

"Now."

As Lady Cresting took her son's arm, Elizabeth could have kicked herself for her tardiness. Courtesy would demand she, at least, share a word with the others present, all of whom were of her and Cresting's social circle. But now, because she'd irritated the marchioness, she would evidently have to wait until after they'd retired from the table to greet the other guests. It was only a slap on the wrist, perhaps, yet it did not augur well for the balance of the evening.

Upon entering the dining room, Elizabeth was surprised—and somewhat terrified—to learn that she was to be seated at the dowager's right as the guest of honor. Peter was seated across the table from her, while Morse sat on her right. Valerie and Lady Fillig were farther down the table.

Elizabeth was about to launch into another apology, this one protracted, penitent, and perhaps untruthful, when the dowager commanded, "Tell me about your family, Lady Pemsley."

Elizabeth squared her shoulders. "I, um, have a son, Oliver—"

"Bah, I have no interest in children. Tell me about your family, your lineage. Peter mentioned that you were raised in the north country? Lincolnshire, I'm to understand?"

Elizabeth reached for her wineglass. *Uh-oh.* "Yes. My father died when I was young—"

"His name?"

A long drink occupied Elizabeth for a blissful second before she answered, "His name was William Moore. A gentleman squire, he lived rather uneventfully—"

"More?" Lady Cresting glowered. "Pray do not tell

me that you are related to that dimwitted radical Hannah More."

"Ah, no, ma'am. That would have been Moore with two 'O's.' "

"Go on, then. What of your mother?"

Elizabeth waited until the footman had served her a plate of turtle soup, reminding herself to keep her facts—or lies—straight. She couldn't allow herself to become flustered. She couldn't.

"My mother was—"

"Of the gentry?"

"I, um, seem to recall that her father, my grandfather, was a Scots earl—"

"Seem to recall?" The marchioness let her spoon fall into her soup plate with a *clang*. "How is it that you do not know?"

Elizabeth felt her fingers give a spastic twitch. "My mother did not often speak of her past. I believe there was a falling-out of sorts with her family."

"Nevertheless, bloodlines must be preserved, Lady Pemsley! They must be preserved at all cost. Families falling out, falling in, falling sideways—it makes no difference.

"Were you aware that a Ballatine served under William the Conqueror? That our ancestors had ties to Russia's own Catherine the Great? Ours is a proud name, Lady Pemsley, a name that has history behind it. Do you think less of your own?"

"I—certainly not."

"Very well, then, you cannot sit back and allow a family rift to deny you and your son of your heritage."

"Yes, ma'am, you are, of course, quite correct."

"Of course, I am."

Elizabeth reached for her wine, drinking deeply to give herself time to latch on to another subject. The marchioness used the respite to slurp her soup.

"Tell me, Lady Cresting," she asked, determined to turn the focus of their conversation. "How did you enjoy the opera last night?"

"Infernal din. It gave me the megrims."

"I am sorry to hear—"

"Where in the Wolds, Lady Pemsley?"

"Beg pardon?"

"Where in Lincolnshire were you raised?"

Elizabeth looked across the table to Peter for assistance. He, however, was engaged in an animated discussion with the Lady Carterling on his left. Eavesdropping, Elizabeth ascertained that the subject was the fall of Constantinople, which meant two things: one, Peter was not likely to take notice of her predicament; and two, what she'd first thought to be a discussion was probably more akin to a history lesson for Lady Carterling.

"Lady Pemsley." The marchioness tapped her fork to her wineglass.

Elizabeth shook herself back to her interrogation. "I am sorry, Lady Cresting, what was your question?"

The dowager pursed her lips unhappily. "For the third time, where in the north were you raised?"

Blinking, Elizabeth realized that her wits had been slowed by the sherry and wine. Her head was swimming, her stomach overwarm.

"Uh, Spilsby, m'am."

"No siblings?"

The questions were coming so fast. Too fast for her to marshal her thoughts.

"As I mentioned, Lady Cresting, my father passed away when I was very young—"

The marchioness waved her hand back and forth, dismissing the loss summarily. "The grandfather, the Scots earl—what did you say his name was?"

A furtive peek to Elizabeth's right revealed that Mr. Morse was engaged with his dinner partner on the other side. Elizabeth briefly entertained the idea of carving "H-E-L-P" into her lamb chop.

"Your mother's father," the dowager repeated. "Although I am not well acquainted with the peerages of Scotland, what with so many MacLeods, Mackintoshes, and Macdonalds running about, I—"

"Macdonald," Elizabeth answered, feeling rather giddy and lighthearted all of a sudden. Because, truly, what was there to worry about? Why should she tie herself into knots of nerves? By Jove, in her day, she had crossed swords with many a character more intimidating than the aging Marchioness of Cresting.

"Macdonald?" The dowager sniffed. "Common enough name, I suppose."

"Yes, indeed," Elizabeth agreed. "Common, common, common," she singsonged under her breath.

The marchioness narrowed her beady, brown eyes. "And how did you meet Pemsley?"

"Ah, Pemsley." Elizabeth sighed, then effusively thanked the footman for removing her untouched soup. "He was visiting friends in the area."

"I see." The dowager drummed her fingers to the side of her plate as it was filled by a servant.

"Turbot?" the footman offered.

Elizabeth nodded, and was served.

A second proposed "Tongue?" which Elizabeth also accepted.

"Church?" the dowager asked.

"No, thank you," Elizabeth said politely, "my plate is rather full."

She giggled, inordinately pleased with her witticism, and glanced across to Peter to see if he had appreciated her quip. But he had yet to surrender Constantinople.

"Your plate . . . ? Lady Pemsley, I asked if you attend church," the marchioness repeated in a huff.

"Oh, yes . . ." Elizabeth started to answer before she was distracted by the glint of gold peeking out from beneath Lady Cresting's silk evening jacket. A button had worked itself loose and—

"Do you attend service?" the dowager persisted.

"Yes. I would say that . . . that—"

There it is again. Elizabeth leaned forward, attempting to get a closer look.

"Lady Pemsley!" The marchioness reared back as Elizabeth's nose was in danger of grazing her bosom. "The impertinence!"

Impertinent or not, Elizabeth knew she could not rest until she identified that article of gold about the dowager's neck.

"Pray tell, what is that?"

The marchioness glanced down, adding another chin to the two she regularly possessed. "What are you talking about, foolish girl?"

"That." Elizabeth stabbed a forefinger in the vicinity of the marchioness's heart. Or where her heart was supposed to have been.

The dowager, looking altogether perplexed, fumbled at her throat. "Do you not recognize a crucifix?" she asked as she pulled from under her jacket a gold, medieval-style cross.

Bloody— "How did you get that? Do you own two?"

A coughing noise came from Lady Cresting. "What did you say?"

Yes, what did I say?

Her head spinning like a top, Elizabeth squeezed shut her eyes. She felt as if she were watching herself from a distance make an absolute and utter fool of herself, without having the first notion as to how to put a stop to the insanity. Unfortunately, the darkness was compounding her dizziness, forcing her to reopen her eyes.

My God. There it was, sparkling against the dowager's dark green gown for all the world to see. The very same crucifix Elizabeth had stolen only days earlier.

"I do not understand," she murmured.

"You are scarcely alone in that," Lady Cresting returned haughtily. "I vow I've never suffered a more peculiar dinner conversation." She turned to her left. "Cresting, I must have a word."

Peter. Elizabeth had nearly forgotten him. Wasn't he sacking some city?

"Cresting, I must insist that you—"

"Elizabeth, are you unwell?"

Across the table, a pair of concerned hazel eyes became the focus of her dizzying world. Murmurs in the background told her she had drawn the attention of the other dinner guests.

"I, um, think that I *am* unwell," she answered, her brain feverishly concocting an explanation for her outlandish behavior. Somehow, she guessed that she was foxed, though, as one who rarely drank, she did not understand how it could have come to pass. A glass or two of sherry, some wine—

Of course, it was the shock of seeing the crucifix that had thoroughly undone her. She clearly remembered placing the cross in the trunk the night that she and Wildcat had . . .

Faith, Elizabeth, she scolded herself, *you mustn't think of that. Concentrate. Concentrate on the problem at hand.* Was it possible for her to gather her wits and salvage this evening? Or should she capitalize on the excuse Peter had advanced?

A brief study of the marchioness's flabbergasted expression convinced her to abort the dinner party. Get out while she still could. It was over. She only prayed that she would be able to conceal her condition from the rest of the party.

"I am feeling warm," she mumbled as Peter came around to assist her from her chair.

"Contagion, Cresting," the marchioness warned. "You'd best have a footman see to her."

"Mother," Peter said in a quelling tone.

Contagion, indeed, Elizabeth thought sourly.

"I would be happy to escort Lady Pemsley home," Mr. Morse offered, rising from his chair.

"Thank you, Morse," Peter answered, "but I will attend to the countess."

Elizabeth allowed herself to be hauled to her feet and, as she rose, the sherry spoke to her.

I couldn't, she answered.

Yes, you can, the sherry urged in an insidiously persuasive voice. After all, she had already botched her only opportunity, hadn't she? It was not as if she had anything more to lose. And wouldn't it feel delicious?

Nothing more to lose . . .

And then, without truly intending to, Elizabeth feigned the slightest of swoons, her hand sweeping across the table to neatly dump her plate of fish and tongue into the dowager's lap.

Seventeen

꒰ ꒱

"No rats," Wildcat muttered.

That, at least, was one good thing he could say about his quarters, after having passed the last twenty hours alternately sleeping and staring at the walls of his room, bored out of his mind as he waited for his stitches to bind.

Since relocating from the Scabbard, he hadn't spent much time in his small, yet clean, hotel room situated within a five-minute walk of Pemsley House. He had been too busy hunting for his bandolier bag and searching for the redhead's Dutchman. But the events of last night had forced him back to the hotel to rest and to convalesce, as he knew that if he did not give the wound enough time to set, he could run the risk of suddenly bleeding out on some lonely London street. He'd seen it happen to other men any number of times.

Drawing back the blanket, Wildcat studied the ugly

black crisscrosses marking his ribs. *No sign of infection,*
he noted with surprise. In fact, the cut didn't look all
that bad, considering the bluntness of the blade. The
wound's edges were a bit jagged, but already he could
see that the skin was starting to close.

Perhaps, he grudgingly conceded, that English doctor
hadn't done such a lousy job, after all.

Wildcat shoved aside the bed linens and pushed to his
feet. Gingerly he stretched, testing his side.

"Hmmph," he grunted. While he didn't feel strong
enough to swim the Delaware, he felt a whole helluva
lot better than he'd felt last night. Climbing out of that
bedroom window had nearly killed him, but he'd been
determined to sneak away before Elizabeth Pemsley realized what she'd done.

What had the crazy woman been thinking anyway?
Did she really believe that she could bring a half-dead
half-breed into her home without stirring up a scandal?
Christ, even the butler had known better. Wildcat had
been on the verge of falling asleep when he had overheard Boyles talking to the doctor, stressing how vital it
was that no one learn the "identity" of their patient, as
the Countess Pemsley was an important personage with
ties to influential people, blah, blah, blah . . .

And even if Elizabeth had eventually come to her
senses, Wildcat wasn't the kind of man who was going
to wait around until he could be thrown out. A Lenape
brave had more self-respect than that.

Granted, he had lost a lot of blood, but he'd suffered
worse. A lot worse. And he sure as blazes wasn't going
to lie around in that snowy-white room and be waited
upon as if he were a child or an invalid.

Besides he still had an obligation to hunt down the

missing brooch for Mockwasaka Valerie. By all rights, he should have told the woman to go to hell after that double cross she'd tried to pull on him. Damn, now there was a female in need of a good dose of common sense. Common sense and, maybe, a strong hand to keep her in rein.

But Wildcat had to accept a portion of the blame. It had been a mistake for him to tell her where Hendrick was staying; of course, he'd never suspected she would go behind his back and make a mess of matters. But, she had. She sure as heck had. And her letter had spelled out her feelings clearly enough, revealing that she never had fully trusted him. She'd put more faith in the white man who'd stolen her damned brooch than the Indian who was helping her get it back.

All the same, Wildcat had given his word and he wasn't going to go back on it. He'd get Valerie her jewelry, just as he'd promised. But first, he needed to take care of another small errand before the night was done.

The evening was warm as Wildcat began his ascent up the side of Elizabeth Pemsley's home. From the tree to the trellis to the wrought-iron railing, the climb took less than five minutes, even in his condition. *Too damned easy,* he grumbled to himself. Anyone could clamber up to Elizabeth's room as he had done, anyone with sinister intentions and enough determination and strength.

He made a mental note to do some surreptitious tree pruning.

Prying open her window with relative ease, he climbed inside, resting for a minute beside the four-poster. Lily of the valley, Elizabeth's favored scent, wrapped around him like a fragrant cloak as he stood there in the sweet-smelling darkness, waiting for the discomfort in his ribs to subside.

Gently he patted his side and found it dry. The stitches had held.

Habit led him to make a quick survey of the room, and as he did so, his gaze alit on the framed silhouette displayed on Elizabeth's nightstand. He picked it up, moving into the scanty light to better view the likeness.

"So you're the lucky SOB," he murmured.

Straight nose, long forehead, weak chin. Pemsley looked like any ordinary Englishman one might pass on the street. Yet this one—this especially fortunate Englishman—must have been more than ordinary to win himself a prize. A prize like Elizabeth.

"How'd you do it?" Wildcat asked with a smile that was, at once, both admiring and envious. His sources had told him that Pemsley had been much older than his wife, a recluse who liked to keep his pretty young wife close at hand. He was also rumored to have been kindhearted, although that heart had supposedly been frail and the reason for his demise.

So what was there about this man that had made Elizabeth fall in love with him? As Wildcat returned the frame to the table, he thought he'd have given his eyeteeth to know the answer.

With a shake of his head, he turned away and headed toward the hidden wall compartment. To the left—or was it to the right? Hunkering down on his heels, he let his fingers skim over the paneling . . .

Voilà.

He pressed the latch and the niche sprang open. Wildcat pulled the small trunk onto his lap, balancing it on his knees. He opened the lid and—

Mitsui. A sound from the hallway had caused him to jerk, so that he'd lost his balance just enough for the trunk to slide back and graze his stomach. Under normal circumstances, he would have recovered in a heartbeat, but the sharp edge of the trunk had caught him directly in his stitches.

He hissed, regaining his balance on the tips of his toes.

Someone *was* coming. In the blink of an eye, Wildcat spun, kicked shut the compartment, and with the trunk tucked beneath his arm, slipped behind the window hangings. He had barely stilled the curtains when he heard the door swing open.

Light flooded the room in shades of soft yellow, saturating the striped silk window hangings with an amber glow. He waited, listening. Whoever had entered was being unusually quiet. Then the door clicked closed again, and all was silent.

But the light remained.

Very, very slowly, Wildcat inched his head around the curtain—

And met Elizabeth's wide-eyed, slightly out-of-focus gaze.

"What are you doing here?"

Wildcat barely heard her, his attention consumed by the way her gold-flecked gown lent a creamy sheen to her skin, highlighting the silvery threads in her pale blond hair.

"You look beautiful."

She stilled, her hand drifting in a totally feminine reaction to her cheek.

"I was worried about you," she confessed, her brows knitting together. "I thought that perhaps you were hurt

somewhere and in need of help. I have even had someone looking for you."

"Well, you can stop looking," Wildcat said as he
stepped out from behind the window hangings to prove
to her that he was perfectly well. Then he saw her gaze
shift a few inches lower.

She drew in a sharp breath that pushed her bodice to
its limits. "H-how dare you!"

Huh?

Her cheeks shone bright pink, and he detected the
faint aroma of spirits.

"I fail to understand why you persist in this," she said
angrily.

"Persist in what?" He glanced to the small trunk he
carried, realization slowly surfacing. "Ah, hell, Elizabeth. You think I'm stealing your collection of trinkets?"

"Stealing . . . ?" Now she was the one who appeared
to be confused as she rubbed at her temple. "I—I
thought that after all this time, you still did not believe
me when I said I do not have your bag. Is that not what
you are doing? Looking for your bag?"

Wildcat shrugged, although the loss of his *pindachsenakan* yet pained him. "Who knows what happened to
it? My theory is that Mockwasaka, the woman you call
Valerie, has spirited it away to her underworld."

He then grinned to indicate that he was kidding. More
or less.

"So then . . ." Elizabeth blinked a half-dozen times,
her eyes a brilliant robin's-egg blue in the muted light.
"Oh, dear God," she suddenly exclaimed. "*You* did it."

Wildcat held his tongue, uncertain as to which "it"
she referred.

"You returned the crucifix to Lady Cresting, didn't you?"

"Oh." He rolled a shoulder. "I figured it would be simple enough."

"Simple?" She gave a short laugh of astonishment. "How could it possibly have been simple to break into the Ballatine home? That house is like a fortress."

"Fortress is overstating it, I think."

"And—" She clapped a hand to her forehead. "You went last night, didn't you?"

He said nothing, his attention wandering to the lush curves of her hips, the tempting softness of her white, plump arms. Was there another woman under the sun half as desirable as this one?

"Tell me, is that why you snuck away?"

"I wouldn't say it was the reason," he answered, "and I wouldn't say I 'snuck' away, but you *were* worried about the old woman discovering the necklace missing, right?"

Elizabeth pressed her fingertips to the vee in her bosom. "So after the doctor had sewn you up, you came into my room, removed the cross, then somehow smuggled it back into the marchioness's possession?"

Wildcat lowered himself into a boudoir chair as he set the small trunk at his feet. "That's about right."

"Oh, my goodness."

Breathing fast, Elizabeth moved unsteadily across the room, before sinking onto an embroidered footstool.

"And this is what you are doing now, isn't it?" she said, voicing the train of her thoughts. "You are returning the items I have stolen."

Wildcat scratched at his jaw. "Well, it's not as if I could return them all," he gruffly admitted. "There are only a few pieces that it's clear where they belong. If I remember, you had mentioned a snuffbox belonging to someone's aunt, and then there was a monogrammed pocket watch you took off a Lord . . . Merriam, was it?"

"Why?" she asked. "Why are you doing this?"

Looping his ankle over his knee, Wildcat used his thumbnail to scrape away a speck of dried grass.

When he did not answer her, Elizabeth asked, "Do you help me as you are helping Valerie? Only instead of retrieving stolen goods, you replace them?"

His jaw went rigid. "Don't fret, princess. I'm not angling for you to pay me."

"Then why? Why risk so much?"

He lifted an insouciant brow. "The way I saw it, sooner or later, someone was going to find that cache of yours and you were going to have to do a bucketload of explaining. Since you seemed so worried about being caught, I thought I could lend you a hand."

Evidently his insouciance was not as convincing as he'd hoped, for her mouth went soft and kissable.

"You do this . . . for me?"

Tension shot into his groin like a red-hot poker. "I warn you, Elizabeth," he said tersely, "if you keep looking at me with those eyes and that mouth, I'm not going to be sitting in this chair a whole helluva lot longer."

Her gaze did not waver as she stood up from the footstool. He swallowed. Didn't she realize what she was doing? Doing to him?

"I mean it," he repeated, making his tone even gruffer and more threatening.

She merely nodded and swayed toward him—

In the next instant, he had her clutched hard in his arms.

Her mouth was warm and sweet with wine, her hands tender as they cradled his nape. She was all softness and womanly flesh pushed up against him, her tongue playing hide-and-seek with his in a game that brought his blood to the boiling point.

There was a joy to their embrace, and also a desperation. A need to hold tight and fast, as if they feared the world would break in and tear them apart.

Wildcat felt Elizabeth start to tremble, her legs weakening beneath her. He scooped her up into his arms, and carried her to the bed, where he laid her down as if she were the most precious of cargo. And she was, he thought to himself. Stretched out across the satin counterpane, she was golden and soft and perfect.

She lifted her ivory arms in invitation. Quickly he shrugged free of his coat, before blanketing her body with his.

"Elizabeth, Elizabeth," he breathed into her mouth. "Do you know how much I want you?"

She pressed herself closer, her hips moving against his in an insistent rhythm that threatened his sanity. The skin of her neck and face was damp and rosy.

"Show me, Wildcat," she whispered. "Show me how much you want me."

He closed his eyes, willing himself control. Willing himself the patience to give her all the pleasure that he could.

Carefully, he nudged aside the sleeve of her gown.

"Like snow," he whispered, trailing his lips along her collarbone. "Soft and white as snow, but, oh, so warm."

As he leaned over her, his hair slipped from behind his ear to brush her shoulder and nape. The contrast between his hair, ink black, and hers, the color of moonbeams, underscored their differences, their dissimilarities, the fact that he came from a place of darkness and she from a place of light. Her world was privilege, his privation, yet together here in the secrecy of her bedroom, they were joined together by need. By desire. By something else Wildcat hadn't the courage to question.

He tugged at her gown's fastenings until her bodice came loose, then pushed the dress and chemise from her shoulders. Above her stays, her breasts swelled, two pearly globes. He dipped his tongue into the crevice between them, tasting her. She was just as delicious as he had remembered.

She pulled his shirt loose from his trousers so that her hands could slide up his back. He bit back a groan, enjoying her caresses too much.

The valley between her breasts beckoned, and lowering his head, Wildcat rubbed his face into her skin. It was not enough, he decided as he shoved impatiently at the edge of her corset, spilling her bosom over the lacy edge.

"Oh, God, Elizabeth," he murmured, before circling one ruby peak with his tongue. It puckered in his mouth, drawing full and tight. The rhythm of her hips increased against his stomach.

He pulled and sucked and bit at her nipples as her nails lightly scored his back, keeping time with her breathless "ahs" and "ohs." His hands were all over her, molding her flesh, filling his palms with her.

"You should not wear this," he told her, yanking irritably at her corset strings. "Never again," he repeated as he shoved aside the stays and gently kissed the red marks they'd left against her ribs.

"*Schiki.*" His voice was hoarse as he drank in the

sight of her nakedness, the perfect round femininity that was Elizabeth.

"Let me touch you," she said.

She did not have to beg. Sitting back on his heels, he quickly shucked his shirt over his head.

"Oh, Wildcat." Her gaze was troubled as she traced with sensitive fingers the stitches in his side. "Was it only last night," she whispered, "that you saved my life?"

"And tonight," he answered, "you will save mine."

For by sharing with him this experience more beautiful than any he had ever known, she gave him a gift—a gift that he knew he would cherish the rest of his days. Forever. For always.

"You are so strong," she said quietly. "Like the statues we saw last week." Skimming her palms across the flat planes of his stomach, she moved upward until her fingertips grazed his nipples, brown and taut. His groin muscles jerked, his breath catching.

"So strong and smooth." Her lids dipped low over her eyes, a small smile curving the corners of her mouth.

As she explored him with her hands, he did the same to her, cupping and shaping. Beneath his trousers, his manhood throbbed until he could no longer tolerate sitting up, so he stretched out on top of her again, her dress bunching at her waist.

"This has to go," he murmured. Together, she wriggled and he pulled until her chemise and dress were lying at the foot of the bed, leaving her clothed in nothing more than a pair of silk stockings and her satin slippers. Above the gold stockings, her thighs glimmered the seductive color of freshly whipped cream. Wildcat could not resist gently sinking his teeth into the thick, white flesh above her knee.

She gasped and he licked the faint mark his teeth had left.

"Damn, you taste good," he murmured as he nudged her legs farther apart. She was breathing heavily now, the soft mound of her stomach rising and falling, her breasts quivering swollen and round.

He bit higher along her inner thigh and she squirmed, crying out. Again he sucked and licked until the redness receded. Purposefully he worked up her leg, filling his mouth and tongue with her perfumed skin. When he reached the apex of her thighs, she was spread open to him, the delicate petals of her woman's flesh pink and moist.

He slid his hands beneath her buttocks, squeezing her softness, closing his eyes with delight.

Then he lowered his mouth to her and loved her. Loved her as she cried out his name in a tremulous voice, her fists clenched in his hair. Her shuddering climax nearly robbed him of the last of his self-control.

When he pulled himself free of his trousers and drove into her, the pleasure surpassed anything he had ever known. She was a goddess, silver and golden and soft and lush. She was a woman, pulsating and hot and passionate.

Her arms wrapped around him, hugging him closer as he thrust into her, wanting it never to end, even as he frantically pushed toward the pinnacle, the point of no return.

"Yes," Elizabeth gasped. "Yes."

Her breathless, disjointed sounds of pleasure urged him on.

"More," she begged. "I . . . I never knew."

And at the point where he thought he would break, surrender to the intensity of all that he was feeling, she arched her back and let out a keening sound much like the call of a bird.

It was a call to set him free. He pushed up and into her with all that he had, her nails drilling into his shoulder blades, as his liquid heat pumped from him in racking waves.

Spent, they collapsed onto the bed, drained of everything.

Wildcat awoke later—he knew not how much later—to complete darkness, the lamp having extinguished itself sometime during the night. After ridding himself of the rest of his clothing, he made love to Elizabeth again, teaching her that the shadows need not hide intimacy, but rather intensify it.

He took her as nature had chosen, her plump buttocks pushed up against him, cool and white. Rocking back and forth on her knees, breasts swaying, she had cried out loud, weeping as he brought her to climax time and time again. Then, she had not been a countess. Then, she had been his woman. His woman alone.

When next he awoke, dawn was chasing night, the shadows no longer dark charcoal, but a filtered lavender gray. Beside him, Elizabeth stirred, her lashes trembling indecisively before they finally lifted.

"You are still here."

Wildcat pushed up onto his elbow. "Did you want me to go?"

"No," she said after a brief hesitation. " 'Tis only that you have a habit of flitting in and out of windows, so I did not know what to expect." A strand of flaxen hair dangled in front of her eyes before she dragged it aside. "And," she added bashfully, "I have never before woken in the morning with a man in my bed."

"Yeah. Well, I would guess that 'never before' might apply to a lot of what we did last night, huh, princess?"

She tugged at the sheet, trying to hide her blush from him.

"You make me out as naive."

"Not naive." He grinned and traced the curve of her breast with his finger. "Just uneducated."

"But learning quickly?"

In answer, he pretended to lunge for her as she dodged to the side.

"Ah," she murmured, wincing.

Wildcat's eyes narrowed. "I was wondering if maybe you'd tipped too many last night."

Elizabeth cautiously lay back against the pillows. "Any discomfort I feel is not from the wine, I assure you. It is only that I am somewhat . . . sore."

Wildcat laughed and was about to offer to rub any sore spots, when he saw her gaze drift inward as she stared up at the ceiling.

"Although, I will confess," she said pensively, "that my behavior at dinner would have led one to believe I had been heavily in my cups. Granted, I did enjoy a sherry or two, but 'tis no excuse for—" She shook her head. "Honestly, I do not know what came over me. I must have been suffering from some sort of madness last night, I believe."

Wildcat tensed. "So you're saying you were insane when you let me make love to you?"

She glanced up at him with a frown. "You misunderstand me. That is not what I said."

He nodded, resenting his defensive response.

Elizabeth reached out and threaded her fingers through his. "Wildcat, I want you to know that last night was . . . special to me. I had not known that a man and woman could—I mean, I am . . . grateful."

"Me, too," he said.

"And I also want you to know that I sincerely regret losing your bag. After all that you have done—that is, you've been so very good—" She bit into her lip, obviously struggling. "I only wish that I could return the bag to you."

"Me, too," he repeated.

Her thumb slid back and forth over the top of his hand as her expression once again grew thoughtful. "Why is the bag so important to you?"

"I don't know," Wildcat cocked his head to his shoulder. "I suppose it was my last link to my heritage. To my past."

Elizabeth's mouth thinned. "I have never understood why people are so tied to the past. What's done is done, is it not? What difference does it make what has gone before? What does it signify?"

Wildcat studied her scowling profile. "Is Jake part of your past?"

It was as if a curtain suddenly dropped between them. Slowly Elizabeth pulled herself into a sitting position, a cold, contained fury blazing behind her eyes.

"How do you know about Jake?"

For some reason, Wildcat was not all that surprised by her reaction. While he'd never actually believed that the old man was her father, he'd had his suspicions.

"I followed you one day to the hospital."

Her nostrils quivered. Her whole body quivered. "You have been following me?"

"Yeah," he said with more than a touch of belligerence. "I started trailing you after you pinched my *pindachsenakan.*"

"But that is—that is reprehensible! How dare you!"

"Hey, princess, I dare what I want. You stole something of mine, remember?"

"But to follow me! To pry into my secrets!"

"Jake is a secret?"

"Oh, God." Elizabeth closed, then reopened her eyes. "What have I done?" she murmured.

Wildcat felt his temper slipping loose. "What the hell is that supposed to mean?"

Didn't she know what she'd done? Or was she already regretting giving herself to a "savage"?

"Go."

He jerked as if she'd struck him full in the face. He swallowed hard, once, then snatched his trousers from the end of the bed and quickly began to yank them on. "Well, hell, if you're you're all done with me, princess . . . I don't want to overstay my welcome."

Her chin quivered as she turned her head aside with aristocratic disdain.

He wanted to shake her. Instead, he said as he headed toward the window, "I'll go out the way I came in since we wouldn't want the servants to know why their mistress was moaning the whole night long, would we?"

She did not look up from her study of her fingernails.

His parting shot as he climbed out into the early morning was a bitter, "Don't forget, Elizabeth, that I am the one who's been cheated here. I'm the one who's been done wrong. You stole my bag and what does it get you? The best damned lay of your life, that's what."

Eighteen
ᘛᘚ

As if turned to stone, Elizabeth sat there, watching the light on her bedroom wall gradually shift from lilac to pink to amber. Outside the window, the birds began chirping their blissful "good morning" song, unaware that her universe had suddenly been tilted on its axis.

"What have I done?" she whispered. "What have I done?"

Last night, in what only could be described as a fit of madness, she had destroyed all that she'd worked for these last long months. She had deliberately sabotaged herself, undermined her hopes and plans, almost guaranteeing that the marchioness would reject her as a proper spouse for Peter. But why? Had the sherry been to blame? Had the shock of seeing the dowager wearing the crucifix ravaged her wits? Or, had there been another reason, unidentified, for her sudden and inexplicable departure from sanity?

She did not know. Honestly, she was sure of only one thing: last night, when she had walked into her bedroom and found Wildcat there, she had realized the truth. She had realized that the passion that smoldered between them would no longer be denied. Since the moment she'd first laid eyes on him, Elizabeth had wondered what it would be like to know Wildcat as a lover. She had wondered and she had wanted it, yet she had denied herself because of Peter. Because of her plans.

But the dinner-party debacle had liberated her. She had already botched everything, so why not take comfort in Wildcat's arms?

Unfortunately that comfort had proved short-lived, not only because of her lingering remorse about losing Peter, but also because Wildcat had ended by giving her a fright. Although she'd been willing to welcome him into her bed, she was far from allowing him admission into her private world. Into her past.

Dragging herself from her bed, Elizabeth slipped into a robe before returning the small trunk to its hiding place. As she knelt on the floor, thinking of all that had passed between her and Wildcat, she suddenly buried her face in her hands. *Good God, he knows about Jake.* And if he knew about Jake, how close was he to learning the rest of it? The rest of her secrets?

Of course, simply to be aware of Jake's existence did not necessarily mean that one was privy to the entirety of her life. Only consider the doctor and the staff at the hospital. For years, she had made her weekly visits to Mr. Morgan's facility without incident, without comment. So why should she now worry if Wildcat, too, knew of her friendship with Jake?

Because, she told herself, she was vulnerable to him.

Because she had always suspected that he had the power to pick apart the puzzle of Elizabeth Pemsley. To unravel her mysteries and lay her bare.

So what now? Where did she go from here now that she'd made havoc of her future?

The answer came but minutes later with her morning cup of chocolate—a note from Peter Ballatine.

> *Elizabeth,*
>
> *I would like to call on you this afternoon regarding a matter of some importance. Kindly send word if one o'clock is inconvenient.*

The letter was signed with a neatly penned, upstanding "B."

"Does the messenger await a reply?" Elizabeth asked, unable to mask her weariness.

"Yes, ma'am," the maid replied.

Elizabeth sent a somber glance to the window. So this was how the courtship was to end. Peter would, no doubt, behave as a perfect gentleman, precisely as he had last night after escorting her home. He would ask no questions, proffer no judgments. His demeanor would epitomize all that was mannerly, reserved, dignified, and benign. Then he would bring down the ax.

"Inform Lord Cresting's man that I will gladly receive the marquess at one o'clock."

"Yes, ma'am."

After the maid left with the message, Elizabeth sat in a chair before the hearth, warming her hands around the cup of chocolate. Although she did feel rather down in the mouth, her mood was not one of total despair or abject misery. In fact, if she had to put a name to her state of mind, she supposed that "resigned" would have done as well as anything else. She was resigned to the fact that she had let Peter go either out of foolishness or folly. Or for some other reason she was not clever enough to identify. And since no one was to blame but herself, she figured the courteous thing to do would be to let Cresting break it off easily.

Yes, courtesy would demand that she be as gracious as possible. As gracious as one could be when informed that one was not up to snuff—that one lacks the qualities required to be a Ballatine.

What then of tomorrow? And the day after? With Peter no longer a candidate for husband, she had to reexamine her options. Who now could serve as a role model for Oliver? Who could teach her son to be a man?

"And whatever will become of me?" she asked, chewing fretfully at her fingernail. Would she never be able to put an end to her pickpocketing? Without Cresting by her side as a steadying influence . . .

Elizabeth jumped up from the chair and clambered back into bed. Then, succumbing to a childish impulse, she pulled the sheet over her head, cocooning herself in darkness. As she breathed in the warm, closed air, a distinctive leathery aroma wafted from the linen sheets.

Wildcat. A pang shot through her stomach up into her heart. Would she see him again? Or had she managed to drive him away with her anger?

She moaned softly and burrowed deeper beneath the covers. As she continued to breathe in Wildcat's scent, she felt her anxieties slowly begin to fade away. A strange sense of peace settled over her, a strange sense of well-being. And despite her emotional chaos and confusion, Elizabeth slipped back to sleep.

She awoke in a panic shortly after noon. Both the upstairs maid and her abigail, Marjorie, responded to the frantic call of the bellpull.

"A bath," she demanded. "Quickly. Lord Cresting is calling in less than forty-five minutes and I refuse to be late yet again."

Although it seemed a small gesture, Elizabeth could not bear the idea of making Cresting wait for her under these highly inauspicious circumstances.

Her abigail dubbed it a "bleedin' miracle," but, through the efforts of many, at five minutes before the hour of one, Elizabeth was bathed, coiffed, dressed, and awaiting the marquess in the parlor.

She had chosen to wear blue, knowing Peter to be fond of the color, and had positioned herself before the window so that the spring sunshine cast a flattering light upon her hair. If she was about to be given the jilt, she preferred to go down looking her best.

"Lord Cresting, m'lady."

Peter entered, his stride slightly less confident than the norm. In his dark gray coat, he appeared to Elizabeth unusually pale—or was that only in comparison to Wildcat's darker complexion? She lifted her chin as she rose to greet him, extending her hand.

"I say, you are looking well this afternoon," Peter said, bowing over her fingers.

In spite of herself, she smiled wryly. Would those few innocuous words ever sound the same to her?

"When I sent the message this morning, I worried that

perhaps you had taken ill and would not be able to receive me."

She invited him to sit down with a quirk of her wrist as she reclaimed her seat, and he took the chair opposite—the chair that had been Oscar's favorite.

"No," she answered, a shade too brightly. "Last evening, as you know, I was not well, but today I am fully recovered." *Recovered from my madness, that is . . .*

"Splendid." Peter's fingertips thoughtfully stroked the gray hairs at his temple. "I app—"

"Regarding the marchioness's dinner party . . ." While Elizabeth knew she should let Peter speak his piece and go, she did feel compelled to put off the inevitable. If only for another minute or two. "I am terribly sorry that I was unable to stay."

"As were we all—"

"And I do hope that Lady Cresting will accept my apologies. How very vexing it is to have a guest arrive late and then disrupt the festivities by taking ill."

"Not in the least." Peter smiled gently. "Mother, of course, was most concerned about you."

Elizabeth nodded her appreciation, although she remembered quite clearly the dowager's suggestion that a footman—not Cresting—see her home.

"However, I did not ask to call on you today to discuss Mother."

"No?" She thought surely her face would crack at the effort it took to maintain a pleasant countenance.

"No," he answered, the gravity in his gaze such that Elizabeth did not feel she could endure it. She thrust a hand toward the table and blurted out, "Tea?"

Peter answered in a patient voice, "No, thank you."

She let her hands fall limply into her lap. *Here it comes . . .*

"Elizabeth." He cleared his throat. "I have had the pleasure of sharing your company for many months now, and although we have never spoken directly of an alliance—"

"No, we never have, have we?" she said, determined to make this as painless as she could. "Therefore neither of us ought to have entertained any expectations of any sort, wouldn't you agree?"

"Well, yes . . ."

"And I believe it would have been the very height of imprudence to view our friendship as anything more than just that: friendship."

"Well, ye-e-s," he agreed, albeit with obvious reluctance. "However, as we both know, friendships will occasionally develop into more meaningful relationships—"

"Of course. On occasion. Although I, for one, would never presume upon a gentleman's feelings."

"And I would hope never to presume upon a lady's," Peter answered carefully.

"No, I am sure you would not." Elizabeth clasped her hands together as her palms started to itch. "You have always behaved exactly as was proper, Peter, and you may rest assured that I am exceedingly appreciative. Therefore, there is no reason that either of us should come away from this conversation feeling as though we have not dealt honorably with the other."

He rubbed again at his temple. "I would like to believe that I have behaved honorably."

"You have, I assure you," Elizabeth said with an air of finality as she pushed to her feet.

Peter, however, continued to sit, his expression bemused. When he refused to stand, she had no choice but to seat herself again.

"I, um—" she stammered. *What more was there to say?*

"Am I keeping you?" he asked, frowning slightly.

"No." She smoothed at her skirts, wishing he would hurry up and be done with it.

"As I was saying . . . Elizabeth, we have been enjoying each other's company for some time now—"

"But without any expectations," Elizabeth insisted.

He nodded jerkily. "Granted."

Oh, heavens. As her anxiety mounted, Elizabeth felt her palms grow itchier, and her stomach begin to growl. In desperation, she selected an apricot tart from the tea tray to keep her hands busy and her stomach quiet.

"Nonetheless," Peter continued, "my expectations aside, I would be most honored if you would accept my proposal of marriage."

Later, Elizabeth would think that 'twas only by the grace of God that she did not inhale the tart whole. A crumb or two did lodge in her throat, requiring Peter to pat at her back as she hacked and wheezed and coughed and made a general spectacle of herself.

"There," she finally gasped, after sipping at a cup of milky tea. "There now, that is much better."

Peter handed her his handkerchief, which she used to dab at her wet eyes.

"I trust that my offer does not come as a complete surprise?" Peter asked, studying her uncertainly.

"Oh, no, not at all." Elizabeth bit into her lip. "That is to say that I didn't think—I mean, it appeared that the marchioness might have taken a dislike of me."

Peter's smile quirked to one side. " 'Dislike' is too strong a term, I should say. Rather, I believe that Mother finds you . . . capricious."

Capricious? "So she approves?"

Peter took the teacup from her hand and placed it on the tray. Then he took her hand in his, his aspect sober.

"Elizabeth, if I were to wait for my mother to approve a bride, I would, in all likelihood, never marry. I only asked her, as a courtesy, to meet with you prior to my declaring myself; never did my decision hinge on her opinion of you."

"Oh." Elizabeth blinked as the room seemed to turn upside down. Or was that her world tilting back on its axis?

"Is it too much to hope that you have an answer for me?" he asked with a tentative smile.

Oh, my God. She held tight to Peter's hand, for fear she'd fall to the floor the way the room was revolving. *Another chance,* she told herself. *Another chance to ensure her and Oliver's future.*

But last night . . . What about Wildcat and those feelings he'd inspired in her? What about that curious ache lingering in the center of her chest?

"It does seem as if you fit well in that chair," she said inanely.

Peter's smile wavered. "Is that a . . . yes?"

Was it? Elizabeth questioned, wondering where in blazes her wits had gone off to. Try as she might, she could not seem to put together two cohesive thoughts. Wildcat and Oliver and tattoos and beaded bags were all whirling about in her head like figures on a carousel.

"I imagine it would be foolish of me to give you any other answer but yes," she said with a shallow, hiccuping laugh.

Peter's fingers tightened on hers. "I am honored."

Elizabeth blinked. Was that it, then? Was she now engaged to be married to Peter Ballatine?

She smiled, laughed once more, and for the first time in her life, fell into a dead faint.

"I've come to see Jake."

Wildcat folded his arms across his chest as the attendant looked him up and down, clearly ambivalent about admitting a stranger in buckskin and feathers.

"I am sorry, sir," the man said, hovering behind the hospital door, "but Mr. Morgan is not in and he normally approves any visitors prior to admittance."

Wildcat sent a quick glance to his boots, before looking the attendant squarely in the eye to lie, "Lady Pemsley asked me to stop by and see him."

"Oh." The man's chubby features relaxed. "My apologies, sir," he said as he stepped back from the door. "You see, I am new to the facility and—"

"I understand," Wildcat interrupted with a thin smile. He followed the attendant into the foyer.

"Mr. Jake has been resting a lot lately," the attendant explained as he led Wildcat down a long, carpeted corridor. "But he just awoke from a nap, so I am sure he will be pleased to have a visitor."

Wildcat wasn't nearly so sure, but refrained from saying so. In fact, he wasn't at all sure that Jake would even speak with him, much less tell him what he'd come here to learn, but he had to give it a try. He had to try to find out why Elizabeth Pemsley had become an obsession with him. Why he could not stop thinking of her, even in his sleep. And why he felt as if their spirits were as one when, in reality, they were as different as two people could possibly be.

Perhaps this man Jake would be able to provide some answers. Because to judge from Elizabeth's reaction earlier that morning, there had to be something here for Wildcat to learn. Something that might help him understand the unfathomable bond that was forming between a half-breed drifter and an English peeress.

"Good afternoon, Mr. Jake," the attendant said as he proceeded Wildcat into a spacious, sunlight-filled room. "You have a visitor, sir."

Wildcat's first thought was that the attendant had led him to the wrong damned apartment. Acres of satins, silks, and brocades vied with mountains of gilt and mahogany and ivory. Rugs so thick a man could drown in them covered the floor from end to end, and the bed approximated the size of a small ship. Surely this could not be the home of a man who'd spent most his life on the London streets?

"Who's there?" a voice called from the bed, in an accent that most *definitely* came from the London streets.

"My name is MacInnes," Wildcat said as he waved the attendant from the room with a polite nod of thanks. He waited until the door closed behind him before approaching the bed.

Older than he'd envisioned, Jake resembled some Middle Eastern pasha as he sat propped up amid a sea of pillows. He was dressed in a lounging robe, his thin white hair covered inexplicably by a gentleman's evening silk top hat.

"MacInnes, MacInnes," the old man muttered, squinting. "Am I supposed to know ye?"

Wildcat sat down in a chair beside the bed. "As a matter of fact, we've never met."

"Ah," he said. "I know me wits aren't wot they used

to be—goin' buffle-headed with age, ye know—but I figured I ought to recollect a singular-lookin' bloke like yerself."

Wildcat smiled slightly. "Singular" was one of the less offensive terms he'd heard used to describe his appearance.

"Can I offer ye a spot of wet?" the old man asked. "Hock, sherry, tea?"

"No, thanks. I actually came to talk with you about a friend of yours."

"Hah!" Jake chuckled raspily, the sound somehow unhealthy. "I ain't got me many of 'em anymore. Most me chums stuck their spoons in the wall a long time ago. I figure it's nearly time for me to be joinin' 'em."

Wildcat questioned how true that statement might be. He'd seen death too often not to recognize its signs, and Jake was a man who looked ready to move on.

"I've come about Elizabeth Pemsley," he said.

The old man's thin brows rose as he pushed out his lips consideringly. Lowering his gaze, he began to fuss with the folds of his pristinely white neckcloth. He tugged and straightened and primped, until Wildcat was convinced that Jake had forgotten his presence.

"So ye've come 'bout Lizzie."

"Lizzie?"

"Aye, I know she's a right proper countess now," Jake said, shaking his head impatiently, as he lifted his faded blue eyes to Wildcat. "But to me, she'll always be me li'l golden-haired Lizzie."

"You have known her a long time, then?"

"Blimey, I'd say so. All 'er life."

Wildcat's chin cocked. He had wondered if Jake might have worked as a servant for Elizabeth's family . . .

"And 'ow long have *you* known 'er?" Jake asked suspiciously.

"Less than a month."

"And I wouldn't s'pose she knows ye're here visitin' me, eh, Mr. MacInnes?"

"No. She doesn't."

Jake's lips pushed out again in that measuring, thoughtful way. "I can't promise ye nothin', but wot is it ye want to know?"

"What can you tell me about her? About her past, her childhood? What's important to her?"

In other words, old man, what can you tell me to help explain why I am kpitscha *enough to fall for a woman who is as unattainable to me as the stars above?*

Jake sighed. "Seems to me ye ought to be askin' Lizzie these questions."

"Would she answer them?"

The old man chuckled again, an ominous rattling audible from deep in his chest. "Only if she was of a mind to, Mr. MacInnes. That li'l bit is as plucky a miss as ye're likely to meet. Plucky and plum full o' heart. When she brought me 'ere, I says to 'er I don't want to be no scroof, I can take care of meself. But Lizzie would 'ave none of it. She sets me up like a king, she does, makin' sure that ol' Jake never wants fer nothin' never again."

Wildcat nodded. The question was "why?"

"I've heard that some people think you might be Elizabeth's father."

"Blimey, why, I'd 'ave given all me teeth—or them's I got left—to be able to say 'at I was," Jake answered hotly, pulling at the brim of his hat. "But—"

His words were cut off as he suddenly grimaced, lowering his hand to his chest.

Wildcat leaned forward. "What?"

The old man's face screwed up into a pattern of fine wrinkles.

"Jake?"

"I—I—" His clawlike hand clutched at the front of the silk robe.

Wildcat jumped up and, in two strides, yanked open the door. "Hey!" he bellowed to no one in particular. "Hey, come here!"

From a doorway down the hall, the attendant came scurrying, his short legs not moving nearly fast enough, in Wildcat's opinion.

"Hurry," he growled as the man scampered past. "Something's wrong."

After a nervous nod, the attendant went to lean over Jake as Wildcat retreated to pace the length of the room. *This isn't good. It's not good at all.*

After a minute, the attendant moved away from the bed, heading for the door. "I need to send for Mr. Morgan," he explained in hushed, worried tones.

"So . . . it's bad?"

The attendant gave a sad nod. "We've been expecting that any day he—"

With a sharp slash of his hand, Wildcat instructed him to say no more. There was no reason to invite death into the room any sooner than they needed to.

"How much longer?"

"I'm sorry, but I don't know."

"Shit." Wildcat glanced over his shoulder, anger and frustration bringing a cold sweat to his brow. "Look, I want you to send a messenger for the doctor and then get right back here, do you understand?"

The man bobbed his head vigorously. Fearfully.

"I'll wait with Jake until you return, but then I need to go fetch someone."

The attendant started to go, but Wildcat grabbed the man by the elbow, gruffly reminding him once again, "And hurry, dammit."

Nineteen
‧⁓⊃⌒⊂⁓‧

The Marquess of Cresting had been gone less than an hour when Elizabeth heard the bell jingle at the front door. She had been sitting in Oscar's old chair, struggling with a note to Oliver, asking him to come home from school.

Informing her son of her upcoming marriage was to be a delicate task, she realized, one which could only be handled face-to-face, with gentle and thoughtful explanation. Even the drafting of this short note was proving excessively difficult—no doubt made so by the fact that her conscience was secretly plaguing her like the very devil.

What of last night? it questioned. *What of—*

The bell pealed again with provoking insistence, forcing her to her feet.

"Dear me," she murmured irritably, "I sincerely hope

that Peter did not disregard my wishes and send for the doctor."

While it had been most silly of her to faint, sillier yet had been the enormous fuss made about it by the Pemsley household. A good thirty minutes had been spent convincing the overly solicitous threesome of Cresting, Boyles, and Marjorie that she did not need the attention of a physician. After all, she'd argued, she had lost consciousness for only a few seconds, scarcely a remarkable event when one considered how many ladies were forever fainting at those overcrowded, overheated society parties.

She had told everyone that lack of sleep was to blame for her light-headedness. Lack of sleep and, of course, the intense and overwhelming emotion resulting from her betrothal to the Marquess of Cresting.

Intense and overwhelming, indeed, her conscience mocked. *How can you pretend that—*

Her self-torment was interrupted by the parlor door unexpectedly crashing against the far wall. Wildcat stood on the threshold, chest heaving, scowling so fiercely that even Elizabeth felt a frisson of fear spurt along her spine.

"Grab your hat or whatever it is you need," he ordered tersely, breathlessly, as his black braid swayed along his jaw. "Boyles is having the carriage brought around. We haven't got a lot of time."

It took a moment for Elizabeth to comprehend his words, for her heart had leaped crazily in her chest when first he'd appeared in the doorway. He was so powerful, so sure of himself . . .

"Time?" She gripped the back of the divan, gooseflesh rippling along her arms. "Time for what?"

Across the room, Wildcat's blue eyes flashed with . . . *Oh, God . . . pity?*

"Jake," he answered quietly.

"No." Her head swam, and she clutched to the sofa back. "What—no! How could you know?"

But he did know. And that was why he had come for her. That was why his forehead was beaded with sweat, because he'd raced halfway across town to tell her. *Please, dear Lord, no. Not Jake.* Not the one person who had loved her always, who had believed in her when she did not know how to believe in herself. She closed her eyes as if she could make the pain disappear inside her head.

She reopened them as a muscled arm encircled her waist.

"Come," he said, and she melted into him, allowing him to half carry her to the carriage.

The ride to the sanitarium was a blur, as Elizabeth dared not permit her thoughts to wander any further than the immediacy of sitting at Wildcat's side, his warmth, his strength. They spoke not at all.

At the hospital, the doctor was waiting for her outside Jake's room. In those few frantic seconds as she searched Mr. Morgan's kind features, she prayed that there had been a misunderstanding. She prayed, God forgive her, that someone else's life lay in the balance— not Jake's.

"And?" she asked, incapable of saying more.

"He is resting easy now, although . . ."

Her breath caught like fire in her lungs. "Although?"

"I am so very sorry, Lady Pemsley. I wish I could tell you differently, but it is impossible to foresee how much longer he may have." Mr. Morgan spoke in the hallowed tones reserved for those already gone. "It could be days, hours . . . minutes."

If not for Wildcat's hand at her elbow, Elizabeth was certain that she would have crumpled to the floor. "Does—" Her voice cracked and she tried again. "Does he know?"

The physician's shrug accepted the inevitable. "I daresay he's known far longer than we have."

Elizabeth heaved a deep, aching sigh. How callous they all were about staring death in the face. How easily they seemed to accept it. She remembered at Oscar's bedside this same insensitivity and matter-of-factness on the part of the doctor, the undertaker, the solicitor. Life, then death. Was it truly as simple as that? And if it was, why did she persist in fighting it so bitterly?

"He's asked for you," the doctor said.

Elizabeth started forward and felt Wildcat's grip fall away from her elbow. She turned back to gaze at him imploringly. "I cannot—"

He appeared to understand without her having to give voice to her plea. Together they entered Jake's room, Wildcat releasing her as she took the final steps up to the side of the bed.

Why, there has been some sort of misunderstanding, she told herself, staring down at the man who'd been friend, mentor, and surrogate father to her. *He looks just as he did when last I saw him.*

"Jake?"

He opened his eyes, and grinned the same special grin he'd reserved for her and her alone since she was no more than an infant.

"Lizzie."

Giddy with relief, she dropped into the chair, almost

laughing. "What do you think you are doing, you incorrigible scoundrel? I fear you have given the doctor a terrific scare."

"But ye're not scared, are ye, Lizzie girl?"

A flutter of uncertainty wafted through her. "Should I be?" Her relieved smile grew stiff when he did not immediately answer her.

"No. Ye needn't be scared. I'm not."

And then she saw it. She saw surrender in his tired eyes.

Grabbing his gnarled hand from the bedsheet, she wanted to weep with shock to find it so cold; but she could not cry in front of Jake. He had once told her, many, many years ago, that her tears were like little knives slicing away at his heart. She didn't believe she had cried in his presence since that day.

"How are you feeling?"

The crepelike skin on his cheeks creased as he smiled again. But this time she saw that the smile took more effort than she'd at first realized.

"T' tell ye the truth, I feel like a man who's 'bout to kick up his toes."

"Oh, Jake . . ."

"Eh, now, none of 'at," he scolded, masking a wince. "So tell me, 'ow's our Oliver?"

Elizabeth bit into her cheek, recognizing Jake's purpose. He wanted this last visit to be like any other, where they would discuss the same array of topics, share the same meaningless gossip about people Jake had never even laid eyes on. There was to be no talk of good-byes or never-agains. No talk of tomorrows.

"He is well," she answered as evenly as she could manage, although her throat felt thick and raw with emotion. "I drove out and saw him at school and he is doing wonderfully well. Despite all my doubts, 'twas evidently for the best to send him away to school."

"Aye, ye know it was. He's goin' to be a first-rate 'un, that lad."

"Yes," she agreed softly. "He is."

And to think, she thought, that her son would never meet this man—this man who had been everything to her.

"And wot 'bout that Cresting fella? Has he come up to snuff yet?"

Elizabeth went perfectly still, knowing that Wildcat stood behind her. But how far behind her?

"Don't know wot's wrong with that fella. Can't he see he's got hisself a treasure in ye, lass? If he 'ad any sense a'tall, he'd 'ave rushed ye to the altar months ago. I tell ye, Lizzie, 'twould ease me mind to know 'at when I'm gone, ye'll be taken care of."

Sweet merciful heavens, I cannot lie to him. She couldn't. She may have lied about every other aspect of her life, but she drew the line at telling falsehoods to her dearest and oldest friend. She simply hadn't the heart—certainly not as he lay dying.

Yet, what about Wildcat? How far behind her did he stand? A few feet away? Out of earshot? Or dare she hope that with her back to the door, she had not seen him as he stepped out of the room?

Jake gave her hand an impatient shake. "Why don't you send fer ol' Cresting now, lass, and I'll set 'im straight afore I go? I'll weasel a proposal out of the bloke—see if I don't."

"I—" With a swollen, salty lump clogging her words, she leaned forward and said quietly, "It is not necessary

to send for Lord Cresting, Jake. He did ask for my hand
. . . and I said yes."

The stillness behind her did not seem natural. Had she
heard a small noise?

"Coo-eee!" Jake chuckled breathlessly with delight.
"And when was ye plannin' to tell me?"

"I—I am not sure," she answered on a shaky smile.

For although she felt as if she were shriveling up inside, at the same time, Elizabeth knew a bittersweet joy,
realizing that she had given Jake this little bit of satis-
faction.

"So, tell me," Jake asked, "when did he finally go to
bended knee?"

Oh, how she wanted to lie then. How very much she
wanted to. For what would Wildcat think of a woman
who slept with one man, then promised herself to another the following morning?

"Today," she whispered.

"Wot's 'at?" Jake strained up from the pillows, but
was unable to lift himself.

Worried, Elizabeth swiftly laid a hand on his chest,
urging him to lie back. Even through the robe, he felt
cold to her. Frightfully cold.

"He asked me today," she repeated.

"Hah." Smiling, Jake let his eyes drift shut. "He's got
hisself a treasure, he does."

"I wonder," Elizabeth murmured.

As she smoothed the lapel of Jake's robe, a spasm
crossed the lines of the old man's face.

"Are you in pain? Shall I call for Mr. Morgan?"

"I don't 'ave no use fer a sawbones now. But would
ye be a good girl, Lizzie, and get me hat? The doctor
took it off when 'e was tendin' to me."

"Which one, Jake?"

"The new 'un."

Elizabeth pivoted in her chair to search for the hat, finally taking a moment to peek behind her.

The room was empty. Empty but for her and Jake.

Oh, dear Lord, when did he leave? Had it been before or after she had told Jake about her betrothal? *Yet what if Wildcat had heard?* she asked herself fatalistically. *What difference would it make?* After all, it was not as if she could break off her engagement to Peter simply because of what had passed between her and Wildcat last night . . .

Could she?

"Lizzie?"

Elizabeth brushed aside a pang of dismay as she retrieved the beaver from the tea table. "Here it is, Jake."

Gently smoothing her hand over the brim, she placed it across the old man's brow at the jaunty angle he preferred.

He touched a finger to her cheek as she leaned over him. "Now listen up, Lizzie girl. I know ye mourned Lord Pemsley somethin' fierce, but I don't want none of 'at, ye hear? 'At black crepe and buntin' is fer ye nob types—we never 'ad no use fer it in St. Giles. Besides," Jake pointed out, his voice growing thin, "ye and me both knows I ain't s'posed t'exist no more, so ye'd look damned queer mournin' fer a man who ain't."

Elizabeth bowed her head, recognizing the sad truth of what he said. Once Jake was gone, she would not be able to properly grieve for her friend since no one was supposed to know about him. No one except those who worked here at the hospital.

For years, Elizabeth had tried to convince Jake to

come in off the streets, but he had resisted, refusing to accept her charity. It had taken deteriorating health and a frightening brush with prison to finally convince the aging trickster to abandon his previous life. Then, once saved from Newgate, Jake had seemed to "disappear," his old cronies believing him to have perished behind prison walls.

It had been safer that way, Elizabeth had decided, protecting Jake from both the courts and his questionable St. Giles's acquaintances.

So, Elizabeth could not don mourning, for questions would arise—questions she would be forced to answer with lies. Lies that would merely belittle the memory of this kind and noble man.

Jake's eyes were shut once again, his white lashes nearly invisible against his cheeks.

"Shall I go so that you may rest?" she asked quietly.

He clapped his hand over hers. "Would ye stay, Lizzie? Stay with an old fool to the end?"

And she did stay. She stayed through the evening and through the night. She stayed until the end.

Unfortunately for Hendrick Henke, the man who burst through his bedroom door about eleven o'clock that night was not in a forgiving mood.

Wildcat had had enough. More than enough. He wanted to finish his business and get the hell out of London as fast as the laws of motion would allow.

"Damn England," he muttered as he planted a left hook to Hendrick's jaw. *Damn England's women,* he silently added, following up the left with a well-placed right.

As the fair-haired Hendrick keeled over onto the bare

floor like a felled tree, Wildcat nodded cynically. "And damn the foolish men, my friend, who don't know any better than to stay away from those women."

Women like the crazed and reckless Valerie and the beautiful, but perfidious, Elizabeth. Women who played with a man's mind, heart, and soul.

But Wildcat was determined to leave them both behind. And soon. After locating and delivering the brooch to Mockwasaka, he would remain in London only long enough to meet his friend's cask shipment, which was scheduled to be pulling into port any day now. Then he would be gone like the wind, putting as much distance as possible between himself and a certain blond countess.

Earlier he had stopped by the stables, where he and the redhead left messages for each other. In a brief note, he'd told Valerie simply, if cryptically, that Elizabeth might be in need of a friend in the days to come.

Because despite his anger and hurt, Wildcat understood that Jake's passing was bound to hit Elizabeth hard. He'd seen her suffering, and though the relationship was not clear to him, he knew what it was to lose a loved one. If she were able to take some comfort from the foolish Valerie's company, then so be it. He'd done what was right.

Crouched on his heels, Wildcat waited until the dazed Hendrick began to stir back to life. Jaw bruised and teeth loosened, the young Dutch artist wisely decided to provide with Wildcat the name of the man to whom he had pawned the famous Ballatine brooch.

Wildcat, already familiar with the name from his inquiries on the streets, nodded and stifled a sigh. If not for Elizabeth and Valerie, he would have already recovered the brooch. In fact, he was supposed to have recovered it the night Hendrick made the sale, but instead he'd been obligated to rescue a pair of women with more hair than wit.

"Ah, hell," he muttered, and released Hendrick's shirtfront so that the man's head fell back with a *crack* onto the wood floor.

At worst, he figured he'd need another day or so to retrieve the brooch—about the same amount of time he'd probably have to wait for the shipment to arrive. Then, once the casks were unloaded, he could head back to Scotland to deliver the goods to his friend Will.

And from there . . . ?

From there, where could he go to free himself from Elizabeth's enchantment? How far, he wondered, would he have to run before he was no longer taunted by the memories of her? Memories of how she'd nibble at the edges of her fingernails when nervous . . . Or how she'd toss her head with false courage, sending silvery-blond strands fluttering across her eyes . . . And most unforgettable, the memories of their night together. A night that he, jaded with experience and age, had believed to be something extraordinary. Something special.

So special that within hours of his departure, Elizabeth had agreed to wed another man.

And why shouldn't she? Wildcat scoffed, angry with himself for caring, for feeling the sting of betrayal.

Granted, what he and Elizabeth had shared might have been special, but it was, fundamentally, nothing more than sex. All right, so it had been great sex. Great, heart-ripping, soul-searing sex. But that was it. Because there never could be any future for the two of them, no hope of anything more than moments stolen under the cloak of darkness.

Truthfully, it wasn't as if he had harbored any delusions of *marrying* the woman. Blue-blooded countesses didn't tie themselves to men with names like "Niankwe." Men who'd been born on muddy riverbanks and who'd sung the *Walam Olum* beneath a harvest moon. Men who'd worn both war paint and tartans and who'd wandered the world for over a decade and still didn't know who the hell they were.

No. Women like Elizabeth married men like the Marquess of Cresting. And that was how it should be.

Staring blindly down at Hendrick, Wildcat suddenly realized that the young Dutchman was gazing up at him as though he didn't believe he'd live to see another tomorrow. His unlined face was chalky white, his dilated gaze watery with fear. His jaw was beginning to take on a light purplish cast.

"I ought to kill you," Wildcat said in a matter-of-fact way. After all, a merciful man would do that very thing, wouldn't he? A merciful man would save young Hendrick from ever having to experience the pain Wildcat was feeling, the pain he was pretending not to feel.

"Take some advice, Dutchman?"

Wide-eyed, Hendrick gave an emphatic nod.

"Stick to women of your own class," Wildcat told him, slowly pushing to his feet. " 'Cause I'll tell you something—those that think they're too good for you . . ." He scratched at his chest, the ache within almost unbearable. "Well, they probably are."

Twenty

❧❧❧

Four days later, Wildcat stood in the dockside shipping office, undecided as to whether he should shout with laughter or with rage.

"I am sorry, sir," the clerk reiterated, tugging at his cravat, "but we've no control over the seas. Ships do go down from time to time and"—he wrenched his neck to the side, as if the neckcloth were strangling him—". . . and this one did."

Lifting a ledger to shield his narrow chest, the clerk explained, "I am certain the bondsmen will settle with Mr. Taggart, sir, but there's naught that I can do." His gaze darted nervously to the fresh cut sliced across Wildcat's cheek. "N-nothing."

Reacting instinctively to the clerk's glance, Wildcat tested his cheek with his fingers and found the wound to be no longer sticky. Thankfully, the cut had been clean and, like the one he had taken in his side last week, was healing quickly. He figured that if he continued at this rate, taking a knife wound a week, he'd not survive much longer in this godforsaken city. It was high time to get out.

"If you like," the clerk suggested, "I could call in my supervisor."

Wildcat grunted, and waved the offer aside. "Don't bother. Taggart can handle it from here."

Outside on the docks, Wildcat stood for a long moment, breathing in the salty, slightly foul smell of the river, the fog the faintest of white whispers as it floated along the ground.

So this is it, he thought. He was now free to leave London. Earlier that morning—much earlier, about three o'clock—he had, at last, hunted down the pawnbroker to whom Hendrick had sold the necklace. In reality, the man was more larcenist than pawnbroker, operating his business from his dirty coat pockets, moving from shadowy street corner to shadowy street corner in order to keep one step ahead of dissatisfied customers.

The man had not easily been parted with the brooch, as Wildcat's torn cheek attested. But he'd eventually been made to see reason. Reason and a prodigious amount of his own blood.

So, with the brooch in his possession, Wildcat had left a message at the stables, instructing Mockwasaka to meet him at four o'clock that afternoon in the same park where they'd met once before. If luck was with him, he hoped that after today he would never again have to meet up with the troublesome redhead. Or evil spirit. Or whatever the hell she was.

Slowly winding his way back to his rooms, Wildcat observed with more interest than usual the furtive glances and not-so-furtive stares that were aimed in his direction as he ambled along the crowded London streets. Over the last weeks, he'd more or less grown accustomed to being viewed as an oddity in this city, and thus hadn't been much affected by the inevitable attention he drew. Truthfully, there were very few cities in this world where he had not drawn notice. In fact, none that he could recall.

But today, walking past the apple vendors and the errand-bound liveried footmen and the young wives searching for a well-priced cheese, Wildcat saw himself—truly saw himself—through the eyes of these *Ingelischmen*. And he did not like it.

Admittedly, if he chose to, he could cut his hair and remove the feathers from his braid and dress himself like any other *schwonnak*. With his Scots blood and his light blue eyes, he might be able to pass for one of these soft, pasty-faced Londoners. If he so chose. But never had he wanted to be one of them. Never had he wanted to identify with these people he'd believed weak and vain and absorbed in their own self-importance. Never, that is . . . until now.

Until Elizabeth.

But how? he questioned scornfully as he climbed the stairs to his rented rooms. *How could I think to belong among these English?*

Yet, had he ever fully belonged to the Lenape?

Throughout his life, there had always been the sense that he was incomplete. That, like pieces of a puzzle divided, the Delaware side of him was unable—or unwilling—to join with the Scots half. His friend Will had once described him as a man straddling two worlds, but Wildcat did not believe that description fit. Rather, instead of straddling those worlds, he felt like a man who had fallen into the chasm between them, into an abyss, a no-man's-land where Wildcat MacInnes was a people unto himself.

No, he told himself, almost angrily. He could not be anything more than what he was and, if he were a stranger to these people, it might very well be because he held himself from them. He held himself aloof, distant. Above.

So where was the "outsider" to go from here? He would have to return to Scotland, if simply to bid goodbye to the friends with whom he'd been staying. But then what? Perhaps on to India? The Orient?

With a long, unsettled sigh, he lay back on the bed, his hands folded behind his head. For so many years he'd wandered, knowing that, someday, he would have to return home to wed Watching Leaves. The knowledge had been both a comfort and a trial, for while he had not honestly wanted to marry the Delaware girl, he had secretly anticipated returning home, knowing that his future had a purpose, a goal. When Watching Leaves had broken their engagement, she had left him dangling, and without direction, spinning like an autumn leaf whose fate lay with the winds.

Perhaps, he reasoned, that was the reason he'd been so very angered by her rejection—because now he was forced to choose his own path. And he did not know where to go. He was tired of wandering. He was ready to settle down.

But not alone.

"Damn you, Elizabeth." He cursed without heat at the beamed ceiling. "Damn you."

From the moment she had stolen his *pindachsenakan,*

his life had descended into chaos: climbing through bedroom windows, and rescuing ladies masquerading as
boys, and taking knife wounds seemingly every other
day . . . and developing emotions that frightened the *mitsui* out of him. Of course, his uncle would have argued
that the bandolier bag had been the repository of all
Wildcat's good fortune and therefore his life could not
be set aright until he reclaimed it. But that was only
superstition—was it not? Besides, the bag was gone. Just
as he would be tomorrow.

He spent the afternoon hours packing his few belong-
ings and booking a seat on a mail coach north. He'd
considered leasing a carriage to himself, as he was not
in the mood for company and would have preferred a
solitary ride back to Scotland; but the first posting house
he'd contacted had no vehicles available, and he didn't
care enough one way or the other to bother hunting all
over the city.

At a quarter to four, as the spring day was at its love-
liest, the sunshine clean and light, Wildcat sat down on
the park bench and stretched out his booted legs. He was
not certain, but he believed that during the walk here,
he might have gone a full ten minutes without his gut
cramping with need for a mere glimpse of Elizabeth.
Hell, that had to be a good sign, he told himself. If he
could last ten minutes today—could he hope for fifteen
next week?

His thoughts of Elizabeth perhaps led him to reflect
on how the blond boy racing through the tall, unkempt
grass resembled young Oliver Pemsley. Although this
youngster was neither so thin nor so pallid, there was
something in the line of his cheek and jaw—

Wildcat squinted across the lawn, recognition pulling

at him. The boy, dressed warmly for the day, had removed his hat and settled against the trunk of an oak.
Propped against the tree's broad base, he withdrew some
sort of trinket from beneath his expensively tailored coat.
A cloth doll or a purse . . . ?

The hairs at Wildcat's nape stood on end. He rose
from the bench and, as if drawn by an invisible string,
found himself slowly traversing the narrow strip of lawn
separating him and the child.

Well, I'll be damned . . .

"Hullo," the boy greeted as he looked up from his
resting place, one hand shielding his brow from the sun.
"I remember you."

With a sense of vague amazement, Wildcat glanced
down at his bandolier bag resting in Oliver Pemsley's
lap. "I remember you, too, Oliver."

The boy grinned, pleased. "I have been away, you
know. At school."

"Ah." Wildcat lowered himself to sit cross-legged on
the grass, moving with a deliberate slowness as he would
while stalking prey. "I imagine that explains why I
haven't seen you around town."

Oliver chuckled. His face had filled out, acquiring a
healthier color. And he seemed to be far more confident
than Wildcat remembered. Far more poised.

"Are you here alone?"

"Oh, no." Oliver glanced to the horizon, his gray eyes
searching. "Aunt Valerie is coming along. She only
stopped to speak with some friends."

Wildcat followed Oliver's gaze and turned to peer
over his shoulder. A few hundred yards away, at the
edge of the park, stood a group of three—two women
and a man. They were laughing, engaged in a spirited

conversation that involved arm waving and parasol twirling. To Wildcat's growing list of grievances against the redhead, he added her lamentable inadequacy as a surrogate nanny.

"So what's that you've got there?"

Oliver's hands protectively cradled the *pindachsen-akan*. "It's my magic bag."

"Magic?"

Oliver dropped his gaze to his lap and appeared momentarily conflicted, as if his intelligence was at war with his need to believe in things magical. "I mean . . . I do not know if it really *is* magic," he admitted. "But it feels to me as if it is."

He pondered a moment longer before lifting his face to Wildcat, his features suddenly coming alive with the exhilaration uniquely and purely honest that children are not ashamed to display, but adults rarely have the courage to reveal. "You see," Oliver confided in a near whisper, "the bag has made of me a different person."

Different? "What do you mean?"

"I mean that now I am able to run around with the other boys without losing my breath, and I can swim across the lake faster than anyone in my class—except for James Saugerty, who is a full two years my senior. And I never cough anymore and I am not afraid of catching fevers. And, of course, you most likely cannot recognize the change, since you did not really know me before, but, you see, I used to become ill rather a lot, and it was terribly plaguesome because I couldn't do all that much."

"I see," Wildcat answered slowly. "And you believe it is the bag that has made you stronger?"

Oliver nodded, his expression that of sharing a momentous confidence. "I do."

Wildcat resisted the urge to grin. The child's earnestness was too poignant for that.

"So where does a fella go to find such a miraculous bag?"

The boy ran his fingers lovingly over the beads on the strap. The beads that Wildcat's mother had threaded by hand evening upon evening for months on end.

"Well, I found this one in my mother's secret treasure chest. She keeps all sorts of interesting things in there. Sometimes, when she's away, I go into her room to play. When I saw this in the chest, I could see straightaway that it was something quite special."

Aha. The riddle of the disappearing bag was finally solved.

"So you took the bag without your mother's knowledge?"

Sober eyes widened beneath a suddenly worried brow. "Oh . . . I suppose I ought to have asked?"

"Yeah, I suppose you should have," Wildcat agreed. Then, as Oliver sighed and dropped his chin to his chest, Wildcat lightly cuffed the boy on the shoulder. "But, hey, there's no reason to act all grief-stricken about it. It's not like you killed someone, you know. Besides, in all likelihood, your mother wouldn't really care that you took it, now, would she?"

Oliver deliberated, his nose scrunching up in a distinctive way that reminded Wildcat very strongly of Elizabeth. "Well, I do not *think* she would mind," the boy said, obviously struggling to come to terms with his conscience, "for she generally allows me to have whatever I want."

With a rueful shake of his head, Wildcat recognized how difficult it would be for the softhearted Elizabeth to deny her son anything. He was a good kid, this Oliver. A bit on the somber side, but nonetheless a pretty good kid.

Casting a glance to the other side of the park, Wildcat observed Valerie still chattering away, completely oblivious to her young charge's whereabouts. Christ, did the woman possess no sense at all? Didn't she realize that Elizabeth would have her lily-white hide as a doormat if anything were to happen to Oliver?

"Irresponsible *ochkweu*."

"What?" The boy's ears appeared to perk straight up. "What did you say?"

"I, uh . . . was speaking in my mother's language."

"And what did you say?"

Wildcat made an offhand gesture to the bandolier. "I was wondering if maybe you wanted me to tell you about that magic bag of yours."

The child craned forward eagerly. "You know what this is?"

"Yup, as a matter of fact, I do. You see, what you've got there is a bandolier bag or, as the Delaware call it, a *pindachsenakan*."

Oliver tried to mimic the Lenape term. "Pend-sunacken."

"Uh-huh. *Pindachsenakan* are made by Lenape women for the menfolk in their family. In fact, most Lenape men usually have two—a fancy one for ceremonial use and one less decorative to take on hunting expeditions or when traveling."

"This one is rather fancy," Oliver pointed out.

"It is, but I've got a hunch that your bag isn't like

most bandolier. It's smaller than most, less bulky. I would guess that this bag was crafted so that the owner could carry it with him at all times."

Oliver nodded, looking for all the world like a sagacious owl. "And what do you think gives it its magic?"

"I—" Wildcat experienced a faint twinge of loss as he resigned himself to the fact that his bandolier bag was no longer his. It had fallen into Oliver's hands for a reason. A reason that, his superstitious uncle would argue, he ought not question.

"I would guess that if a Lenape brave had carried the bag with him for many years, the bag might possess some potent *mantowakan* power."

"Mantowakan?" Oliver was nearly falling onto his face in his determination to catch Wildcat's every word.

"It's like a spiritual power. Or good luck."

"Of course," Oliver agreed breathlessly. "That would explain my newfound strength."

Despite himself, Wildcat's lips quirked to the side. It was only right that the boy should keep the bandolier. After years of viewing this small bit of leather and beads as a symbol not only of his heritage, but also of his identity and manhood, Wildcat recognized that it was time to let it go. It was time to pass it on to another. To one whose need of it was far greater than his own.

"You know," Wildcat said, "I received a bag a lot like this one when I was about your age."

"You did?"

"Hmm-mm."

"Did you feel different after receiving it?"

Wildcat scratched at his temple. "You know, I think I did. I seem to remember that once I started to carry the bag, I felt like . . . like—"

"Like what?" Oliver asked, practically sitting in Wildcat's lap at this point.

Wildcat bobbed his head in silent remembrance. "I began to feel like . . . a man."

It was as if a lamp had been lit behind Oliver's eyes. He sat back against the tree, his spine straight and tall, his childishly round jaw set high and proud.

"Yes," he whispered solemnly. "I know precisely what you mean."

And, there in a quiet London park, Wildcat took a lesson from a nine-year-old earl. He saw that from this day forward, it wasn't going to matter a whole helluva lot to young Oliver Pemsley how others defined him, because he had just defined himself. He knew who he was. This skinny little owl-faced boy in silk stockings knew that he was destined to be a man.

"Tell me more," Oliver pleaded. "Such as how did you come by those tattoos?"

"These?" Wildcat rotated his wrists to better reveal the patterns that traveled up his forearms. "Tattooing is a common practice among my people. First, one takes a needle and outlines the design with tiny pricks, deep enough to draw blood. Then you rub some poplar bark that has been burned and powdered into the—"

"Oliver!"

Together Wildcat and Oliver turned to gaze toward the center of the park, where Valerie was spinning around in a frantic circle.

"That's Aunt Valerie."

"Uh-huh."

Oliver stood and waved until he'd caught the woman's attention. A faint sagging of her shoulders revealed Valerie's evident relief.

As she started toward them, Wildcat pushed to his feet, brushing bits of grass from his deerskin leggings.

"Oliver, you see that bench over there? I'm going to have a private word with your aunt and I'd like you to stay right here where we can keep an eye on you, all right?"

Curiosity flickered across Oliver's features, but he merely nodded, his pale hair flopping over his forehead, as he sat back down to admire his prize.

Taken aback by an unexpected rush of emotion, Wildcat froze in his tracks as a feeling of envy—*envy* of all things—washed over him. To his amazement, he was suddenly envious of the man who would be a father to this child, who would be responsible for leading this interesting, intelligent, and somewhat quirky little boy into manhood.

Damn. Never would Wildcat have believed that the prospect of paternity would cause him to feel jealousy for another being. Much less a dull starched shirt like the Marquess of Cresting.

"It's these blasted Pemsleys," he grumbled to himself. Clearly they had an extraordinary aptitude for getting under his skin.

Whirling around, Wildcat was yet muttering to himself as he grabbed the elbow of a red-cheeked Valerie.

"Oh," she gasped. "Good aft—"

"Oliver is going to wait by the tree," he curtly interrupted, his grip on her tight, almost punishing.

"I—I should speak with him."

"Right," Wildcat mocked, his back teeth grinding. "But after *I* speak with *you*." He pushed her toward the bench.

"What happened to your cheek?" she asked.

Barely able to hold his anger in check, he did not, at first answer her.

"I was party to a disagreement," he said, once she'd sat down and he'd taken a seat beside her.

"A disagree—"

"What the hell are you doing?"

She blinked at him as if he'd spoken to her in Lenape. "I—I beg your pardon?"

"Just what are you thinking to let a child run around loose while you giggle and gossip? Fercrissakes, don't you know how dangerous this city is? Don't you know that there are people out there who earn their living by selling children? Selling them for purposes so evil your imagination can't even stretch that far?"

"Goodness! Oliver was not going to come to any harm here."

"And how do you know that?" Wildcat countered, dropping his hand meaningfully to the knife at his waist. "You could not see that it was me he was talking to, could you? Not from that distance, you sure as hell couldn't."

"Why, I—I—" Her expression a comical mix of guilt and arrogance, Valerie yanked at her bonnet brim. "Why, I do not see how this could possibly be any concern of yours, Mr. MacInnes."

"You don't, huh?" Privately, Wildcat asked himself the same question. Why should he care? Because the boy was Elizabeth's?

"Why did you bring him?" he asked.

Valerie's pout was more suited to someone of Oliver's age.

"If you must know, I offered to take Oliver this afternoon as a favor to Elizabeth. She has been nothing but a bundle of nerves these last few days, and I thought she might benefit from some rest before the celebration this evening."

"Celebration?" A tic spasmed near his right eye.

"Yes. Did you not know that Elizabeth and my brother are affianced? Lady Herndon is hosting an engagement party for them this evening."

Wildcat managed an incoherent grunt as a thousand invisible blows landed on his chest.

"In any event," Valerie said, fluttering her hands in an impatient gesture, "you surely must have had a reason to ask me here this afternoon. Dare I hope that you've brought me the brooch?"

He answered her flippancy with a steady stare. "I have."

"You—"

Her slack-jawed incredulity was worth all the torment she'd put him through these last weeks, he decided. Or close to it.

From his coat pocket, he withdrew a small linen bag.

"Oh, my heavens," Valerie breathed. "I do not believe it."

"Believe it," he said, tossing the bag into her lap. "For there it is."

"I thought I was done for," she murmured. "The Regent's fete less than a week away . . ." Lifting her eyes heavenward, she let out a long, shuddering sigh before turning to Wildcat to ask somewhat sheepishly, "I apologize for ever doubting you, Mr. MacInnes. How much do I owe you?"

Wildcat sniffed, folding his arms over his chest. "I have no use for your money, Mockwasaka."

"But you must allow me to compensate you. You must."

"Don't worry about it. It sounds like you're already taking care of evening the score. Provided," he added, "that in the future, you keep a closer eye on the boy."

Her long neck craned to one side, Valerie studied him over her needle-sharp nose. "The note you left for me last week about Elizabeth being in need of a friend— how did you know?"

"Know what?"

"How did you know that her spirits were low?"

He did not look at her, instead picking at a splinter in his palm. "I just did."

"And you left me the message because . . . ?"

He shot her an irritated glare. "Well, hell, she needed to talk to someone. Isn't it obvious?"

Valerie's freckles wriggled as her foot tapped against the gravel path. "You know," she said quietly. "It is now."

Twenty-one

"*Elizabeth, I beg* you. If you've one merciful bone in your body, you will hand over that shawl this instant so that I may use it to tie shut my dear mother's mouth."

"What has she done now?" Elizabeth asked through facial muscles that ached from hours of smiling and accepting good wishes.

"What has she done?" Valerie smacked the heel of her hand to her forehead, doing little to improve the state of her coiffure. Her feathered headdress wobbled drunkenly. "Why, just this minute, I overheard her tell Sir Wyecroft that he'd do well to offer for me if he held any hope of lifting his family's consequence to the lofty levels of the Ballatine name."

At the other end of the ballroom, the orchestra launched into a sprightly country dance, and Elizabeth watched as Lady Herndon paired off with Major Poage, who was about half her size and one fourth her age.

"Gracious, that is rather direct, isn't it?" she commiserated.

"Rather. I do fear that the terrified Wyecroft is packing his bags for the Continent as we speak."

Elizabeth gave her friend a wan smile, her tired gaze continuing to roam over the crowded ballroom. *Who in heaven's name are all these people?* she wondered. Was it possible for one man to have so many friends and family? One would have believed half the population of London to be in attendance, with a goodly number of additional guests having been shipped in from the outer shires.

"It's quite a crush, isn't it?" Valerie said at her ear.

"Overwhelming. I had not realized that Cresting's social set reached so far."

"Oh, yes. 'The Professor' travels in a myriad of diverse circles, none of which I find the least bit appealing. His interests, as you can tell, lean to politics, academia, finance—frightfully dull stuff. But I suppose you will learn to accustom yourself to it, won't you, dear? After all, this is all destined to be yours."

Elizabeth surreptitiously rubbed at her temple, in an effort to ease the pounding therein. Although she enjoyed a celebration as much as anyone, she was not in the habit of attending grand soirees on as regular a basis as Cresting seemed to fancy. During the last year, she would have guessed that she'd been to at least fifty or more parties with the marquess—certainly more than she had attended in the entire eight years previous.

She and the late Earl Pemsley had preferred a quieter existence, cultivating but a few important friendships, and spending the majority of their time at home with Oliver. Any entertaining had been done on a small, intimate scale—not like this. *Good God, not like this.*

"If it brings Peter pleasure . . ."

"But does it bring you pleasure, Lady Pemsley?"

The note of challenge in Valerie's tone caused Elizabeth to slide her friend a sidelong glance. "I do not understand what you could mean."

Valerie hoisted a white shoulder, left bare by the daring cut of her lavender evening gown. "If you'll pardon my presumption, uncharacteristic as it is—" she said, winking broadly.

Headache notwithstanding, Elizabeth smiled. At least, there was one person in this room whom exhibited a sense of humor.

"—I have noticed," Valerie continued, "that ever since the engagement was formally announced, you've not been exactly the picture of a happy, blushing bride."

Elizabeth glanced to the tips of her ice-blue silk gloves. "As you know, I have had much on my mind. There have been Oliver's feelings to consider, of course . . . And you must not forget that I have been down this path once before. Not only have I been married, Valerie, but I have been married *and* widowed."

"Ah. So, then, it is your advanced age that is to account for your subdued demeanor?"

Elizabeth pursed her lips. "If you must put it in those terms . . ."

As an older lady in puce satin passed by Elizabeth's place of refuge, Valerie returned the woman's greeting with a cordial flutter of fingers. "A cousin, I believe," she explained to Elizabeth sotto voce. "Perhaps on Father's side of the family—the sane side, you know."

Elizabeth responded with a disinterested nod, having abandoned well over an hour ago any hope of remembering the names of every Ballatine to whom she'd been introduced.

"So . . ." A saucy toss of Valerie's head sent a violet ostrich plume swinging along her jaw. "Speaking of Oliver, has he begun to come around yet?"

"Why? Did he say something to you this afternoon?"

"No, no. I only ask because I know how important it is to you that he approves."

Elizabeth shrugged, feeling moderately guilty for having inflated Oliver's unfavorable reaction to the engagement. But how else was she to have justified her sadness in the wake of Jake's death? Particularly at a time when she was supposed to have been floating on air?

To account for her case of the dismals, she had seized on the excuse that Oliver was having a difficult time reconciling himself to the marriage plans. Which was not a total fabrication, after all. He had expressed dismay to learn that they would be moving from Pemsley House, and he had commented that he didn't "really know" Cresting very well. But, like his father, Oliver had been too much the gentleman to voice any strong objections, especially when he was of the belief that his mother's future happiness lay at stake. Therefore, upon being told of Elizabeth's plans to wed, he had asked two or three pertinent questions, wished her much joy, and then retired to his room for the remainder of the day. Elizabeth's efforts to draw him out since then had yielded almost nothing.

"Oh, I say, did Oliver happen to mention that we met Mr. MacInnes at the park today?"

Elizabeth's stomach lurched. Hopeful that her faint exhalation of surprise had not given her away, she kept her gaze trained straight ahead. "No. He, uh, did not mention it."

"Ah, well . . ." Valerie leaned forward as if to examine Elizabeth's expression more closely. "I thought that perhaps you'd be interested to know that he and I have concluded our business."

"Satisfactorily, I trust?" Elizabeth said, with what she hoped to be the proper degree of lightness.

"Yes, indeed." Valerie brushed the annoying ostrich plume back from her face, adding archly, "Although I was taken aback by the unconventional form of payment he chose."

"U-unconventional?"

"Hmm-mm." Valerie's smile bordered on the nauseatingly coy. "Instead of money, he requested a boon. A *personal* sort of favor, if you take my meaning."

Jealousy rose like hot bile in Elizabeth's throat. "And did you grant him this boon?"

"Of course." In the light of a hundred candelabra, Valerie's eyes flashed a wicked silvery gray. "I assure you, darling, it was no hardship."

Elizabeth clasped her hands, fighting an almost uncontrollable urge to put her fingers to work. Either by stealing something or by throttling the life out of her favorite friend.

"Goodness, Valerie, is it any wonder, then, that your mother is pushing you to wed?" Elizabeth asked, knowing that she was being horrible, but unable to stop the bitter words from pouring forth. "If you persist in provoking her with such fast behavior—awarding 'favors' to every man you meet—why, then you must expect that she'll try to rush you to the altar if only to safeguard your reputation."

Valerie arched one auburn brow. "Touché, Elizabeth."

Instantly, she was overcome with regret. "Oh, my. I am so exceedingly sorry, Valerie. I did not wish to suggest—"

"I know precisely what you wished to suggest," Valerie said, her grin genuine despite Elizabeth's nastiness. "You wished to suggest that I go straight to hell."

"Oh, no!"

"Oh, yes," Valerie retorted, laughing. "Yes, indeed, it's all quite clear to me now."

"Valerie—"

"Come, Elizabeth, you needn't apologize. I baited you, you see."

"You wh-what?"

Beaming like the orange cat who had swallowed the canary, Valerie explained, "The favor your Mr. MacInnes asked of me was to keep a friendly eye upon you. Somehow he suspected that your spirits were low, and he requested that I stay close in case you needed a congenial shoulder to lean on."

Elizabeth covered her eyes with her hand. "Heaven help me, Valerie, I feel so foolish. Can you forgive me?"

"Ooh, now, no time for that." Valerie pulled Elizabeth's hand from her brow as she nudged her in the side. "Here comes Cresting."

While Peter wove a course through the masses, Elizabeth tried to regain her composure, but her heart was galloping as if it was about to burst from her chest.

"So this is where you two have been hiding," Peter said. "Quiet little spot you've found."

As always, Cresting epitomized understated elegance in his conservatively cut charcoal evening coat and cream marcella waistcoat.

"Yes, here we are," Valerie said, "hiding behind the orange trees. I felt it my duty to drag Elizabeth away from the dance floor before she danced her feet to bloody stubs."

"Lovely image, Valerie," Cresting said dryly, accustomed to his sister's frank way with words.

"Were you looking for me?" Elizabeth asked. Perhaps she'd absented herself too long from the festivities.

"As it happens, my dear, I was searching for this imp at your side."

"Me?" Valerie's eyes rounded and she resembled no one as much as a child caught with her fingers knuckle-deep in the sugar bowl.

"Yes, Mother has been trying to get a word with you all evening. Have you been avoiding her again, Valerie?"

"Goodness, Cresting, now, why on earth would I want to do that?"

Peter's lips tightened in response to his sister's mockery.

"Very well, since Mother is unlikely to corner you, I may as well inquire—do you know what might have happened to the Ballatine brooch?"

"The b-brooch?"

"Evidently," Peter explained, "she intended to wear the pin tonight, but when she went to retrieve it, it was not in the vault."

Instinctively Elizabeth placed her arm around Valerie's back, for her friend had suddenly acquired a startling verdant hue.

"I . . . Oh, for God's sake, I have it!" Valerie blurted out.

"You have it?" Peter's gray-flecked brows fused together. "With you? Tonight?"

Fumbling at her waist, Valerie untied the lavender lace reticule attached to her gown. "I, um, know that Mother likes to have her gems cleaned prior to wearing them, and since I was certain she'd want to wear the brooch to the Regent's gala next week, I thought I'd do a good turn by seeing to the cleaning myself."

"But to bring it to the soiree?" Peter asked. "Was that wise?"

"I know, silly of me, wasn't it? You see, I became so absorbed in planning for this evening that I forgot all about calling the jeweler and then simply didn't have time this afternoon to return the brooch to the safe." Valerie jerked at the purse's strings. "However, you may assure Mother that there is no reason to—"

It was as if a mason had taken a chisel to her face, for suddenly Valerie's features appeared to crumble to pieces.

"Valerie?" Elizabeth asked. "What is wrong?"

"I—I . . ." Her eyes filling with tears, Valerie looked up from the bag and stammered, "I-it's gone."

"Gone?" Peter echoed, his legendary composure deserting him for the moment. "By Jove, Valerie, are you saying that the Ballatine brooch has been stolen?"

Stolen? Oh, dear . . .

Elizabeth's breath rushed from her lungs and she nearly doubled over at the thought. The mere idea.

Oh, God, I couldn't have. I simply couldn't have. Please, please, do not let me have pinched the Ballatine brooch. Not from Valerie. Surely, surely not.

While the world around her slowed to half speed, Elizabeth dimly took note of the crowd gathering in response to Valerie's tears. The orchestra had ceased playing as murmurs of "the Ballatine brooch" circled the room, growing louder and louder with each passing second.

"Lock the doors," someone called.

"Everyone must be searched," another man shouted.

"No," Elizabeth whispered in the tiniest of voices. "No, I could not possibly have done such a thing."

But had she?

Am I that powerless over my compulsion?

Obviously, the theft of the famous Ballatine brooch was tantamount to social suicide. It was the most blatant act of self-sabotage she could imagine. Why in God's name would she have stolen it? Why?

All about her, people were talking and moving and yelling. All about her there was chaos and confusion. But Elizabeth paid no heed to the ever-increasing mayhem. She was focused and intent, concentrating on only one purpose: the opening of her reticule. She had to know. She simply had to.

Drawing her purse into her hand, she pulled at the delicate strings, her pulse roaring in her ears.

I did not, I did not, I did not . . .

The pale blue silk fell open, revealing a gold guinea, two hairpins, and . . . the single ugliest piece of jewelry Elizabeth had ever seen.

I did.

When the gasp went up from the hundreds of party goers, she did not glance up. When she heard Valerie call her name, she did not glance up. When Peter quickly snatched the brooch from her palm, still she did not glance up.

Then a man's voice, accented and familiar, sliced through the cacophony: "I stole it."

Elizabeth finally raised her eyes as her legs went weak.

"No," she whispered without anyone hearing her.

"I stole it," Wildcat announced to the stunned assemblage. "And I hid it in her reticule to avoid detection."

Through a haze, she watched a half-dozen men, both gentlemen and servants, converge on Wildcat.

"No," she whispered again, but her voice was nothing more than hot breath. Her knees began to melt. A hand gripped her upper arm, holding her erect.

And as she stood there, numb and mute, Wildcat was led away.

Twenty-two
꙰꙰꙰

It had been a damn-fool thing to do. Stupid. And selfish.

With his ticket to Scotland tucked securely in his coat pocket, and his bag packed and sitting by the door, Wildcat had stared out into the warm June night and said to himself, "Well, hell, what harm could it do? It's not as if it means anything."

His final night in London, and he was plotting to see Elizabeth one last time, if only from a distance, if only for a moment.

Admittedly, his pride held him back at first. His pride and his hurt. Because, whatever his feelings might have been for Elizabeth—and he hadn't yet put a name to them—it was pretty damned obvious that she had made her choice. Five days had passed since he'd delivered her to Jake's bedside. Five nights since he'd delivered her to the stars. Had she tried to contact him? Had she thought of him at all? As she made preparations for her wedding?

Yet . . . could he fault her?

Let's see. A rich and powerful marquis or a half-breed drifter? Yeah, that was a tough decision, all right.

But whatever emotion was compelling him, Wildcat knew that he could not leave London without saying good-bye to Elizabeth. He didn't have to say good-bye to her face, or even speak to her, but he had to end it. End it for him.

Thanks to an informed hackney driver, Wildcat had easily located the Herndons' home on Hanover Square. Not that it would have been any great challenge to find the house on his own, he'd realized. The noise, the music, and the carriages lined up down the street offered ample clues as to the site of a celebration.

Trailed by a skinny black cat that had decided to follow him from his rented rooms, Wildcat had slid over the back courtyard wall with ease.

"Let's make this quick, huh, MacInnes?" he muttered, uncomfortable with the manner in which his pulse was already accelerating. In anticipation.

He had promised himself that once he had found her, he would take a good look—one last look—then promptly head off for a few tankards. And maybe a woman.

Yeah, maybe another warm body is the answer.

But, then . . . Then he'd seen Elizabeth dancing, her pale blond hair more luminous and golden than the moonlight, her gentle smile more soothing than a spring rain, and suddenly his feet had refused to cooperate. They hadn't wanted to carry him off to a riverside tavern so that he could drown his sorrows in stale ale and a strange bosom. They'd wanted to stay.

So, for over an hour, Wildcat had hidden in the shrubbery, spying upon Elizabeth.

Robed in a shimmering gown of palest sky blue, she'd looked to him unusually lovely, the light violet circles under her eyes not detracting from her beauty, but rather underscoring her vulnerability, her delicacy. She had appeared fragile and frail. And frightened.

And the longer Wildcat spied upon her, the more convinced he became that something was wrong. There was a sadness about her—a sadness that he could not wholly contribute to Jake's passing. She appeared skittish, as always, but skittish in a different way. There seemed to him a desperation in the fast, furtive movements of her hands, a hopelessness in the constant tugging of her shawl around her shoulders as if she wanted to bury herself beneath the silky wrap. When he'd expected to find her positively glowing with happiness in the arms of her fiancé, instead he watched, confused, as she retreated behind a cluster of potted trees, her eyes clouded and uncertain.

Then the mood had shifted. Cresting had joined them, and Valerie had responded to her brother like an animal cornered. An urgency entered the scene, a sense of jeopardy. Reacting solely on instincts, and disregarding the risks, Wildcat had entered the ballroom unnoticed as all eyes had turned to Elizabeth.

She opened her bag.

The brooch.

It had taken less than a heartbeat for Wildcat to piece together what must have happened. He did not hesitate.

"I stole it."

Separated by ten yards, perhaps twenty people—and differences too numerous to count—Wildcat observed Elizabeth mouth the word "no."

"I stole it," he repeated defiantly. "And I hid it in her reticule to avoid detection."

No one chose to question why he stepped forward to confess. No one asked how he might have slipped the jewelry into Elizabeth's bag when it was tied to her gown. Not a single person present examined the likelihood of a man in deerskin leggings infiltrating the party without anyone having taken notice. Seriously, why question when it was far easier for all to believe guilty a feather-wearing red man than one of their own? A lady of quality?

Instantly he was surrounded, rough hands pulling at him from every corner. "Easy," he grumbled. "I'm not going to give you any trouble."

"If you like, Cresting, I can take care of this," offered a young man with longish sideburns.

Cresting? Driven by a need to face down his rival, Wildcat twisted in his captors' grip. As he glanced over his shoulder, his gaze met a pair of green eyes, intelligent and mildly curious.

"That's considerate of you, Morse," Cresting said quietly, although his gaze did not break contact with Wildcat's. "I will see Lady Pemsley home, then catch up with you later."

"Very good," Morse said. "Let us go, men."

Braced on either side by two burly footmen, Wildcat was led from the Herndon ballroom. But before he could be hauled through the large double doors, he pulled up short on the threshold, searching for one last glimpse of Elizabeth. To his dismay, he was unable to find her.

He started to turn back around when, from the corner of his eye, he spotted Cresting in the middle of the room. The marquess had not moved, although people were milling around him like agitated ants. As the footmen cursed at him, dragging him through the doorway, Wildcat realized that Cresting had been staring after him. Staring and frowning.

Somehow, amid the hubbub, Valerie ended up at her mother's side, indisputably the very last place on earth she would have chosen to be. Her wrist clamped firmly in the dowager's clawlike grasp, she was being pulled along like a child's toy, bumping into and bouncing off of whoever happened to cross her mother's path.

"Come along, Valerie," the dowager hissed. "Stop dallying. I must get to Cresting."

"Pardon," Valerie said as she plowed into Mrs. Townshend. "My apologies," she sheepishly offered, after stomping on Major Checkering's toes.

Feeling rather like a croquet ball careening from post to post, Valerie reached Peter dizzy and disoriented, and nursing a sore wrist.

"The brooch, Cresting," the marchioness demanded, whipping her flat palm to within an inch of her son's nose. "Where is it?"

Peter glanced first at the dowager's splayed glove thrust toward him, then at her reddened cheeks and quivering jowls. "Pray, do not overset yourself, Mother," he cautioned. "I promise you, the brooch is in safe keeping. Collinsworth has it at the moment."

"Unfortunately," he added as he peered past her to the other end of the room, "I must now excuse myself to find Eliza—"

"Collinsworth?"

To judge from her mother's horrified reaction, Valerie would have believed that Cresting had said he'd handed the brooch to Lucifer, instead of the renowned gemologist, Edmund Proctor, the Viscount Collinsworth.

"Yes," Peter answered, checking his steps.

Undoubtedly, Valerie decided, he was just as perplexed as she by the near hysteria evident in their mother's features.

"He offered to examine the piece for any damage," Peter explained, "which I thought a very generous gesture."

"Generous?" the dowager shrieked.

Goodness, was the woman flirting with an apoplectic fit?

"Where is Collinsworth?" Lady Cresting demanded in a piercingly shrill voice. "Where is he?"

Peter laid a soothing hand on their mother's forearm. "Here he is, Mother. Right here."

Pushing a path through the throng came the viscount, his spectacles perched low atop his nose. He lifted a finger as he approached, in an attempt to draw Peter's eye.

"Cresting, a word, if you please," the viscount called over the heads of those straining forward, hungry for gossipy details.

With more courtesy than Valerie would have employed, Peter asked those milling about them, "Friends, we appreciate your concern, but would you kindly excuse us?"

Disappointed, and perhaps even contrite, the gawkers retreated, allowing them a spot of privacy amid the chaos. In the background, conversation continued to buzz as the room seemed to grow smaller with so many crowded into one corner of the ballroom.

As Lord Collinsworth joined them, Valerie noticed Peter's gaze circle the periphery again, and she knew that he must be impatient to locate Elizabeth, who had been visibly distraught by MacInnes's shocking revelation.

Shocking . . . and utterly inexplicable. *Why,* Valerie asked, *would he have stolen the brooch when he'd only just returned it to me a few hours earlier?* It was illogical. It made no sense. Yet, with all the confusion, she'd not had enough time to think it through, to try to sort out just what in the blazes had taken place here.

"I, um . . ."

Collinsworth interrupted her. "I have some very distressing news, Cresting."

"You have lost it?" the marchioness asked, sounding almost . . . *hopeful?*

"Oh, no, your ladyship, you may rest easy on that score: I have not lost the brooch the marquess handed to me, I assure you. However"—his sparse little eyebrows waggled—"that particular piece of jewelry is a fake."

Valerie's sharp intake of breath set off a bout of coughing as her mother moaned something about the "Lord" and "forgiveness."

"It is an excellent forgery," the viscount hurried to say, as if that would be of comfort to anyone. "One of the best I have seen. The craftsmanship is exquisite, the attention to detail unparalleled. But, sadly, the stones are worthless glass."

"I do not understand," Valerie finally managed to say.

"Evidently your thief must have exchanged the Ballatine brooch with this reproduction."

Peter's forehead furrowed thoughtfully as he smoothed a hand across his temple. "Pardon me, Collinsworth, but, like my sister, I am unable to understand how such an exchange could have taken place. The man would have to have been familiar with the brooch's design in order to forge a reproduction, and since Mother has not worn the piece in many years, and since the brooch has been sitting in the family safe during that time—"

"Might he have viewed the piece in a portrait?" the viscount asked.

"I daresay it is possible," Peter conceded, tapping at his chin. "But, if the thief had successfully made the exchange, what was his purpose in confessing to the theft of the counterfeit?"

Collinsworth shrugged. "To be frank, old man, I can't say why the fella owned up in the first place."

"Wait," Valerie broke in, her head spinning in every which direction like a wind-tossed weathervane. "None of this adds up, does it?"

Could Wildcat have found the brooch earlier—perhaps sometime last week—and arranged for a counterfeit to be made? But if he'd had a fake brooch in his possession, wouldn't he have tried to pass it off as the genuine article this afternoon, instead of attempting to make the exchange this evening? And how could he have managed to slip it into Elizabeth's reticule? And why—

"I can explain."

The sound of her mother's voice gave Valerie a start. "You, Mother?"

Good heavens, how can Mother hope to explain when

she doesn't even know the half of it? Unless, of course,
she did know all along that the brooch was missing . . .

Rouged lips pursed tightly, the marchioness fluffed
the swansdown trim on her gown. "You," she told the
viscount with a cavalier sniff, "may leave us."

Collinsworth obediently melted away as Cresting
murmured appreciation and thanks.

More fluffing of the swansdown followed until Valerie thought she'd go mad with waiting.

"I am most displeased with you, daughter."

Aha. Now they were treading familiar ground.

"Your brother has tried to rationalize your reckless-
ness by telling me you thought to have the brooch
cleaned. As a kindness to me. Poppycock! You had no
business removing the brooch from the safe. No business
whatsoever."

"I believe that Valerie recognizes her error in judgment, Mother," Peter agreed in a conciliatory tone.
"Now, you said that you have an explanation for us, as
to how the brooch proved to be a fraud?"

"Do not rush me," she said, snapping closed her fan.
"I do not relish this, Cresting."

A muscle in Peter's cheek bulged, and Valerie saw
him yet again search the ballroom for Elizabeth.

"Well, I suppose there is no other way to say it," the
dowager grumbled sourly. "The brooch is a fraud because we are."

Peter jerked his gaze back to their mother faster than
one could utter the word "panic."

"You see, Cresting, prior to your father's death, rumor
held that he was one of the wealthiest men—if not *the*
wealthiest man in all of England. As the sole living heir

to the Ballatine fortune, he lived on a grand scale, which I never thought to question, for I had no reason to do so. I was only the wife, you understand. However, upon his death, I soon learned that the rumors of your father's wealth were just that. Rumors."

Sniffing again, the marchioness reached for the crucifix around her neck.

"Evidently the family had been living off the Ballatine name for decades, amassing enormous debt, spending frivolously, with no regard whatsoever to the future of the estate. As the solicitors so clearly explained to me at the time of your father's passing, the life of luxury we had enjoyed had been nothing more than an illusion, a pretense. The coffers were empty. Empty except for the brooch."

"So you sold it," Peter said.

"I had to. I sold the brooch and had a copy made by a reputable jeweler. I had no choice, don't you see? I had to begin somewhere, and I could not allow my son, the Marquess of Cresting, to be raised as an impoverished nobody, as if he were no better than anyone else."

Flabbergasted, Valerie could not think what to say. All these years, she'd been taught that they *were* better than anyone else. That by nature of their superior wealth and breeding, their family sat atop the highest peaks of society like the very gods atop Olympus. A Ballatine attended the right schools and parties, married the right people, said all the right things. To be a Ballatine was to be at the supreme pinnacle of England's aristocracy.

And for Valerie, it had been too much. Too much to live up to.

Yet, it had all been false. Even the acknowledged symbol of their family's preeminence, the Ballatine brooch, was nothing more than common colored glass.

Raking a quivering hand through her hair, Valerie thought of the anguish she had suffered these last weeks, the torment of waiting for the brooch to resurface. So much effort and worry. So many sleepless nights. Why, she and Elizabeth had nearly been killed, and Wildcat twice had been wounded in his quest to find the brooch. In his quest to find a few bits of meaningless glass.

"So you have spent the last thirty years rebuilding the fortune," Peter said softly. "Little wonder then that I've not been privy to all your financial dealings."

"I didn't want you to know, Cresting," the dowager huffed. "I did not want you to know the shame of having been born virtually penniless."

"The shame?" Valerie whispered. Was it shameful to be poor or shameful to take consequence from something as insignificant as the name to which you were born?

"Mother, you must know how deeply grateful Valerie and I both are for what you have done," Peter said, raising her hand to his lips. "It could not have been easy."

Valerie shook her head, unable to categorize the myriad emotions rioting through her. Did she feel angry, betrayed . . . proud?

For truthfully, how extraordinary it was to think that the prestige and wealth she had forever rebelled against had not been a birthright, after all, but instead had been earned through her mother's determination and will.

"Well, now you know," the dowager muttered. "So let us hear no more of it, as I refuse ever again to participate in a discussion of this same subject. The brooch, as it is, will be returned to the vault and it will *stay* there."

Valerie nodded, thinking that although the mystery of the fake brooch had been solved, she still did not comprehend the entirety of the evening's events. For, now that her initial shock had subsided, she was beginning to suspect that Wildcat MacInnes had not stolen anything this night. That—

"Pardon me, m'lady."

A young serving girl cowered at Valerie's back.

"Yes, what is it?"

A scullery maid of some sort, the girl was obviously unaccustomed to speaking with her superiors. "Lady Pemsley asked me to come get you quietlike, miss. She says it's fierce important."

Peter must have overheard—or been eavesdropping— for he stepped forward, nearly jostling Valerie aside. "Where is Lady Pemsley?"

The maid waffled timidly. "I was only supposed to fetch Lady Valerie—"

"Never mind that," Peter said. "Be a good girl and lead us to her, will you?"

Twenty-three

❧❦❧

By the grace of God—and a particularly sympathetic footman—Elizabeth had managed to escape the ballroom within minutes of Wildcat being led away.

"Anywhere," she said as she followed the servant into a narrow corridor. "Anywhere at all. That noise—it was unbearable, maddening." She lifted her hands to ears that were still ringing with the clamor of so many voices. "If I might only catch my breath . . ."

And she *was* breathing hard. Breathing deeply and far too rapidly, until she felt as if she were about to suffocate on the very air in her lungs.

"Here, m'lady?" The footman hesitantly directed her to a plank table in what looked to be a servants' dining hall. The smell of yeast lingered in the air, and the stone walls were blackened with soot and age. The hearth nurtured the dying embers of a recent fire.

Elizabeth sank gratefully onto the table's bench. Her

skin felt clammy along her arms and neck.

"May I get you anything?" The footman, who appeared to be no older than eighteen, was a sweet, gangly-limbed boy, clearly worried about his role in Elizabeth's flight. After all, was it entirely acceptable to sneak the guest of honor away from her own party?

"No, thank you," Elizabeth answered as she shivered and reached for her shawl. Alas, she found it gone—no doubt having slipped from her shoulders at some point during the mayhem.

"Shall I strike the fire?"

Elizabeth shook her head. "If I might just have some time in which to collect myself. Again, I am most appreciative of your help . . . ?"

"Roger."

"You may rest assured, Roger, that Lady Herndon will hear of your kindness."

The boy's relief was evident as he backed out of the room, bowing a number of times in the process. He left her with the single fat candle he'd plucked from a hall sconce.

Once he was gone, Elizabeth lifted her face to the ceiling, wrapping her arms around herself.

"Oh, God," she whispered. "Oh, God, what have I done?"

Bouncing off the cool stone walls, her voice returned to her as a mocking echo. *Done, done, done . . .*

How could she have stood there and allowed Wildcat to be taken away? How? She had been suffering from shock, of course. That was the only possible explanation. First, the discovery of the brooch in her bag, and then the surprise of finding Wildcat in the Herndons' ball-room—

Why, the entire episode had been overwhelming. Overwhelming and shocking and strange, really. Strange, because, in the midst of the chaos, in the midst of unthinkable emotional turmoil, she had looked up and seen Wildcat and suddenly . . .

Suddenly the world had seemed right.

Elizabeth let out a faint sound of wonder. "I love him," she said softly. "I love Wildcat MacInnes."

No wonder then that she'd been senseless with surprise, for the realization had hit her in that very instant when he'd charged into the ballroom like a knight on a white steed and saved her from herself.

My goodness, how long have I not realized? Did I love him the night that we spent together? She could not be certain. But she did see quite clearly now that she had loved him as they had stood, hand in hand, outside Jake's sickroom. Yes, she must have loved him then, when she had turned to him for comfort, knowing that she could trust him with her secrets. With her pain.

But what good had her love brought to them? From her acceptance of Peter's proposal to this night's catastrophe, she'd done naught but make a muddle of their relationship. And make trouble for Wildcat.

But how shall I set it right? How?

"Oh! My apologies, ma'am." A girlish voice broke into Elizabeth's deliberations as, from around the door, a white-capped head popped into view. "I didn't know anyone was in here."

"Wait!" Elizabeth called out before the head disappeared. "I need a favor of you, please."

Waved into the room, the young scullery maid listened carefully as Elizabeth sketched a description of Valerie Ballatine.

"Purple feathers on orange hair," the girl said, her thin face solemn. "Yes, ma'am, I've got it."

"Kindly ask her to hurry," Elizabeth said. "Inform her that it is urgent."

Very urgent, Elizabeth silently repeated as the maid hastened from the room. *Very.*

She did not believe she'd waited even two minutes before the door flew open again, this time to admit both Valerie and Peter.

"By Jove, Elizabeth, I was beginning to worry," Peter said, rushing to take her hand as he sat down beside her on the bench. "Ridiculous, I know, but I had visions of you overcome and untended in some dark corner of the house." He glanced around, adding wryly, "Although, I daresay, this could qualify as a dark corner, eh?"

"I am sorry, Peter, but I simply had to get away. So many people shouting and talking—"

"I know, I know," he soothed, patting her fingers. "Quite a stir, I fear. There is nothing like a touch of excitement to bring out the worst in a supposedly civilized people."

Mustering her courage, Elizabeth was about to introduce the subject of her own "worst," when she was distracted by Valerie. Or more specifically, by the intensity of Valerie's regard.

Standing behind Peter's back, her gray eyes wide and intent, Valerie was staring at her with a fervor and an energy that Elizabeth simply could not ignore. She tried to shift her focus back to Cresting so that she could confess all her sins, but Valerie's gaze continued to hold her like a mesmerist's spell.

It is as if Valerie is trying to tell me something—

A sudden tingle shimmied up Elizabeth's spine. Her

own eyes grew round and dry. *You . . . know?*

Although wordless, her question was understood and answered with a quick wink and a shallow bob of Valerie's chin.

But what did she know? Of Elizabeth's thievery or of her newly discovered love for Wildcat?

Unconsciously, Elizabeth started to rise from the bench to go to her friend.

"Yes, indeed," Peter said, also coming to his feet. "Let us get you out of this damp air." Turning to his sister, he said, "I am going to escort Elizabeth home, Valerie. Would you like to come along or wait for Mother's carriage?"

"But, Peter, I cannot go home!" Elizabeth said, grabbing at his sleeve as if to stop him. "That is, I . . . I—" She let her hand fall away from his arm, suddenly self-conscious. "I must . . . speak with you."

"Is there a reason we cannot talk in the carriage?" he asked with a calm and smiling courtesy that only compounded Elizabeth's growing sense of remorse.

She sent a frantic glance to Valerie, stammering, "I s-suppose not."

"I believe," Valerie said cautiously, "that I will wait and go home with Mother."

Peter tugged at the scalloped edges of his waistcoat. "I am sure she'll be glad of the company, Valerie. Particularly in light of all that's transpired this evening."

As he reached across the rough-hewn table to retrieve the candle stand, Valerie leaned over and half whispered, half mouthed to Elizabeth, "It doesn't matter, you know."

Elizabeth blinked. *What? What does not matter?*

She did not have the time to ask before Peter's light

touch settled against her lower back, guiding her toward the door. But Elizabeth could not let it go. She had to know her friend's meaning. Desperately, she twisted around, dodging a peek around Peter's elbow.

Behind him, Valerie was nodding, her smile lopsided, as she pointed to the feather in her headdress.

It does not matter.

Approbation? Was that what Valerie had been trying to convey with her cryptic message? Had she been attempting to pass on her approval? And what precisely did she believe would "not matter"—the jilting of her brother by her closest friend for a man such as Wildcat MacInnes?

When considered in those terms, Elizabeth concluded that she must have misunderstood. Valerie *was* a Ballatine, and despite her defiant flirtations with artists and the like, she was not apt to endorse a serious relationship with a man she had once dubbed a "savage." A man so far beneath them in social standing that he might as well not have existed in the shortsighted view of the *ton*. A man who, by the very nature of his character and heritage, stood at the extreme opposite end of the spectrum from a Marquess of Cresting.

Yet, unlikely as it seemed, Elizabeth could not escape the notion that Valerie had just given her . . . her blessing.

"Mind your step, dear. The walk appears slick from the drizzle."

Elizabeth started, abruptly made aware of the light rain falling around them. As a footman trailed behind, holding a parasol overhead, Peter hurried her to the coach.

"Pemsley House," she heard Cresting instruct the coachman.

"Oh, no, Peter, I cannot go home," Elizabeth protested, feeling herself in danger of being swept away on a tide of normalcy. Cresting would escort her home, bid her good night with a chaste kiss, ask to call on her tomorrow to discuss wedding plans—all without a thought for what had taken place this evening. "Peter, you do not understand."

His regard was inquisitive. "I do not?"

"I cannot go home." Her stomach lurched, but she persevered, "I must surrender at Bow Street."

"Surrender . . . ?" Peter's astonishment was quickly replaced by a look of concern as he sent a warning glance to the attentive footman standing at the carriage door. "Why don't we wait to discuss this, Elizabeth?" he asked quietly. She then listened as he instructed the coachman to drive around town until they had decided on a destination.

As soon as the wheels rumbled into motion, Elizabeth burst out, "It was I who stole the brooch, Peter. Not the man they took away from the party. *I* stole it and I cannot allow another to take the blame for my offense."

His face as still as a death mask, Peter did not speak for at least a minute. "Why would you steal the brooch, Elizabeth?"

Oh, dear. This was more difficult than she had imagined.

"Because I"—she tucked her head into her chest—"cannot help myself."

Incapable of meeting his gaze, she contemplated her fingers tangled like knots in her lap. The same treacherous, perfidious fingers that had brought her to this unfortunate pass.

"I have an affliction of sorts," she explained. "I have tried to conceal it, I have tried to conquer it, but it seems that no matter what I do or what promises I make myself . . ." She peered up at Peter from beneath her lashes, thinking how deucedly complicated it was to put this to words. "I, um, pinch things."

"Ah." He steepled his hands together, slowly tapping the tips of his gloves in a methodical, thoughtful rhythm. "I see."

"Although I have been terrified of discovery," she rushed on, "I am not so great a coward that I can allow another to suffer for my crimes. Therefore, I must ask that you drop me at Bow Street so that I may surrender to the authorities."

"And what would motivate you to do such a thing?" he asked without any hint of judgment or censure.

"Peter, I must," she insisted. "Do you not recognize that I have no choice in the matter? I must do what is right."

"Is it right for Oliver, Elizabeth?"

"I—" She swallowed hard, thoughts of her son beating away at her resolve.

"I think we must be very careful not to respond rashly to this situation," he said, his words precise and deliberate. "In fact, perhaps 'twould be better if we were to wait until morning—"

"No!" She shook her head adamantly, a curl coming loose from above her ear. "I cannot let him spend even one night incarcerated when it is I who ought to be behind bars."

"Him?"

Guiltily, she let her eyes flutter shut for one brief moment. "I am acquainted with the man. His name is MacInnes."

"I see," Peter said again, without truly saying anything at all.

"Please, if you will only leave me off at the night court, I will set matters straight."

"Elizabeth, you must appreciate my position," Peter said, with a gentle, almost fatherly smile. "While I admire your courage and your desire to behave honorably, I could never forgive myself if I were to allow you to pursue this course. My dear, you must first think of Oliver. Putting aside the issue of the familial disgrace, what would become of him if you were sentenced to serve prison time? How do you think the boy would get on without you?"

An unseen fist seized Elizabeth's heart, squeezing it dry. "But I have no choice," she whispered. "Like you, I could never forgive myself if another were punished for my wrongdoing."

"But marching into the Bow Street offices is not the answer." He reached across the cabin and took hold of her hand. Her knuckles ached with tension and there was a spot of blood upon her glove where she had earlier chewed a nail to the nub.

"At the risk of appearing boastful, you must know that I am not without some influence," Peter said, his manner as unpretentious as one could imagine. "If you insist on pursuing this plan, will you, at least, allow me to help you?"

Hope licked to life in Elizabeth's breast. Perhaps Cresting might be able to arrange for a lighter sentence, one that avoided imprisonment.

"I don't know," she answered. "Do you think that there is anything that can be done tonight? I understand that it is late, but I must see this issue resolved, Peter. I must see it resolved tonight."

A question flared behind his gaze, but he said nothing, merely directing the coachman to carry them back to the Ballatine home.

"I do not suppose," he said, after an awkward moment's pause, "that I might coerce you into returning to Pemsley House while I negotiate with the magistrate."

Elizabeth bit into her lower lip. "I would rather not." She didn't dare return to the safety and sanctuary of her home, lest she be tempted to flee with Oliver in the night, like the criminal that she was.

"As you wish," Peter said, his lips flat with resignation. "Although I hope you know what you are risking, Elizabeth."

And what am I risking? Was she placing her pride before Oliver's future? Was it more important for her to act with morality than with common sense? Or was she finally seizing control of her life, refusing to hide any longer behind the screen of lies Oscar had made for her?

As they arrived at the Ballatines' Mayfair town house, the hour was approaching three in the morning, the streets almost empty except for the occasional stray carriage. The butler greeted Peter at the door, informing him that Valerie and the dowager had returned home and already had retired to their rooms.

After settling Elizabeth in a wing chair with a "medicinal" glass of sherry, Peter sat down at his study desk and began to write. Watching him, her fists clenching and unclenching with nerves, Elizabeth eventually set aside the sherry glass for fear she would shatter its delicate crystal stem.

"To whom are you writing?"

Peter glanced up from his inkwell, his expression somehow both impatient yet tolerant. "I am drafting a request to the Bow Street magistrate, asking him to attend me as soon as possible."

"Will he come?" Instantly Elizabeth thought herself to be the very silliest of women. Of course, the magistrate would come. He was being summoned by the Marquess of Cresting.

"I believe that he will," was all that Peter said as he sealed the note with a drop of wax, then rose from his desk. "Will you excuse me, Elizabeth, while I see to the delivery of this message?"

He left the room, and she downed her sherry in one hasty gulp. She then proceeded to pace. When Peter did not immediately return to the study, Elizabeth concluded that, once again, Cresting was exhibiting a great deal of empathy and sensitivity. Undoubtedly, he had wanted to provide her with some privacy in these difficult hours following her painful confession. Either that, she decided, or her fidgeting was driving him berserk.

The clock had just struck four-thirty, and Elizabeth's feet were sore from the miles she'd trodden over Cresting's Axminster carpet. She could not bear the suspense any longer. *Where was the bloody magistrate? Did he not realize that her very existence lay in the balance?*

With half her hair falling loose about her face and the other half struggling to stay in its pins, Elizabeth swept from the room, her once-stunning ball gown wrinkled and spotted with sherry. She had to find Cresting.

Approaching the front hall, she heard a pair of male voices.

"Thank God," she murmured. "At last."

But as she entered the foyer, she saw Peter pulling closed the front door, affording her only a glimpse of a retreating back.

In surprise, she asked, "Peter, who was that? Was that the magistrate?"

"It was," he confirmed, pivoting slowly toward her, his shoulders more bent than was his habit. The late hour notwithstanding, Peter looked to Elizabeth unusually tired, older than his years.

"But why has he gone?" she asked, hurrying forward. "Why did you not tell me when he arrived? Was I not supposed to have gone with him?"

"It has all been taken care of, Elizabeth."

"But am I not to be taken into custody?" She lowered her voice, cognizant of how it carried in the vast foyer.

Reaching her side, Peter lightly cupped her elbow, the scent of cigar smoke clinging to his superfine coat. "As I said, the matter has been resolved. I simply explained to the magistrate that there had been an unfortunate misunderstanding among the family regarding the brooch. He understood and agreed that the charges against MacInnes will be dropped."

She pulled up short. "He is to be released?"

"Yes. Very shortly."

"Oh." Elizabeth's pulse fluttered wildly with relief and she was forced to avert her face.

"I realize," Peter said, "that you thought a confession was required of you but, frankly, I did not see how your admission of guilt would benefit anyone. Not you or Oliver. Therefore, I took it upon myself to handle the matter as I saw fit. I hope you understand."

Elizabeth vacillated. Of course, she had no burning desire to see herself incarcerated, yet she also felt that this time, for once, she had to face her problem head-on. This time, she could not merely sweep her sins under the carpet—or drop them in a hidden trunk.

"But, Peter, what I did was wrong. I ought to make amends."

With an almost inaudible sigh, he let his head list to the side, the silver strands at his temple glimmering in the meager light. "Yes, Elizabeth, it was wrong. However, you and you alone will have to decide on the penance. Not the Bow Street night court.

"Personally," he continued, "I think it best for all concerned that we close the chapter on this episode. No one was harmed and the brooch has been recovered."

"And when it happens again?"

Peter's grip on her elbow slid slightly higher, assuming a more intimate position on her upper arm. "I don't think it need happen again, Elizabeth. I have been giving this a great deal of thought, and I feel strongly that together we can triumph over this affliction of yours."

Her astonished gaze flew to his. "Y-you still wish to marry me?"

"I do."

He meant it. He truly meant it. And in that moment, Elizabeth felt as low as she had ever felt in her life. She was a fraud, a cheat, an impostor. And even worse, she was an idiot. During all these many months, she'd not once perceived the depth of Cresting's affection for her. But there it was. There, in his painfully earnest gaze, she saw that he genuinely cared for her. Perhaps even loved her. And she, God help her, was going to wound this kind, noble man. Wound him with what she must tell him.

Fleetingly, she questioned if she did need to wound him. But only fleetingly. For then she realized that Peter deserved a wife who was capable of giving him love. Not one who would forever be haunted by memories of another.

"Peter, I—" Tears welled in her eyes and she swiped them away inelegantly with the back of her hand.

Bending down, he looked at her with a quizzical smile. "I fear those are not tears of happiness you shed."

"Oh, Peter, I am so sorry," she implored, "but it is I who am to blame. Never will I be deserving of you, never. No, please—" she said as he started to protest. "You cannot understand—how could you?—but I am not the woman you think me to be. Goodness, I am not even the woman I *want* to be. It's all terribly complicated and I suppose I owe you the truth—"

"Elizabeth."

Peter's hand dropped slowly from her arm, not as if he no longer could bear to touch her, but rather as if he understood that she was not his to hold.

"Elizabeth, you owe me nothing." He straightened, his shoulders once again squaring with the proper marquess-like dignity. "I have enjoyed your company and I thank you for having shared it with me. That is all that need to be said."

Her tears flowing freely now, Peter handed her his monogrammed kerchief.

"It is late. May I have John Coachman drive you home? Or," he asked, his voice faintly rough, following a clearing of his throat, "would you prefer to be taken to the Bow Street offices? Mr. MacInnes ought to be released within the hour, and I daresay you might like to . . . offer him your thanks."

From beneath the kerchief, Elizabeth glanced up, eyes wide. Although Peter had not questioned Wildcat's motive in taking the blame for the theft, neither was he obtuse. Or were her feelings so transparent?

"That would be most kind," she murmured.

After arranging for Elizabeth to borrow one of Valerie's cloaks, Peter walked her to the curb in front of the Ballatine home. The sky had taken on a violet hue around the edges of the horizon, and a bird or two had begun to twitter an early-morning song.

As she made ready to enter the coach, Elizabeth faltered, remembering one last thing she needed to do.

"Here," she said, careful to shield her actions from the footman. Wrenching her glove from her hand, she handed Peter the diamond engagement ring he had given her only that afternoon. "And thank you, again, Peter."

He pressed her hand gently, his eyes soft and sad, before releasing her. "Thank you, Elizabeth. And goodbye."

Twenty-four
༺༻

Wildcat studied his manacled wrists, thinking not of the chains' weight or significance, but instead remembering the night Elizabeth had traced a dainty fingernail along the diamond-patterned tattoos circling his forearms. That night had been the closest to heaven he'd ever come, and the closest he figured he was ever likely to get. That night also had signaled the beginning of the end.

Of course, he should have known better. The minute he'd first laid eyes on Elizabeth, he had recognized that he was more likely to steal a star from the skies than to steal a woman like her from her privileged white world. She, in her diamonds and fine, ivory lace, with her silver-spun hair and come-hither eyes. Was it any wonder he had been unable to resist?

And yet, he'd resisted before, hadn't he? It was just that Elizabeth had been . . . different. He'd had no choice. Despite everything in his gut that kept warning him to back

away, he had not been able to. His heart had won out
over his better judgment. He had fallen for her. Fallen
for her hard. And he'd landed with a messy *splat*.

Which was why he now sat, waiting to be tossed into
an English prison by a white-wigged magistrate who
didn't much give a damn if some half-breed fancied
himself in love with a countess. But Wildcat harbored
no regrets about what he'd done. Not a one. Because,
really, what did he have to lose when compared with
Elizabeth? His future held very little promise, while hers
held so much. She could be happy. She and Oliver both.

The sharp rattle of keys brought Wildcat's head up as
the warden ambled into view.

"Let's go," the man said, his words slurred, his head
lolling loosely on his neck.

Ah, time to be remanded to Newgate . . .

With an ironic sense of calm, Wildcat came to his feet
and followed the warden, who careened back and forth,
his keys jangling with every drunken step.

Suddenly he lunged to a stop, and only Wildcat's
quick reaction prevented him from colliding into the
man's back.

"Now, let's s-shee here," the jailer said as he leaned
forward, squinting over Wildcat's bound hands.

Whoa— Had the man been drinking max all night
long or swimming in it?

Holding his breath, Wildcat kept his wrists still as the
jailer attempted to jab a key into the manacles' lock. On
the fourth or fifth attempt, his efforts met with success,
and Wildcat watched in mild surprise as the chains were
removed from his hands and set upon a hook on the
wall.

Then, further confounding him, the warden produced Wildcat's knife.

"Here ye go," he mumbled.

. Suspicious, Wildcat accepted the knife, his movements slow and cautious as he returned it to its belted sheath. *What the hell is going on here?* he asked himself. Was the warden so soused that he'd confused Wildcat with another prisoner?

As he followed the man around the corner, the answer became immediately apparent.

"Elizabeth."

Cloaked in a navy-blue mantle, she stood just inside the front doorway, fatigue rimming her eyes and mouth. She gave him a weak, wobbly smile.

"No!" Wildcat whirled around, grabbing the warden by the upper arm. "Look, I don't care what this woman told you, *I* was the one who stole the brooch, do you understand? It was me. Come on," he said angrily, attempting to drag the jailer back to the row of manacles. "It's me you want. Not her."

The warden blinked, as if Wildcat's outburst had roused him from his gin-induced daze. "Blimey, it's been a long night," he whined. "Can't ye just go peaceablelike?"

What? Wildcat glanced over his shoulder at Elizabeth, who beckoned him with a wave of her fingers.

"You are free to go," she said. "The charges have been dismissed."

"And what about . . . you?"

She tucked a strand of hair back under the hood of her cloak. "I, too, am free."

He hesitated a moment before dropping his hand from the jailer's arm. The man let out a relieved hiccup.

"Oh, my. Your cheek." Elizabeth's brows furrowed as she glanced to the side of his face.

"A scratch," Wildcat answered, shrugging. "It's nothing."

Her features were still set with worry as she urged, "Come. You and I have to talk."

"I don't think so," he muttered. The time for talking was done.

Nonetheless, he followed her from the Bow Street office out into the quiet, predawn hours. Beneath a dark, rose-streaked sky, a crested carriage awaited, manned by a driver and two footmen, all of whom appeared nervous to be lingering in this part of town. Their livery Wildcat recognized as belonging to the Ballatine house.

Elizabeth started toward the carriage. Wildcat pivoted on his heel and headed in the opposite direction down the walkway.

"Wildcat!"

He did not turn around, but kept on walking. Fast. If he hurried, he could still make the scheduled departure of the Scotland-bound coach.

"Wait!" she called again.

But he had no intention of waiting. He had no use for apologies or good-byes or expressions of gratitude. Or whatever it was Elizabeth thought she needed to say to him. Sure, he was glad she'd kept him from a prison sentence, but he figured that just evened the score between them. He'd saved her last night; she'd saved him this morning. Nothing more to be said.

He'd gone about a hundred yards, when the Ballatine berline drove past on his left, the horses moving along at a healthy trot. For a brief second, he wondered whether the driver would pull alongside; but the coach continued down the street, with a whiff of ashen dust.

"Good-bye, Lady Pemsley," Wildcat murmured. *"Wawullamalessil."*

Then, before he fully recognized what was happening, a threatening shadow, moving swiftly, flashed in his vision's periphery. His fingers clasped the hilt of his knife as he spun around—

"Goddammit, Elizabeth!"

He'd been that close to slicing her open. . . . Evidently the noise from the passing carriage had smothered the sound of her approaching footsteps.

She was panting, holding her side with her hand. The wind had blown free her hood, and her hair was spilling in pale disarray past her shoulders.

"What the hell are you doing?" he cursed. "This isn't exactly Mayfair, you know."

Her mouth lifted to one side as she glanced across the street to the murky outline of low-rent, tumbledown shops lining Long Acre.

"You're quite right," she said, recovering her breath. "We should turn up here."

"Here?" Although Wildcat didn't know London as well as he might have, he could tell by the looks of Mercer Street that it was no place for a lady. Heck, it was no place for him. Refuse littered the walk, and the stench of decay hung thickly over the unlit lane. Shadows shifted. Dogs growled. Not far ahead, at the next corner, two unsavory-looking characters were engaged in some manner of dispute, one threatening the other with a bottle.

"You've got to be kidding," Wildcat murmured, fingering his knife. "We're sure as hell not going down there."

"Come on," Elizabeth said, drawing her hood over her hair. "I have something to show you."

And before Wildcat could stop her, she'd crossed over to the opposite side of the lane, across from the two filthy beggars who'd begun to trade profanities.

Mitsui. Was she mad? More than anything, Wildcat wanted to put a whole lot of distance between himself and Elizabeth Pemsley. He wanted to be on that Edinburgh-bound coach in a few hours, and to forget that his heart had ever been trampled to bits by this woman.

But he couldn't walk away and leave her *here*.

With three long strides, he caught up to her. He made a move toward taking her hand, but then reconsidered, reluctant to touch her lest he succumb to temptation and drag her into his arms. And, in this quarter of town, he needed to keep both his hands free.

"Elizabeth, look around," he said tersely. "Do you know where you are?"

She sidestepped a furry lump—something that looked to be an animal carcass. "Seven Dials," she answered.

Wildcat tensed, casting a careful eye around them. Though fear wasn't an emotion he often encountered, he felt a jolt of it then. Fear for Elizabeth. What if they were attacked? Could he protect her from a mob of assailants?

"Fercrissake," he hissed, "even the watch refuses to come down here."

"I know," she said quietly.

Above them, the sky continued to grow lighter, sunrise perhaps a half hour away. A baby wailed. Glass shattered. On their left, they passed a narrow alley, from which emerged a trio of sleepy young boys, their faces nearly black with soot.

"Chummies," Elizabeth explained as the threesome went by without even looking up from their dirty bare feet. "Chimney boys."

Wildcat watched them shuffle along, their ragged clothing hanging from their cadaver-thin bodies. If ever, he thought, there was a picture of utter hopelessness . . .

"Look, Elizabeth, I don't know what you want to show me, but I think I've seen enough. Can we please now get the hell out of here?"

"May I tell you a story?"

His eyes narrowed. "To be truthful—"

"A long time ago," she interrupted, her voice hushed, "there was a skinny little girl who lived with her mother in the back alley and underground courts of Seven Dials. Her mother worked as a Covent Garden nun, a prostitute—she always had—and so it was anyone's guess who the girl's father might have been. I suppose it was a hard life they led, but since the girl didn't know any other, she didn't mind it all that much. Until her mother died."

Elizabeth stopped walking and calmly pointed to her left. "They found her body down that way, not far from the chapel, a wire wrapped around her neck."

Wildcat followed her gaze, a sick feeling descending into his stomach.

"At any rate," she continued, "the girl's mother had been friendly with a certain rum diver—" Smiling crookedly, she turned to Wildcat, explaining, "That's St. Giles's cant for a pickpocket."

"Jake?"

She nodded. "He was well respected in these parts

because of his skill and his cunning, and for the fact that he'd eluded the gibbet more times than anyone could remember. So when he took the little girl—me," she clarified unnecessarily, "under his wing, no one thought much of it. After all, it wasn't as though anyone in Seven Dials wanted to go to the trouble of dropping me off at the foundling home. I was only about six or seven at the time. So Jake took me in. And he taught me the tricks of the trade, the footman's maund and sham patents. And the foyst."

"To pickpocket?"

"Yes, to pickpocket. And as luck would have it, I turned out to be a natural. By the time I was ten, I could snatch a gentleman's pocket watch from inside his coat in less than six seconds."

"Huh. I have often wondered how you were able to lift my bag."

Elizabeth exhaled on a shallow laugh. "Jake called it a gift. But, as good as I was, *you* found me out. Just as Oscar Pemsley did."

Wildcat's brows rose. "The earl caught you in the act of stealing from him?"

"He did. But before handing me over to the authorities, he gave me a choice. Either I could take my chances with the courts or I could agree to go away to his cousin Louisa's house in Lincoln Wolds."

"Why? Why would he choose to send you away?"

Elizabeth lowered her gaze. "He found me pretty, despite the grime and tattered clothes, and decided to make me into a lady. A marriageable lady." She shrugged, her cheeks growing pink in the dusky light. "And, you see, I had only just turned fourteen. Oscar was thirty-nine."

Well, hell, Wildcat thought in amazement. *The sainted*

Oscar Pemsley hadn't been a saint at all. He'd been nothing more than a lecherous old man.

"So, for two years, I lived with Louisa, learning how to speak properly and eat properly and play the pianoforte and embroider and . . . and—" She ducked her head. "Read and write."

"And where was Oscar?"

"Oh, Oscar continued to live in London, but he would come north to visit every few months and we would review the history he had invented for me—the lies I was supposed to tell once he brought me back to London. Which he did," she said softly. "On my sixteenth birthday, we were wed. And, then, the following year Oliver was born."

"I see," Wildcat said. And what he saw was that old Oscar had taken advantage. For, really, what other opportunities had Elizabeth had?

"I think that after Oscar died, I began to feel unsafe. Without him to guide me, I didn't trust myself to keep up the pretense, and so I began to steal. Out of anxiety, I suppose."

"And married to the Marquess of Cresting, you can once again feel safe," Wildcat said without bitterness.

"No, not at all. Don't you understand? It was Oscar who held the illusion together. He was the one who made it possible. Then, after he was gone, it became too much for me. I couldn't keep it going."

Her blue eyes caught an early ray of sunshine as behind them a coarsely dressed woman drew open a window and shouted to a man on the far side of the street.

"Yes," Elizabeth said, "I admit that, for a short while, I believed Peter was the answer to my problems, but then you proved to me how very wrong I was."

Wildcat ran his hands over his thighs, refusing to believe what he was hearing. Elizabeth belonged with a man like Cresting. She did.

"But all this changes nothing," he argued, indicating the decaying buildings and filthy alleys surrounding them. "No matter what went before, you are still the Countess Pemsley and I am still Niankwe MacInnes."

"Yes, but I am also Lizzie Moore. And with you, I can be both Lizzie *and* Elizabeth. I don't have to pretend any longer to be only half of myself."

Wildcat looked away. *No. It could never work. Never.* Elizabeth's hand on his arm drew his gaze back to her, and his pulse quickened with the emotion he saw shimmering in her eyes.

"I love you, Wildcat. Won't you please give us a chance?"

His teeth and fists clenched. "Dammit, Elizabeth, even if I were willing to, do you think anyone else would give us a chance? Look at me." He flicked the tip of his braid. "This is who *I* am and I sure as hell don't belong among your society friends."

"But does either of us have to belong anywhere?" she asked in a near whisper. "Is it not enough that we belong to each other?"

"And what about Oliver?"

"Oliver and I will go with you. Wherever you decide to go."

Hope clawed at Wildcat's chest. "You would be giving up so much."

The muscles in his forearm flexed under the increased pressure of her fingers.

"On the contrary," she said. "I would finally be gaining the other part of me, the part of me I have lost. And

I truly do believe that once I can accept Lizzie again, then I will no longer feel the need to pinch things. And *that,* I am only too happy to 'give up.' "

Wildcat swallowed, looking out on the scarred building faces and refuse-swollen alleys that surrounded them. How, after rising above this, could Elizabeth throw away all that she'd gained? For him?

When he did not answer, her fingers slid from his arm. "Oh, God," she said. "Perhaps I have presumed too much. Do you not . . . feel as I do?"

Wildcat's chest swelled with a deep, painful breath. "Elizabeth, if your love for me was even one tenth of what I feel for you," he said, his voice husky, "I should consider myself the damned luckiest Indian who ever walked this earth."

She laughed softly, her head falling onto his shoulder. "Well, then consider yourself lucky, Mr. MacInnes. Very lucky, indeed."

"I will consider myself luckier yet, if we get out of here in one piece," he said, gesturing to the motley group of men gathering across the way.

"Yes, I see what you mean," Elizabeth agreed. "Fortunately, I recall a convenient little shortcut behind the chapel," she said with a subtle jerk of her head. "Shall we be off?"

Wildcat nodded, reaching for his knife with one hand, her fingers with the other. "The sooner, the better."

And, as dawn fell on the filth and poverty of London's most dangerous slum, the seemingly unlikely duo of Niankwe MacInnes and the Countess Pemsley made a run for their lives. And neither of them had ever been happier.

Epilogue

ᙣᙏᙣ

"*M*itsui, *woman, will* you sit down? All that pacing is making me dizzy."

Elizabeth swiveled from the front window, her smile nearly as wide as her expanding tummy. "Hah! You cannot convince me that you're not just as eager to see Oliver," she teased. "Thrice now, you've broken off that pen nib you're sharpening."

Wildcat looked regretfully at the shattered pen in his hand. He had been found out. "And where are the *auwesiak?*" he asked, rising to come join her at the window. "It is too quiet. A bad sign."

Smirking, Elizabeth nodded her chin to a large, spreading oak that shaded the front lawn of their Scotland home. "Our 'little beasts' are planning a surprise for their brother. I am not certain, but I believe it involves some variety of flying machine Michael invented."

Wildcat grunted softly. "It is our fault for naming him Mechkalanne. The crazy boy actually believes himself a hawk." Leaning forward, he spoke to the mound of Elizabeth's stomach. "Now, you will have some common sense, won't you, little one? You will go to university like your brother Oliver and bring pride to the MacInnes family."

Elizabeth laughed and rested her hand on her husband's bent head. Thin streaks of silver had begun to thread the thick blue-black hair, which he now wore in a simple queue.

"You will see," she said, smiling. "All of our children will make us proud. Mr. Donelly says that Katherine is his most gifted student. He confided to me last week that he has high hopes for her musical career."

Wildcat took Elizabeth's hand in his, raising it to his lips. "And why do you think she plays the violin so well?" he asked, lifting a teasing brow. "She has inherited her mother's dexterous fingers."

"Do you think so?" Elizabeth asked archly. "Then, Richard, I daresay, possesses his father's glib tongue. Would you believe that this morning he told me that I have hair like moonbeams? And that from a four-year-old!"

Wildcat chuckled and glanced out to the tree, where three dark heads were just visible bobbing among the sage-green leaves. "Perhaps then I shall put him to work for me when he is older. He can sweet-talk the distilleries into paying higher prices for our grain."

"And why on earth should he do such a thing?" Elizabeth asked in surprise. "We have all that we need."

"Yes, but maybe I wish to drape my lovely countess in priceless jewels, hmm?"

Elizabeth leaned back against Wildcat's chest as his arms came around to circle her. "You have already given me jewels," she said, sighing with contentment. "And one of them just fell out of the tree."

Here is a special sneak preview of Casey
Claybourne's next novel . . .

A THING OF BEAUTY

Coming in October 2000 from Berkley Books . . .

With the lights dimmed, the violinist took bow to instrument, casting the first shimmering notes adrift across the hushed ballroom like musical petals floating upon the wind. Although Belinda felt herself drawn to the haunting melody, she dared not tarry to enjoy it. This was her opportunity. Her opportunity to slip away under the cover of darkness.

Aunt Phoebe and Sissy would understand—wouldn't they? She had, after all, done her duty. For an agonizing two hours and twelve minutes now, she had endured the unspeakable torment of a grand society function only by pinching her thigh each quarter-hour to keep from falling asleep. *I shall have bruises in the morning,* she thought as she edged quietly toward the exit. *Bruises to show for my familial loyalty.*

Moreover, Belinda rather thought that she served as more hindrance than helpmate to her cousin's cause. Surely even Sissy could see that Belinda's lamentable social skills did little to enhance the family's standing among this elite crowd. Why, the entire evening, she had done naught but hide behind a pot of orchids, sending yawn after yawn into her silk fan, while stuttering the infrequent inanity to the occasional passerby. Really, how could it possibly benefit poor Sissy to be associated with such an inept relation?

Indeed, in the time it took Belinda to sneak from the darkened ballroom, she had convinced herself that she was doing her cousin a favor by fleeing the party. *A favor,* she repeated gleefully.

She rounded the corner into the shadowy hallway—

"Ow!"

Her chin connected sharply with a shoulder, as something wet landed upon her forearm.

"Goodness, I am so sorry," Belinda started to apologize, before realizing that she had collided with none other than their illustrious hostess.

But Lady Fitzmartin scarcely even glanced at her, as she whirled past, glowering, her gloved fist clenched around a small bottle.

Belinda coughed and lifted her arm to sniff at the dampness on her shawl. *Carnations? Ugh* . . . Evidently Lady Fitzmartin had been refreshing herself with a dab of perfume at the time of the collision.

"Awful French stuff," she muttered. "Why don't people simply learn to bathe every once in a while?"

Wrinkling her nose, Belinda glanced down the corridor as the music from the ballroom dipped and swayed. She hadn't much time. Soon the soloist would be done and the lights would be raised and people would again begin to roam the halls.

"Perhaps 'twould be best to sneak out the servants' entrance," she murmured, not wishing to draw any more attention to herself. Or to her flight.

Snuffing a last guilty twinge, she tiptoed down the hallway, veering first left, then left again, hopeful that she was headed for the back of the house. But as the corridors grew darker, Belinda began to feel as though she traveled in circles, gauging her course by the fading strains of the violin. When she finally entered a small rotunda that opened onto four different hallways, she paused, uncertain which direction to choose. . . .

"This is not wise, you know."

Her breath caught like a jagged fishbone in her throat, as Belinda jumped, one hand splaying protectively over her heart. Across the rotunda, the figure of a man could be seen leaning against a column, his silhouette tall and sleek.

"I, um . . . it isn't?" she stammered in a whisper.

His head cocked to the side, and she heard him sigh. "You must realize that I came tonight for one reason only; to settle this between us once and for all. It is over, Clara. Over. Our time together was enjoyable, but now it is done."

Clara? Belinda's eyes drew wide, as she breathed in the spicy scent of carnations. Had this man—this man with the elegant accent and unnervingly masculine voice—mistaken her for his lady love? Lady Clara Fitzmartin, perhaps? They were of a similar height. . . .

"I do not wish to hurt you, but the simple truth is that I am no longer interested. I am sorry."

But he did not sound sorry, Belinda thought, her toes curled tight in her slippers. He sounded tired. Or bored. And not at all the sort of man who'd take kindly to a stranger prying into his personal affairs.

After a short silence, in which Belinda stood perfectly still, he burst out, "Blast it, Clara, please don't let us make fools of ourselves."

Belinda swallowed a nervous, hiccupy laugh. *I fear it is too late for that,* she thought. For not only had he mistaken

her for his ex-paramour "Clara," but she had already stood
there far too long without correcting his misconception.
What should she do? Should she tell him the truth? Or
would it be best to simply wait it out?

Then he sighed once more and pushed away from the
column. Her pulse leaped.

Oh, my stars, he is coming toward me! Quickly she
whirled around, averting her face. Were the shadows deep
enough to conceal her? *Please, God?*

As he drew close, the heat of his body warmed her back,
his breath light upon her neck and scented of whiskey. In
the far distance, Belinda heard the violin swell to its cres-
cendo.

"Come now, Clara. Can we not savor the memories of
what we once shared without sullying them with bitterness?" The husky timbre of his voice set Belinda's cheeks
on fire. "I, for one, will never forget the evenings we spent
wrapped in each others' arms—the passion, the pleasure,
the promises kept."

A sudden dizziness forced Belinda to shut her eyes.

"Your kisses were ambrosia, my darling. Your caresses
the sweetest I've known."

*I ought not be listening to this. I ought to tell him the
truth—* And yet, she said nothing, unable to move, waiting
helplessly for his next words . . .